T. T. MONDAY

THE SETUP MAN

T. T. Monday lives in San Jose, California.
The Setup Man is his first thriller.

Praise for T. T. Monday's

THE SETUP MAN

"Don't shy away from this mystery if you're not a baseball fan. The industry is seamlessly interwoven into the story and you'll pick up all you need to know without any effort. If you are a baseball fan, dive in headfirst." —*Suspense Magazine*

"Monday has a *Dragnet*-like, just-the-facts style and offers lots for baseball fans to enjoy as well."
—*New York Post*

"Monday delivers an all-star performance with this series debut. Here's hoping that [Major League pitcher and private investigator] Adcock has more than a few innings left in him."
—*The Chronicle Herald* (Halifax, Nova Scotia)

"Monday's plot is inventive, but it's the verisimilitude of Adcock's baseball life that makes this one a delight. Adcock is a solid MLB citizen. . . . Here's hoping he has many more seasons and many more cases." *Booklist* (starred review)

"T. T. Monday's prose is wry, funny and just smart-ass enough."
                                                    —*Toronto Star*

"A throwback Southern California mystery in modern pinstripes. . . . A treat for readers of mystery or baseball novels, this debut will be especially enjoyable for fans of both."
                                                    —*Kirkus Reviews*

THE SETUP MAN

A NOVEL

T. T. MONDAY

Vintage Crime/Black Lizard
Vintage Books
A Division of Random House LLC
New York

FIRST VINTAGE CRIME/BLACK LIZARD EDITION, DECEMBER 2014

The Library of Congress has cataloged the Doubleday edition as follows:
Monday, T. T.
The setup man : a novel / T. T. Monday.—First edition.
pages cm
I. Title
PS3620.A95945S48 2014   813'.6—dc23   2013033289

Vintage Trade Paperback ISBN: 978-0-8041-6982-0
eBook ISBN: 978-0-385-53846-6

Book design by Michael Collica

www.weeklylizard.com

Printed in the United States of America
10 9 8 7 6 5 4 3 2

For my daughter, who loves baseball
And my wife, who loves baseball players

1

My dad wasn't a ballplayer. In his teens he did some boxing, but he spent his adult life in the straight world, inspecting aircraft welds at the McDonnell Douglas plant in Long Beach. He told me that if I wanted to make easy money—and he always believed this was the best kind of money to make—I should look into relief pitching. I remember one afternoon we were sitting in the den, watching the Dodgers get clobbered by the Cincinnati Reds on TV. A left-handed reliever named Matt Young had just bounced a curveball off the plate, walking home a run. "Look at this fool," Dad said. "Guy couldn't find the strike zone with a pebble. He works ten minutes a day, and he's making a killing. I bet his kids will never have to work a day in their lives."

Dad was almost correct. This was 1987, a few years before the agents grabbed the owners by the balls and journeymen like Matt Young started buying vacation homes with cash. I did some research, and in 1987 the Dodgers paid Matt Young $350,000. He appeared in forty-seven games, pitched fifty-four innings, and posted an earned-run average of 4.47. Believe it or not, those are decent numbers. I put up a similar line last year. But times have changed. Last year I made a million five.

My name is Johnny Adcock. I am a thirty-five-year-old

American man, six feet two inches tall, 190 pounds, with a cholesterol count on the high end of normal. Women have told me I'm handsome, but I know not to listen. Even ugly ball-players get compliments. Here are the facts: I have gray eyes, a straight nose, and one slightly pronounced canine tooth. I wear a uniform to work. I travel the country on a chartered jet. I'm divorced, with a thirteen-year-old daughter who lives with her mother in Los Angeles. For now they live well—a house in Santa Monica, private school, organic groceries—but let's be realistic, I am one torn ligament away from permanent unemployment. Ginny, my ex, knows that. She sends me vitamins to prevent injuries. That's her idea of work.

In an average week, I spend approximately two hours throwing a baseball, including warm-ups. Roughly every other night I get called upon late in the game to face a single batter, always a lefty. Conventional wisdom says that it is better to have a left-handed pitcher face a left-handed batter, because the curveball will break down and away, out of the batter's reach. I don't throw a curve, but baseball is an orthodox religion, and orthodoxy resists exceptions. I can count on one hand the number of right-handed batters I have faced this season.

Here is a typical night's work: I walk in from the bullpen, throw my eight warm-up pitches. The batter, too, takes his time to get ready. He says a prayer, checks his grip, maybe does a little baton flip with his bat. If he's at home, he might check out the crowd. Then he steps into the box and we go at it. I throw my strikes and he takes his cuts. The whole dance lasts ten minutes, tops. If I get him, they pull me and put in the closer. If I don't, they probably pull me anyway. Ten minutes a night, seventy-plus nights a year, plus the playoffs if we're lucky.

If you look at this backward, you'll notice that I have a lot of free time. Enough to stun an average man. The best relief pitchers are ruminants, men who desire nothing more than a seat on a bench, a game to watch, and a half-pound bag of David Sunflower Seeds. In college I read a poem about a man who measured out his life in coffee spoons. Good relievers measure theirs in seeds. But I am not a good reliever, because I'm restless. Maybe if I had been a position player—a shortstop, let's say—things might have been different for me. I might have taken extra batting practice in the cages under the stands. I have that option. I carry in my wallet a magnetic card that gets me into the clubhouse twenty-four hours a day. But relievers don't bat enough to make extra batting practice worthwhile. The last time I batted was four years ago. Nightcap of a doubleheader, the starter got in trouble early, and Skipper gave me the ball in the second inning. I went four frames, batted twice, and struck out both times, once on a foul bunt.

You might imagine that ballplayers go out and party after games. Some do, but there are lots of games, and the next is usually tomorrow. After a game, the next day's starting pitcher goes directly to sleep. Most guys go back to the hotel and watch TV, maybe Skype with their kids. But hotel television has never been enough for me. I need something more stimulating— especially after those hours waiting on the bench. I could have taken graduate courses through the mail, studied for life after baseball. Lots of guys talk about doing that. This is my thirteenth year in the bigs; I probably could have had a Ph.D. by now. I could have read every book ever written. But reading requires a still mind. Mine darts around like a knuckleball. I suppose I could have written books like Jim Bouton, great tell-all books about baseball and America, but again there is the problem of stillness, and also the question of why readers would want to peek inside my head.

Luckily, I found something better to do with my free time.

Ten years ago, my teammate Charley DeAngelo took me aside and told me his wife was fooling around. He had no evidence, but there were plenty of hints—jewelry he didn't remember giving her, strange numbers on the caller ID. He was going to follow her around for a day, see what he came up with. Could be boring, he said, so did I want to keep him company? I was recently divorced and had nothing better to do in the endless mornings before reporting to the stadium. So I rented a car and drove to the rendezvous spot. But DeAngelo never showed. There I was, parked across the street from the wife's gym, waiting for her to finish Tae Bo or whatever. What the hell, I said, I'm here, I will follow her, and, lo and behold, I discovered she was cheating—and not even hiding it. She went to an Italian restaurant for lunch, where she was joined by a gentleman in a business suit. They ordered Prosecco and oysters. Afterward they went to a hotel. I remember that I debated whether to tell DeAngelo. In the end I did, but only on the condition that he pass my name around to anyone else who needed this kind of help. DeAngelo thanked me for my effort and said he would put the word out.

An hour later, the phone rang. Word spreads fast in the major leagues.

A decade in, this sideline has earned me lovers and haters. The former are the guys who have required my services, at this point a cast of several hundred. The latter are those—managers, front-office folks, team PR personnel—who would prefer to ignore the ugly side of baseball. My detractors think the investigations represent a conflict of interest, even though I would never do anything to affect the outcome on the field. Mostly I think they're scared. They know sometimes I find dirt that implicates the wrong people. We're a tight group, baseball people, and our lives tend to touch like paper dolls. To some of us, that is frightening.

The appeal for me is the same as it ever was. Playing a child's game for money can be hard on your self-respect. Even now, I'm still not a doctor or a diplomat, but I'm more than I was. I'm more than a guy on a bench cracking seeds, waiting for a lefty to bat in the eighth.

God help me if a man's not entitled to that.

2

We are in Denver, last game of a road trip that started two weeks ago in Houston. The Bay Dogs of San José (that's my club) have been playing surprisingly well; if we win tonight we will be seven and five on the trip, but we're still buried in the standings thanks to a shit-poor first half of the season. Tonight's contest starts at 7:05 p.m., which means the bus leaves the hotel at three. I don't even think about these things anymore, I just feel them like tides. At two-forty-five, I am pulled magnetically to the lobby. The clubhouse guys are scurrying around, tagging our luggage. After the game we will go directly from the park to the airport. I am early, as usual; most of the other guys are still upstairs packing. I spent the morning and early afternoon down on the Sixteenth Street Mall, looking for a birthday present for my daughter, Isabel. She wants a certain kind of jeans, a brand called Miss Slinky. I did not find them.

Let me rephrase that: I spent the early afternoon looking for jeans. I spent the morning in bed with a young woman named Constance O'Connell. Connie is the cousin of my buddy Jerry Simmons, who pitches for Detroit. Three or four years ago, when Jerry was still with the Bay Dogs, a bunch of us were drinking beer by the pool after a day game. It was this very same hotel, now that I think about it. Anyway, this group of half a dozen girls shows up, college-aged but well dressed. Jerry waves them over and buys their drinks. We assume that he has ordered in some talent, but it turns out the girls are strictly volunteers. Jerry introduces us around, and right away I'm drawn to Connie. She has these inky black eyes, a perfect little upturned nose. She laughs easily and often. We talk about northern California—she has just graduated from Sonoma State, where she ran track and earned a degree in library science, whatever that is. I ask if she does experiments with books. She says she does, and gives me her number. She tells me to call her next time we are in Denver. I do call, but it isn't until the Division Championship Series in October that we actually meet for drinks. The Bay Dogs lost that series, but I gained a friend. Life is funny that way. Did I mention her hair smells like a pine forest? I love Denver.

Our backup catcher, Frankie Herrera, takes the seat next to me on the bus. Frankie's about twenty-five, in his second year in the bigs. Like me, he grew up in L.A., but on the opposite side of town. It might as well have been another country. He tells me about gang fights and cockfights and cat fights—basically, his whole neighborhood was fighting all the time. He may have become a catcher just for the protective equipment. But Frankie is about as clean-cut as they come. In this era of gaudy tattoos, of Matt Kemp and Yadier Molina racing Mike Tyson to the last unmarked patch of hide, Frankie has just one decoration: the word "Granma," misspelled just like that, across his right hip. It was a casualty of high school, he says—a friend was practicing to be a tattooist and Frankie volunteered his ass. He never told his grandma about the tattoo, but he did donate money to build a new baseball diamond in her village in Sonora. He strikes me as uncommonly generous for such a young kid, and it's obvious he values his family. He and his wife have twin sons, a big house in San Diego near her folks. He's just genuinely nice, no drama.

"What's the good word, Adcock?"

I exhale. "Not 'cutter.' But I've been working with Phil, and I think we found the problem."

Phil Sutcliffe is our pitching coach. After I gave up the go-ahead run our first night in Houston, he watched me throw and said I was snapping the wrist too early when I released the cutter. A cutter, or cut fastball, is a pitch thrown more or less like a fastball, but with most of the pressure on the middle finger. I have made the adjustment suggested by Sutcliffe, and we'll see what happens. The body forgets, so you have to remind it. The problem is that it forgets again.

"Bad night," Frankie says. "Don't worry about it. Actually, I need to talk to you about something else. Something besides baseball, if you know what I'm saying."

Even though everybody on the team knows what I do in my spare time, they speak about it only in whispers.

I slide in closer to Frankie.

"What's your mind?"

"That's it? I just tell you?"

"How did you think it worked?"

"I thought we'd meet in an alley or something."

"An alley, Frankie?"

"I don't know—"

"This isn't Boyle Heights. I'm not selling drugs."

Herrera pulls a phone from his jacket pocket, checks for new messages, puts it back.

"It's my wife," he says. "I got a problem with my wife."

"I'm sorry to hear that."

He looks at me sideways. "Why are you sorry? I haven't even told you the problem."

"Listen, buddy, you're not the first, and you won't be the last.

We're on the road a lot. Everybody knows how it goes. Sixty to seventy-five percent of my work is guys who think their wife is fooling around."

"And are they?"

"Most of the time."

"Well, that's not the problem."

"Lucky you."

He checks his phone again. When he looks up, his expression is suddenly paranoid. He grabs my arm with surprising force and says, "This has to stay on the down low, Adcock. You can't tell nobody. I need your word."

"You have it," I say. "That's what I'm here to do."

He releases the grip and just looks at me, giving himself one last chance to bail out. Everyone does this the first time. A problem isn't a problem until you tell it to me. After that, it's a straight line to the solution. Not everybody wants their problems fixed.

"When I met my wife," he says, "she wasn't, you know, such a good girl."

"How do you mean?"

"She worked in clubs."

"Okay."

"You know the kind of clubs I mean?"

"I think so."

"And also, a couple of times, she needed money at the end of the month. For rent and bills. So she made some movies."

I could have told Frankie the rest of the story myself, I've heard it that many times, but I let him finish. A guy wants to be heard first of all. I sometimes think that is half the service I provide.

"Of course, now she's different. She is a different person since she had the twins."

"Sure, I bet."

"I thought everybody forgot about the videos. But then, the day before yesterday, I got this message on my phone."

"What kind of message?"

"A text message with a link to a Web site. One of those free porn sites."

"And the video was hers?"

Frankie nods.

"Do you know who sent it?" I say.

"The number was blocked."

"There are ways to get around that."

"I was hoping."

"On the other hand," I say, "anyone can buy a prepaid SIM card. She's not still in touch with the photographer, is she?"

"He told me he'd never do anything with the files. Maria doesn't know this, but I paid him a nice chunk to just sit on them. But I swear to God, Johnny, if I ever find that motherfucker . . ."

"Easy, Frank. You have a lot to lose."

"I know. Maria tells me the same thing."

"Good woman."

"Tell you the truth, all I want to do is find the files and erase them. I don't need revenge or nothing. I just don't want my boys to grow up and find out their mom was, you know, that kind of actress."

"How old are they now?"

"Gonna be five in October."

"Time flies, huh?"

"That's what everybody says."

"So it was just the link, no message with it? Normally, you get a demand—not necessarily in the same package, maybe by mail, or a phone call?"

"You've seen this kind of thing before, huh?"

"Unfortunately."

This seems to make the kid feel better. He pulls out his phone again but doesn't even look at the screen before putting it back in his jacket.

"Nah, there's no demand. You think they want money?"

"Maybe. I'm going to need the phone."

Frankie's face drops. "For real?"

"Sorry, Frank, but I need to see the video. You can transfer the number to another phone, but I need the message, in its original form."

"Promise you'll keep your hands by your sides?"

"Come on—"

"She's my wife, Adcock."

"I know she is, and I promise to give her video the respect it deserves, regardless of how effective it may be."

"I appreciate that. So—how does this work? Do you charge by the hour?"

"We can talk about that later."

"Okay. I'll have my agent call yours. You're with IMG, right?"

"It doesn't work like that, Frank."

"Oh. Right."

"Don't worry about it. Just get me the phone. Call Verizon or whoever, tell them you lost your handset."

"Yeah, okay. I can do that."

"The sooner the better," I say. "You know where to find me."

3

Tonight our starting pitcher, Tim Harlingen, scatters six hits over seven innings. The Rockies' only run comes in the bottom of the seventh, when our center fielder loses a routine fly ball in the lights. Harlingen is a prideful guy, he wants to finish the game, but the score is tied, 1–1, going into the top of the eighth, and Skipper pulls him for a pinch-hitter (who strikes out, but that's how these things go). Bottom of the eighth, we send out Mitsu Yushida to face the top of the Rockies' order. Yushi gets the first two on grounders, but then he loses his concentration and walks the third and fourth guys on something like nine pitches. I have been warming up for exactly this scenario, because the Rockies' number-five hitter, Tom Kelton, is a classic Adcock adversary: a lefty batting thirty-five points lower against left-handed pitching.

As I jog in from the pen, I go over Kelton's scouting report in my head. You're supposed to jam him inside to start the count, maybe he fouls off one or two, and then put some junk on the outside corner and hope he chases. Kelton and I broke into the league the same year. We have faced each other dozens of times. Like most scouting lines, this one is factual but insufficient. The truth is that if Kelton is feeling good he will put your best pitch in the cheap seats. Inside, outside—it doesn't matter. He's a drinker, though, and it is after ten o'clock. I cross my fingers and hope he's jonesing.

Skipper puts the ball in my glove. "See you in a few," he says. I nod.

Our starting catcher, Tony Modigliani, the third member of our little committee on the mound, goes over the plan: "Let's start him with fastballs up and in. Got it?" Physically, there are two types of major-league catchers. First is the short, stocky guy with a thick skull, the Mutant Ninja Turtle. Frankie Herrera fits this mold, along with greats like Yogi Berra, Mike Scioscia, and the brothers Molina. Most Turtles took up the position when they were young because it suited their physiques. Growing up, they spent the vast majority of their practice time behind the plate, not beside it, so they tend to be only average hitters. But catching is the most specialized position after pitching—just handling pitchers and their egos takes a degree in psychology—so a guy like Frankie Herrera can expect to enjoy a long career if he stays healthy. Tony Modigliani is the other kind: tall and lithe, maybe six four and 220, with the long, strong arms of an outfielder. In fact, Modigliani played outfield until college, when his coaches told him to try catching. Less competition, they told him, more chance to stand out if you can hit. With those long arms he hits for power—forty homers in his rookie season alone— and because he trained as a hitter, his eye is well developed (he led the National League in walks last year). The problem is that these long-limbed guys are not cut out to be squatting four hours a day, two hundred days a year. Eventually, their knees give out, and they have to move to first base, or join an American League club, where they can DH. There are plenty of examples of this type, too: Mike Piazza, Benny Santiago, Joe Mauer. Everyone loves them—when they're healthy.

One more thing: for some reason, long-limbed catchers tend to be dicks.

"Up and in," Modigliani repeats, "you got that?"

"Got it," I say.

He trots back to the plate, flips down the mask. I take my eight warm-up pitches while the crowd watches bloopers on the big screen. Then the ump gives the signal, and Kelton steps into the box.

I do as I am told, spot a fastball up and in. It has good velocity, a little trailing movement, and it is headed right for Diggy's waiting mitt when Kelton turns and jacks it over the right-field wall.

The runners come home—one, two, three—and the score is now Rockies 4, Bay Dogs 1.

"One pitch," Skipper says to me as he takes the ball. "I think that's a record."

"What can you do?" I say. "Line on Kelton is up and in."

Skipper taps my ass. "Maybe it's time we rewrote the line."

On the flight home, I hide behind my headphones. One of the problems with being on the road with a baseball club is that you're never alone. There's always someone around—teammates, coaches, trainers, writers, video crews. If you want the world to disappear after a bad night on the mound, you can't just put a blanket over your head. The best you can do is crank up the music and shut your eyes. Most people respect that, even if the sulking player is far too old to be wearing a purple headset labeled "EarCanz™ by Weezy."

Know what I'm really too old for? Late-inning homers. If a kid with a triple-digit heater hangs a slider and loses the game, you forgive him. You take the long view and trust he will work out the kinks by his next outing. After all, he's still bringing the heat. With me it's another story. My hard-throwing days are long gone. My game is about location, changing speeds, and outsmarting the hitter. The moment I lose the ability to fool a drunk like Tom Kelton, I become expendable. No headphones can drown that out.

When we reach San José, Herrera finds me in the players' parking lot.

"So, hey," he says, "do you think maybe we could erase the link before I give you the phone?"

"Afraid not, buddy."

"Do you really have to watch the clip?"

"Lucky me, right?"

"Look, Adcock—"

"I'm just kidding. I'll close one eye, how's that?"

He hands me his iPhone. The case is decorated with children's drawings.

"Great," I say. "Let's see what we can find."

"I've got my fingers crossed. Thanks for your help, by the way."

"Don't thank me yet."

Frankie laughs and pulls out his keys. "Yeah, I guess that would be smarter." His black BMW chirps. He flips his suitcase into the trunk, slips behind the tinted glass, and disappears into the night.

4

My own iPhone starts vibrating around seven the next morning. I am in my apartment, on the twenty-first floor of a building in downtown San José. It's not a glamorous address, but it suits me. The ballpark is walking distance, so I don't need a car. I keep a motorcycle in the garage for emergencies. The view is a nice bonus. From my living room I can usually see the hills on both sides of Silicon Valley, the little horsetail clouds above the ridges, the windmills in the passes. In front of me, northward, are the backwaters of the Bay, the toxic red sludge in the evaporating ponds, the stinking marshland, the abandoned railroad trestles. On a clear day you can see all the way to San Francisco. This morning, though, I see nothing. We are fogged in.

"This is Adcock."

"Johnny, it's Bil Chapman."

Bil is the Bay Dogs' clubhouse manager, a middle-aged man trapped in the body of a teenager. Though he must be over forty, his face is ravaged by acne and he sweats through his shirt most days by noon. Bil still lives with his mother, but he claims that it is the other way around, that his mother lives with him, in a house he owns. As though that makes any difference: Bil's life is a series of small, almost unnoticeable rebellions, for example leaving the last "l" off his first name. He tells me that's edgy.

"You know what time it is, Bil?"

"Johnny, I have some bad news. Frankie Herrera died in a car accident last night."

I wind up to tell him it's too early to be fucking around, and then it occurs to me he's serious.

"Skipper is asking everyone to report two hours early," Bil says. "We're going to have a meeting, and then there will be time with grief counselors—"

"Grief counselors. What happened?"

"It was a car accident."

"Yeah, you said that. How? Where?"

"We got a call from the Highway Patrol at five this morning. They found Frankie's car on the road to Half Moon Bay. Highway 92. He went over the edge."

"Half Moon Bay? Frankie's apartment is in Santa Clara."

"Yeah, I know. Maybe he went for a drive? I mean, he went for a drive, obviously."

"When did it happen?"

"They're saying around three a.m."

I go back in my head. We landed at SJC at twelve-thirty or one. Back at the stadium parking lot, one-thirty. It occurs to me that I may have been the last person to see Frankie Herrera alive.

"So there's a meeting?"

"One-thirty sharp."

"Yeah, I'll be there."

"I'm really sorry, Johnny. I know Frankie liked you a lot."

By eight-thirty, I'm in San Mateo, teasing my bike through the gridlock on 101. The interchange with Highway 92 is a giant flyover weaving between office buildings emblazoned with the names of Internet companies selling electronic real estate. This is the suburb where Barry Bonds grew up, where he was the only black kid in his high school. I bet even today he would be the only one. This is still mostly a white area, but it has been filling up lately with Indians and Chinese pushed north out of the deeper parts of Silicon Valley. I think about Barry's childhood friend, a white guy, who went on to become his trainer and is currently serving time for refusing to testify in the steroid trial. I wonder if any Indians or Chinese would have done that for him. Not that I approve, of course.

As the road winds uphill into the Coast Range, I leave suburbia and plunge into the redwoods. The temperature drops ten degrees. It occurs to me that I do not know exactly where along the next ten miles the accident occurred. I don't even know what I am looking for. I pass a peloton of cyclists in DayGlo Lycra—computer geeks and bankers who just remembered they have bodies. Every year at least a dozen of these guys go over the edge on this road. The county has installed guardrails on all the curves, but nothing like that is going to stop a cyclist careening downhill at sixty miles per hour. Might stop the bike, but not the rider.

I get plenty of nasty looks as I pass the cyclists. It makes me feel better to know that I could strike out any one of them on three pitches. Of course, a couple are probably rich enough to buy my contract. I think it must be better to be a pro ballplayer in Cincinnati or Pittsburgh or Milwaukee, where the league minimum salary puts you near the top of the local pecking order. Here in the Bay Area, a million five a year makes me solidly middle class.

Three curves after Skyline Drive, I find the spot. There's no mistaking it: a section of the guardrail has been replaced with yellow police tape, and three uniformed cops stand next to their cruisers, shooting the shit. Two Highway Patrol and a San Mateo County sheriff. I ride past them, around the next bend, and hide my bike in the bushes. I lock up my helmet and open the goody box, a stash of Bay Dogs paraphernalia I take with me everywhere, because you never know when you might meet a fan.

When the sheriff's deputy sees me walking toward the yellow tape, he comes over and shakes his head.

"You can't be here," he says.

Very politely I ask, "Is this where Frankie Herrera's car went off the road?"

He looks at me like I just told his five-year-old daughter where babies come from. "No comment," he says, waving his hand. "You have to leave."

"Because he was my teammate," I say. I put out my hand. "Johnny Adcock."

"No shit." The deputy loses himself for a minute. I wait while he regains his cop composure. "I'm really sorry about Mr. Herrera," he says.

"Yeah, he was my wife's favorite." I smile like I'm embarrassed. "She liked 'em young."

"My old lady likes Modigliani. But they all do, right?"

I pull a baseball from the pocket of my leather jacket. "Give her this."

The cop turns the ball, finds Modigliani's signature, smiles. "So, Mr. Adcock," he says, "you want to see where it happened?"

"I do."

He goes over to the two patrolmen, and they chat for a minute. Then he waves to me. "Sorry for your loss," says the CHP captain, a middle-aged white man with a handlebar mustache and thighs that push the capacity of his golden uniform tights. I've always marveled at how much cops look like out-of-shape second basemen—or maybe how much second basemen (Jeff

Kent, for example) look like in-shape cops. "Tough luck yesterday," he says. "One pitch."

"Scouting report called for a fastball high and tight," I explain. I shake my head to indicate (hopefully) that I would like to leave it at that.

"That Kelton is a killer," says the captain.

"You're telling me."

"Guess they thought you might get him this time, huh?"

I bite my tongue. "Guess so, yeah."

I give the captain and his partner autographed balls, and they walk me over to the guardrail. On the way, we cross a set of fresh-looking tire tracks cutting across the road from the eastbound lane to a point just a few feet from the rail. Looks like Frankie was on his way home when he died.

"These from Frankie's car?" I ask the cops.

"Most likely," the captain says. "Though, to be honest, those look a bit wide. What was the deceased driving, Cam?"

"BMW 328," the partner replies.

"I guess you can get those with wide tires, right? Anyway"—he puts his gloved hand on the mangled steel rail—"here is where he went over." This stretch of Highway 92 is set into a hillside that has been encased in concrete to halt erosion. Imagine a miniature Hoover Dam; add fog. The cop nods to a spot downhill a hundred yards, on the next curve, where two more police cruisers are parked, with their lights flashing soundlessly. "And that is where he ended up."

"Can you take me down there?"

The captain rolls the baseball in his hand. "I don't know, Mr. Adcock. That would be against our procedures."

"Where are you from?" I say. "You want to see the Giants? I can comp you a pair of tickets."

He smiles at his partner. "The real question is, will you win?"

"Is this about last night? With all due respect, officer, if you want to try to throw a baseball past a hulk with a club, go right ahead. I wish you all the luck in the world."

The cop retreats from his pose. "I didn't mean it like that. I know how hard it is. I played ball in high school."

"And?"

"And I joined the Highway Patrol the week after graduation."

To save the guy's pride, I look away.

As we pick our way down the hill, I hear the captain cursing me under his breath: "Fucking left-handed assholes. . . . One pitch! Fucking jerkoff thinks he's such hot shit. . . ."

At the lower site, Frankie's BMW is a mess of twisted, smoking steel. The air smells like gasoline, burning hair, and plastic. I try to breathe through my mouth.

The captain points to a gash in the roof where the metal has been pried open. "See that aperture? That's where the crew removed the bodies. They sent the Jaws of Life, but this was no salvation job, I'm afraid. Sorry if that sounds insensitive, Mr. Adcock, but that's just the truth."

"Did you say 'bodies'?"

"Two. Your friend Mr. Herrera and an unidentified female."

I try to act cool, as though this is what I expected to hear.

"Actually, Captain," the partner pipes in, "she had ID."

The captain fixes him with a withering stare. "We can't say her name," he says slowly, "because she was a minor. Seventeen years old."

"Oh yeah?" I say.

"Mr. Adcock, I could lose my job if I told you her name—"

"I understand."

"—but because you were his friend, I will tell you this much: they weren't family."

5

Before the evening's game, the stadium honors Frankie with a moment of silence. For us, though, the silence has been going on since the early afternoon. The grief counselors, two overweight librarian-looking women in cable-knit sweaters, sit for hours in the trainer's room without any takers. No surprise there. I could have summarized the players' sentiments like this: Number one, it wasn't fair, the kid was only twenty-five. Number two, holy shit, it could have been me. And number three—but this is only my concern—who the hell was the girl in the car? Is there a connection with the video? I used to believe in coincidences, but that was before I started doing investigations and realized that "coincidence" is just another way to say "I give up."

Ironically, our bats choose this somber occasion to explode with an orgy of runs. Fifteen, to be exact, on twenty-five hits, the highest totals of the season. Every man in the lineup scores. Modigliani has two homers and a double, for six RBIs. Skipper decides to air out the bullpen, giving all of us a little work in this rare glimpse of garbage time. I get the whole eighth inning, and our closer, Big Bob Schneider, pitches a perfect ninth. The closer normally does not pitch unless he has a chance for a save, but we've been playing so badly that there haven't been many games to save. Skipper figures Schneider needs work, so he brings him in anyway. I like a blowout win as much as the next guy, but it takes a long time to score fifteen runs. It is eleven-forty-five when Big Bob records the final out. Thanks to the continuing somber mood in the clubhouse, there is no chitchat tonight, and by twelve-thirty I am a free man. Donning a pair of Oakleys and a 49ers hat for cover, I take the light rail to Japantown. There is only one place I want to be, only one man who can help me sort out the events of the last twenty-four hours.

Marcus Washington pitched sixteen years in the bigs, the last four in San José when I was new to the league. He comes from a bygone era when all pitchers trained to be starters. The guys in the bullpen—especially the long relievers and setup men—were either failed starters or starters whose prime had come and gone. The pen was a kind of back pasture where old horses were put out to graze. By the time I met Marcus, he had not started a game in eight years. "The game is changing," he told me. "Soon there will be seventh-inning specialists, eighth-inning specialists, first-out-of-the-ninth specialists." I told him that had already happened. "Look at me," I said. "This is my first year, and already I've got my slot. I'm destined to pitch the eighth for my entire career." Marcus leaned back on his folding chair and said if that was so then he was finished.

Marcus's retirement plan had always been to open a bar. (The writers of *Cheers* were right to make Sam Malone a relief pitcher—bartending is a pretty common dream in the bullpen.) But after the Bay Dogs cut him loose, he realized that he was not quite ready to retire and accepted an offer to play in Japan for the Kintetsu Buffaloes. Thus our man Makasu (Japanglish for "Marcus") enjoyed a second career in Japan, where, in addition to several years' worth of top-quality Asian trim, he gained an important grain of inspiration: it was not just a bar he was supposed to open, but a sushi bar.

Sushi Makasu opened right after the dot-com bust in a storefront on Jackson Street once occupied by Kozmo.com. Marcus pulled out all the stops in infusing the vibe of his native West Oakland into the neat order of San José's Japan-town. The lighting is subdued, even dark, and the sushi bar is a long zinc-topped number with rotating stools. All the waitresses are African American: Marcus calls them his "Afro-geishas." They wear black Lycra tube dresses, platform heels, and cat-eye mascara. Hair pulled tight in a bun. Marcus trains the girls on what he calls "properness." Properness means no talking back to a customer, no matter what he said, or what you think he said. It means apologizing if the food takes too long, or if the order was incorrect. Marcus told me these notions of service were foreign to the girls he had grown up with in Oakland—girls whose daughters he now hires. At first Marcus rolled all the sushi himself, but that got to be a bottleneck as the restaurant's popularity grew. Eventually, he hired his brother Rich, a recent parolee, and showed him the ropes. Rich brought in another old boy, and so on. Marcus joked that the state should make him a parole officer. These days, with the restaurant humming along, Marcus mostly sits in his office, a windowless cell next to the restrooms, behind a door marked with a framed, autographed photo of his idol, the pitcher Vida Blue.

I wave to Rich as I walk through the restaurant. He nods, no smile. On the stereo, Bill Withers laments that there "ain't no sunshine when she's gone." All night I have been thinking of Frankie's wife, how the problem of the porn film is still unsolved, and how I should be the one to solve it now that

Frankie is gone. But when I think of calling her up—especially now that I know Frankie had a secret of his own—I start to smell tar. Maybe I don't want to touch this baby. ("I know, I know, I know, I know, I know," wails Withers.)

I rap on the office door. Vida shivers in his Oakland A's cap with his hard stare. Marcus opens the door all smiles, as jocular as his brother is dour. He has the classic pitcher's physique—tall and lanky, wide shoulders, long legs. Marcus was famous for his herky-jerky delivery on the mound: the extra-high kick, limbs flailing out in all directions, before the ball shot forth like a rocket from a cloud. In retirement, he still moves that way. I see his motion as he swivels his desk chair and rises to greet me. His close-cropped natural and Cab Calloway mustache are shot through with silver, but his personal gravity is undiminished. He has been retired from baseball for ten years, and you would think his appeal would dim, but Marcus's appeal was never just about baseball. He is one of a handful of players I have known over the years who would have gotten just as much action if he had never touched a baseball. Dark skin, bright eyes, a voice like Lou Rawls's: Marcus was the original hound dog. He never married—says he never needed to. Even now his orbit is thick with impossibly young women. When I was new in the league, he showed me the ropes both on and off the field. He partied hard. Like a lot of ballplayers who came of age in the eighties, Marcus developed a weakness for coke, but unlike Doc Gooden (to name just one of his contemporaries), he never let it ruin him. By the time we met, his days of dissipation were largely behind him. He speaks of the late eighties like a veteran recalling combat. And he keeps his nose clean, mostly.

Marcus of course has seen the night's box score.

"Now we know, Johnny Adcock," he says as he pumps my

hand. "Now we know what it takes for you to go a whole inning. A ten-run lead. That is your handicap, my friend."

"I appreciate your confidence, Pops."

"Come on, young man. After that one-pitch thing in Denver, I would have thought you needed at least twenty runs up. But, no, it turns out the skipper is a forgiving man, a kind and loving man. Like Jesus Christ."

"What could I do? Modigliani called it high and tight."

"And you couldn't shake him off?"

"My cutter is in dry dock. He wanted a fastball. Would you have shaken him off?"

Marcus cranks up the wattage on his smile. "I shook everyone off."

"Yeah, well. Those were different times."

"Yes, they were."

"Marcus, I need a favor."

"Hold it," he says, and then he reaches down and pushes a little button on his desk. It looks like a doorbell.

"What's that for?"

"You want some tea?"

I shrug.

"You come in here, you drink tea. My rules."

"You're the boss."

"You are goddamned right about that."

Just then there's a knock on the door, and one of Marcus's waitresses walks in. She is a sister, of course, with dark brown eyes and an ass from here to Hunter's Point.

"Thank you, Miyako," Marcus says as he takes the teapot and cups from the tray. The girl bows and leaves without saying a word.

"Miyako?" I say.

"Miyako. That's her name."

"You gave it to her?"

"She chose it. I gave her some options, and she chose that one. It means 'beautiful night child.'"

"Don't you think it's strange that you make them change their names? I mean, who changes their name to work in a restaurant? Besides strippers."

"Common misconception," Marcus says. "Geishas are not hos. Their job is to make the customer comfortable, that's all." He pours steaming tea from the cast-iron tetsubin pot into the two porcelain cups. "The geisha is there to help her client relax. I don't doubt some geishas get down. But more often than not, they just serve tea."

"Isn't tea a stimulant?"

"My girls ain't hos, John. Now tell me what's on your mind."

"You heard about Frankie Herrera?"

"I did. You know, Roberto Clemente was taken before his time. Thurman Munson also. Not bad company, come to think of it."

"Herrera was a good kid. Looked up to me, for some reason. He was always coming to me for advice."

Marcus smiles. "What comes around goes around."

"I guess so. The night before the accident, he came to me with a problem."

"Like, a *problem* problem?"

Marcus knows all about my sideline. In fact, from time to time he has helped me out, serving as my local eyes and ears when I am on the road.

I nod. "A matrimonial problem."

Marcus sips his tea. "I see."

"It seems his wife made some videos when she was younger. Herrera thought they had disappeared, but a few weeks ago someone posted one online and sent a link to his phone."

"Blackmail?"

"That's what I'm thinking. And one more piece of the puzzle:

Turns out Herrera wasn't alone in his car last night. He had a girl with him. Seventeen years old. You won't read that in the papers."

"You put the gag on?"

"Baseball fans are everywhere."

Marcus nods knowingly. "And you got the girl's name, I assume."

"I could have, if I hadn't pitched Kelton high and tight. Bastard patrolman ribbed me worse than you for that."

"How long are they going to keep it quiet?"

"They said they were going to contact the girl's family first, and then make a decision."

"So a day. Two tops."

"That would be my guess."

"Have you talked to the wife?"

"Not yet. She's flying in tonight to claim the body. I expect she'll turn up."

"I expect that's right. So what do you need me for?"

"Are you still in touch with Bam Bam Rodriguez?"

Javier "Bam Bam" Rodriguez had been the Tony Modigliani of the late-nineties Bay Dogs—the team I joined when I came up from the minor leagues. We were not a great team, but Bam Bam, a Puerto Rican import, was the star attraction. His was the face on the car-insurance billboards, the filthy dreadlocks pulled back into a semi-respectable ponytail, the bulging eyes Photoshopped to look trustworthy. Like most ballplayers, Bam Bam had plans beyond the baseball diamond. His particular ambition was to move south to the San Fernando Valley and become a pornographer. "I jus' love the fucking," he would explain with a shrug. Because I was new and did not want to be rude, I would let him bend my ear for hours: in the trainer's room, while he was getting his daily massage; in the hotel lobby, waiting for the bus to the airport; in the moldy visitors' clubhouse in Philly, waiting out a rain delay. "Lord Jesus, he want me to have two life, Johnny, the *béisbol* and the fucking. Two life, ju understand?"

Last I heard, his dreams had come true. Fancy that.

"We're friends on Facebook," Marcus says.

"Track him down. Tell him you're looking for a girl. Don't tell him she's Herrera's wife until you're sure he's for real."

"Oh, he's for real," Marcus says. He swivels in his chair, grabs the mouse on the desk, and shakes the computer awake. "Take a look at this. . . ."

"That's okay—just tell me what you learn. I want to know who posted that clip."

"Am I allowed to pay for this information?"

"He won't need our money," I say, "if he's got any information worth buying."

"Gotcha."

I rise to go, but Marcus stops me.

"Do yourself a favor," he says. "Shake off Modigliani once in a while. Don't let him think you're his bitch."

"What if I am?"

Marcus clicks his tongue. "You young fellas are too conservative. Too damn conservative."

"Tell that to Frankie Herrera," I say.

6

By the time I leave the sushi bar, the light rail has stopped running, so I walk home. I take shit from my teammates for not having a car, but on nights like this I'm glad I don't, because I have the city to myself. At 3 a.m., even the homeless in St. James Park are bedded down for the night. The only waking soul in sight, a lone hooker on the corner of First and St. James, peers into the white glow of her cell phone. For better or worse, this is San José at full tilt. A hooker texts her pimp, a relief pitcher leaps across the trolley tracks, and in the office parks north of town millions of computers cycle and whir, turning electricity into money.

I touch my keycard to the scanner in front of my building, and the door clicks open. In the elevator, I start thinking about Marcus, and whether it was wise to get him involved in this case. He has a tendency to get in too deep, and he usually ends up expanding the mess rather than helping to mop it up. But I love the guy. He is the reason I'm still playing ball. You burn out if you take anything too seriously, baseball included. I never understood that until I met Marcus. Now I worry that I understand it too well.

I am so wrapped up in this line of thinking that I do not even notice that the deadbolt on my apartment door has already been opened. I just turn the knob, flip the lights, head straight for the bedroom. We have a matinee tomorrow; I have to be at the park by ten-thirty in the morning.

"I thought you'd never come home," says a voice from the bed.

"Oh, hi," I say, too tired to be surprised.

"That's all I get? I'm nude."

"You're always nude."

"I am not. Today I wore a pantsuit."

"A pantsuit?"

"A Dolce & Gabbana pantsuit. And a silk blouse."

"And under that?"

"Under that, I was nude."

"See?"

I throw my jacket on the back of a chair, start unbuttoning my shirt.

"How was work?" she says.

I love it when she says that. It makes me feel like an honest man.

"A little better than usual," I say. "Skip gave me more outs than I expected, but it went well. Better than the last night in Denver. You?"

"I heard a pitch from a couple of Stanford biochemists who have developed a pill for BO. They're calling it 'medical deodorant.'"

"Are you going to fund it?"

"Not sure yet. I have to see if it works."

"I know some guys who sweat a lot."

"Maybe they can help."

"We have rules against taking drugs not prescribed by a doctor. Are you a doctor?"

"Actually, yes. But not the kind you need."

"What kind of doctor are you, then?"

"Come here and I'll show you."

The conversation goes on like this until she gets tired of talking and stuffs a sock in my mouth. As promised, she is naked. Soon enough, I am, too. We do the needful, and the next thing you know it is four-thirty.

"Don't you ever sleep?" I ask.

"You know I'm bionic, Johnny."

This is the truest statement I have heard all day. Bethany Pham is not only the most intelligent woman I have ever met, she is also the best lay, and it's not even close. The best part—or worst, if you've had a long day—is that she requires zero sleep.

"I'm not complaining," I say. "It's just that I may have to work for ten or fifteen minutes this afternoon."

"Poor baby. Come here and let me make it up to you."

"Again?"

"Do you have a problem with that?"

"No, I just—"

At five-fifteen, garbage trucks rumble in the alley behind the building. The window pinks and then turns gray. Bethany reaches over and gently squeezes my cock, then swings her legs over the edge of the bed. She stretches her arms above her head, sniffs her pits. Her back is sculpted by the mile she swims every morning, which itself is only a warm-up for a ten-mile jog. Her glossy black hair shines with a hundred colors in the angular light.

I push myself up on my elbows.

"Go to sleep," she says. "You need rest, weakling."

Bethany is a San José native, the only daughter of Vietnamese immigrants. Officially, she is a seismologist with a Ph.D. from Caltech, but she makes her living sniffing out bullshit. As a partner at a venture-capital firm in Menlo Park, she hears a thousand business plans a year and invests in less than five.

She has never thought it's strange that I face one batter per game. She understands about making it count.

I watch as she pulls a black Speedo up her lean, muscular legs, writhing like a snake until the straps snap over her shoulders. She keeps a full set of workout clothes in my apartment and little else. Like me, Bethie is divorced and swears she will never marry again. Like me, she supports her ex with generous monthly checks. Also like me, she is secretly glad she has an ex to support, because she does not know what she would do with her money if she were allowed to keep it all. She lives her life at the poles of intellect and physicality: pie-in-the-sky technology and punishing exercise. If Bethany has a problem, it is that she has little patience for anything in between. I don't know if I love her, but I do feel something for her that I don't feel for the rest of the women in my life. It might just be proximity. I may never know. Neither of us wants to ruin a good thing with too much scrutiny.

"Will you be around later?" I say.

"Around where?"

"Just around. I may need to ask you for something."

She shrugs. "You know my number. No promises."

"Of course not," I say.

I watch her gather her things into a big, expensive-looking handbag with a small gold clasp. She slips a wide cloth band over her head to keep her hair out of her eyes.

"Farewell," I say.

"You are too sentimental, John. Had I known that when I met you, I might never have . . ." Her voice trails away. I hear the front door open, and then, quite unexpectedly, another woman's voice.

"Is this Johnny Adcock's apartment?" The voice is young and slightly squeaky. It belongs to no one I know.

"It is," I hear Bethany answer.

"Is he here?"

Bethany yells, "Next!"

I scramble. The jeans are on the floor, where I left them last night. This morning. A few hours ago.

Heels click in the hall. The squeaky voice calls out: "Mr. Adcock?"

I have my pants on and half my shirt buttoned up when she appears in the bedroom doorway.

"What time is it?" I say. That's as good as any other first line, considering.

"Six o'clock. I'm sorry it's so early, but I have a flight. My kids are waiting for me at home."

I realize I am standing before the widow Herrera.

7

The widow is petite, not more than five feet and a hundred pounds. She looks to be about Frankie's age, certainly not more than thirty. All her parts are real, although her coffee-colored hair may have been straightened. She has neat, sculpted brows, black eyes, and dark tones on her lips and lashes. This morning she wears a black silk blouse, black jeans, and a pair of dark slingback sandals. Open-toed shoes seem like a strange choice for a woman in mourning, until I notice that her nails are painted black as well.

"I'm Maria Herrera," she says. "Frankie's wife."

"Johnny Adcock."

"Your wife let me in."

"My wife?" I finish the last few buttons on my shirt. I don't correct her. "Listen, I'm sorry about Frankie. He was a terrific guy and a hell of a ballplayer. I hope you'll accept my condolences."

Mrs. Herrera wipes the corner of each eye with the back of her wrist, taking care not to smear her makeup. "Would you believe I'm already sick of hearing that? Everybody has been trying to tell me who my husband was, how wonderful he was. He was no angel, that's for sure. But neither was I, as I assume you know. Frankie told you about our problem?"

"He did."

"He assured me you would take care of it."

"I'm going to do my best."

"You have his phone. Have you watched the video?"

"Not yet."

"Frankie would have wanted to know who was behind it," she says; then she pauses, as though weighing her next statement. "I should tell you that I don't care who sees that video. Not now. My husband is dead. What could be worse than that?"

Plenty of things, I want to say. He could have been a gardener and left you with squat instead of a major-league pension.

"The reason I came to see you," she continues, "is that I suspect my husband was murdered, and I want you to find out who did it."

"You realize it was an auto accident."

The widow takes a deep breath and lets it out slowly. "Something was wrong with Frankie. He was preoccupied."

"And from that you conclude he was murdered?"

"I know my husband, Mr. Adcock."

"Of course you do. I didn't mean to imply otherwise." This is where I might have mentioned the girl in Frankie's car, but something holds me back. Loyalty to the brotherhood of ballplayers? Maybe I just can't stomach the bullshit about Frankie being "preoccupied." Whatever it is, I resolve to keep that bit buttoned up, at least until I sort out this mess. "Do you have any idea who might have wanted him dead? Did he have gambling debts?"

"Frankie never gambled."

"Drugs?"

"None that I know of."

"I would say it might be the person who was trying to blackmail him, but you have to wonder how they expected to get money from a dead man."

The widow's gaze is insistent, bordering on desperate.

"I assume since you're standing here that you don't want to go to the police."

"I'm not ruling it out," she says. I know she doesn't mean it. I've had clients wield police investigations like a goad, as though the threat would spur me to reach a speedy and amenable conclusion to the case. I just ignore them. If they were in a position to call the police, they would have done so before they called me.

"Let me ask you something, Mrs. Herrera. Do you have any idea who might have sent that link to Frankie's cell phone?"

"Would I be standing here if I knew that?"

"Probably not. But if you had to guess?"

"The guy who made the film was named Steve Doubilet. I guess you'd call him the director, although he didn't do much directing. But, you know, Steve's not a very good suspect."

"Why's that?"

"For one thing, he found Jesus five years ago. I'd lost touch with him by then, but I heard from a friend that he'd been saved. A couple months later he killed himself."

"Just couldn't wait, huh?"

No reaction from the widow. I make a note that she is not amused by wit.

"Who else knew about the film?" I ask.

"Just us. Steve promised Frankie he'd never upload the file."

"Yeah, Frankie said the same thing when he gave me the phone. You must have realized, though, that there was a chance it would get out at some point."

"We figured. But Frankie was in rookie ball. We had nothing to lose."

"So why make the film at all?"

The widow raises her brow. "What's that expression? Young, dumb, and full of . . . ?"

I think back to when I was in rookie ball. Ginny and I were newly married, living in a one-bedroom shit trap in Tucson. It was 110 degrees outside, and the window-unit A/C in our apartment worked only for about ten minutes before it blew the circuit. We used to go to department stores and screw our brains out in the dressing rooms. We did it in a public bus once, too. But that was a more innocent time. People weren't packing video cameras on their cell phones back then.

"Watch the video," she says. It seems like she is going to say more on the subject—she opens and closes her mouth a couple of times—but then she says, totally straight, "You're a good man, Adcock."

"With all due respect, Mrs. Herrera, you don't know that."

"Frankie said if the league were filled with guys like you it would be a much more civilized place."

"He said that?"

"He did."

"Well, that was a nice thing to say."

"Yeah, Frankie surprised me sometimes with his niceness."

I notice for the first time the way the widow's chest presses against the inside of her blouse, stretching the fabric so you can see her bra in the space between the buttons. I can't help wondering what she looks like without clothes. Nude, as Bethany would say. It seems I'll find out soon enough.

"I'll call when I have news," I say. "What's the best number to reach you?"

"You have Frankie's phone," she says. "Let's hope my number is in there."

"Let's hope," I say. I show her out and close the door, and I do not watch her little half-moon ass sway down the hall through the peephole. I promise I do not.

8

So much for sleep. I dial a cappuccino from the machine on my kitchen counter. The device cost me two grand, but it is hardly an indulgence. I would sooner give up my bed. Use it often enough, you don't even need a bed. To be fair, the brew is not as good as they make in the café downstairs, but the convenience is worth it. This I can drink in my underwear.

While watching a dead teammate's wife have sex.

I prop the phone on the kitchen table, sip my coffee, and settle in. When the film begins, a young Maria Herrera is in someone's living room, looking at the camera over one shoulder and then the other, kissy kissy. Her hair is dyed black, which makes her complexion look lighter than it appears in person. She is also younger, of course, but otherwise she's the same woman who was just standing in my front hall. She curls her finger to beckon someone from behind the camera—the film has a kind of shaky, grainy, home-movie conceit. A man in a red nylon tracksuit walks into the frame. However, the shot is set up so that his face is not visible. You can see that he is black, muscular, somewhat overweight. Reminds me of the ball-player Prince Fielder. When Maria Herrera stands before him, you see that he is at least a foot taller and probably outweighs her three to one. She looks up at him, takes hold of the zipper on his jacket, pulls it down. Same with his pants. His endowment is as large as you would expect. The widow kneels down, and the camera comes in for a close-up. After five minutes of polishing the pole, she stands and walks over to an overstuffed leather armchair. She removes her tank top, licks her nipples like ice-cream cones, moons for the camera. She removes her shorts and drapes herself across the chair, legs akimbo. The Prince of Power (back turned to the camera) crouches down between her thighs. She looks down and says in a cloying, girlish voice, "I've never done this before." I laugh in spite of myself. "Don't worry, baby," the Prince says, "I'll be gentle."

Upside, downside, frontside, backside: you know the routine. After twenty minutes you start to wonder how much longer it will be before the Prince anoints her with his royal jelly. Then a telephone rings. Maria reaches over and fetches a massive, bricklike cellular from the side table. She pulls up the antenna and flips it open. "Hello?" she says. "Oh, hi, Pablo. No, I'm not doing much. Why don't you come over?" The big guy stops thrusting for a minute, asks who it was. "Just my cousin," she says. "He's coming over."

"Cool," says the Prince, "I'm sure we can find something for him to do."

A minute later, you hear a doorbell, then footsteps. A new man walks onto the set. His face, too, is kept out of the shot. Quickly he sheds his clothes, and Maria Herrera kneels between the two gentlemen, a cock in each hand. A few minutes later, she changes positions so the new guy is on her back door. The shot tightens around their midsections—hers is the smooth unblemished brown of a Coppertone ad, his thick with ropy muscle, a few pimples, and an amateurish tattoo. The camera pans out a bit and I see that the tattoo reads "Granma" in crude Old English script.

I nearly drop my cappuccino.

I rewind to the moment when Pablo enters the apartment, replay the banter between the "cousins." No question, the male voice belongs to Frankie Herrera.

My mind races to the consequences: Bay Dogs management would have been furious if this clip hit the Internet. Frankie's endorsement deals, if he had any, would have been terminated as well. No energy drinks or breakfast cereals want to be associated with a porn star.

The trouble, as Frankie surely understood, was that the video was already online. Its only saving grace was the anonymity of a DIY porn site. All it would have taken to ruin Frankie Herrera was for someone to identify the actors and post the link on a Bay Dogs message board. Anyone who had ever seen Frankie Herrera in his underwear—years of teammates and half the sportswriters in the Bay Area, for starters—would have recognized him instantly.

I pick up the phone and call Bethany's office. Her assistant, a deadpan Korean American kid fresh out of Harvard, answers on the first ring.

"Good morning, Johnny," he says. "May I offer congratulations on last night's win? Fifteen runs is six standard deviations from the Bay Dogs' median production."

His tone is astonishingly flat. The voice in a GPS has more affect.

"Thanks, Jun. I guess we got lucky."

"I was going to mention luck, but I was worried it would offend you."

"No offense taken. We'll take luck."

"Just a moment, please, while I transfer you."

When she comes on the line, Bethany sounds as busy as always. I hear men chuckling in the background.

"Done with the Latin babe?" she says. "I thought for sure you'd beg fatigue."

"It was Maria Herrera," I say. "Frankie Herrera's widow."

I assume she cups her hand around the phone, because the background noise is suddenly gone. "Wow, John. Is she already auditioning replacements?"

"Listen, I have to be at the park in half an hour. Do you still have that project with the morgue? The one where you take DNA from stiffs."

"You mean DataShape?"

DNA collection was only one part of the company's business. A minor part, if I recall Bethany's explanation correctly. The project that got her to pull out her wallet was DataShape's operations at the sewage-treatment plant. Someone at Data-Shape got the idea that if you were to sequence human DNA from a city's raw sewage, you could assemble a statistically representative model of human genetic diversity. According to Bethany, this has plenty of valuable implications—for example, the ability to pinpoint genetic variations that cause diseases. If you find that 1.91 percent of the DNA in the sample has a particular genetic mutation, you might look for a disease that also occurs in 1.91 percent of the population. This is called analytics. It's not just for ranking draft picks.

"First of all, Johnny, it's not a project, it's an investment. I am on the board of DataShape. I don't work there. Do you understand the difference?"

"Could you work there if you wanted to?"

"If you don't tell me what you want in five seconds, I am hanging up."

"Okay—I need to find out who was in the car with Frankie Herrera. The girl. I need her name."

"There was a girl in the car with Herrera?"

"It's a long story. The police are calling her an 'unrelated minor.'"

"So you want me to go to the morgue and pose as an employee of DataShape."

"If it wouldn't be too inconvenient."

"What's in it for me?"

Fortunately, I am prepared for this question. "I watched the video," I say.

"And?" Bethany is trying to mask the curiosity in her voice. And failing.

"It was surprising," I say. "Surprisingly good."

"Oh yeah?"

"It kind of put me in the mood."

"Fine," she says, "but this is the last time."

"You always say that."

"I always mean it."

"Then why do you—"

"Do I have to spell it out?"

"I don't know, it might be nice to hear."

"Goodbye, Johnny."

9

There are two pieces of news when I arrive at the clubhouse later that morning. First is that the new backup catcher has arrived from our triple-A affiliate in Riverside. Sad how quickly we are replaced. Already the kid has made himself comfortable in Frankie's old locker. In the major leagues, lockers do not look like the ones you used in high school. In fact, they do not even have locks. Picture a wide, open-faced booth with a bar for hanging clothes, a chair or two for entertaining guests, and, in the case of our friend Modigliani, a flat-screen TV. The rookie will be allowed no frills, but you can tell he feels pampered just by the space. He has taped up photos of his folks—an overweight and sunburned couple on vacation in Hawaii—and an innocent-looking brunette who might be his girlfriend but could just as easily be his sister. On the shelf above the clothes bar, he has arranged a mini-library of self-help titles: *The Seven Habits of Highly Effective Athletes, The Purpose-Driven Career,* and so on. I see that he also has a few detective novels up there, classics like Chandler's *The Long Goodbye,* James M. Cain's *Double Indemnity,* and Dashiell Hammett's San Francisco classic, *The Maltese Falcon.* The spines look worn. I am impressed, but not enough to break my stride. The kid sits with his head down, intent on a text message. I try to walk past unnoticed, but he feels me somehow.

"Hey, Johnny Adcock!"

His exuberance reminds me of my daughter, Isabel, at two years old, the time I took her to Disneyland and she met Cinderella in the flesh.

"That's me."

The kid puts out his hand. "Jerry Díaz. I can't tell you how excited I am to meet you. I'm a huge fan."

Díaz is a stocky kid, another Ninja Turtle, maybe five ten and two hundred pounds. His dark hair is cut military-short, and his cheeks are rosy and dimpled when he smiles. His voice is colored by a surprising country-and-western twang.

"Díaz, huh? Where you from?"

"Fort Stockton, Texas, sir. It's about halfway between El Paso and—"

"I know where it is. I played in the Texas League once upon a time."

"I grew up on a ranch out there."

"Yeah, I heard your voice, and figured—"

"You figured what? That I wasn't a wetback? Thing is, my family has been ranching in Pecos County longer than yours has been in this country, so—"

"I was just asking where you're from."

"Damn it, I didn't . . ." Frustrated, he mumbles, "Can we start over? I'm really sorry I jumped on you. I was hoping to make a good impression, and now I've screwed it up."

"Look, kid, don't get too comfortable here. Chances are you'll be bounced between the bigs and triple-A half a dozen times before you stick. Happened to all of us."

"I know that, sir. I am totally prepared for that eventuality. It's just that . . ." He pauses, looks me in the eye. His sincerity is flattering, but it also makes me uncomfortable. "When I say

I'm a big fan, Mr. Adcock, I'm not referring to your pitching. That is to say, you're a great pitcher and all, but . . . Aw, damn, I really jacked this, didn't I?"

"I think I see where you're heading."

"You do?"

"Sure, but the answer is no. I work alone."

"I wasn't asking—Mr. Adcock, please believe me that I wasn't asking for you to take me on, or not right away. I want to learn from you however I can. I mean, you're famous! Everybody in baseball knows what you do. I want to be a major-league catcher for sure, but I want more, if you hear what I'm saying."

"I hear you. And the answer is still no."

"Okay, okay. I came on too strong. Something I got to work on, I know." The kid steps around his chair and into the aisle. He puts out a thick, callused hand. A rancher-turned-catcher's hand. "I'm just damned glad to meet you, Mr. Adcock."

"Welcome aboard, Díaz. Like I said, don't get too comfortable."

I cross to the end of the aisle. My locker is relatively spartan—just a school photo of Isabel, an unopened bottle of B vitamins from Ginny, and a charger for my phone. I plug in the phone and begin changing out of my street clothes. My white home uniform, number 39, hangs from the bar, laundered and pressed. I wonder if young Díaz realizes that he belongs to one of the largest castes on earth—workers in uniform. At the low end, our group includes maids and fast-food cooks, janitors and airline baggage handlers. It moves on to nurses, members of the military, cops, and firefighters. At the very top, even higher than pilots, are professional athletes. Basketballers earn the most at present—an average of $5.75 million per year. Baseball players average three and a third. But no major-league ballplayer earns less than the league minimum of four hundred grand. That includes Díaz (although his salary will be prorated because he was called up midyear). Is it right that a twenty-year-old kid makes more than San José's chief of police? You could argue that he deserves it, based on the value our society places on entertainment. Hell, for an autographed bat, the chief might make the argument himself.

I am lacing up my cleats when Phil Sutcliffe comes to see me. Like all pitching coaches, Sutcliffe is a compulsive counter. To a certain extent this pathology makes sense—someone needs to keep track of how many pitches we have thrown—but Sutcliffe, in my opinion, takes it too far. He wears a pedometer on his belt, a little electronic fob emblazoned with a black-and-yellow Bay Dogs insignia. Between innings you see him looking down at the thing, as though his fitness hinges on the number of times he paces the dugout over nine innings. We joke in the bullpen that he gives his wife a hundred pumps a night—no more and no less—and after that he rolls off, whether he has blown his load or not.

"Skip wants to see you," Sutcliffe says. He scratches his lumberjack beard with both thumbs.

"What about?"

"You're not in trouble."

"Why would I be in trouble?"

"Good work last night, Adcock. You looked sharp out there."

I shrug off the compliment, but it is nice to know that someone is paying attention.

"Tell him I'll be right in."

Sutcliffe walks off and I finish lacing. Say what you will about my side job; at least it means I will never have to become a pitching coach.

In the back of the clubhouse, Skipper's office looks like the chief's office on cop shows: a glassed-in cube with venetian blinds for "difficult" meetings. The blinds are open when I

47

arrive, which I take as a good sign. Skipper is hunched behind his desk. The scouting binder on the Padres—there's one for each team—is open in front of him.

"Come in here, Adcock."

He has not even looked up to confirm my identity, but that is one thing about Skipper: he has eyes on the top of his head.

"You wanted to see me, Skip?"

"Sit down and close the door."

I do as I am told. Easing into one of the metal folding chairs, I put my feet up on the corner of the desk.

"Don't do that."

"Sorry—"

"How old are you, Adcock?"

"Thirty-five, sir."

"Pretty old for a ballplayer. My knees were shot by the time I was your age."

Skipper was a catcher in his playing days. Lots of managers were catchers: Connie Mack, Joe Torre, Bruce Bochy, Mike Scioscia. You might say this is because catchers know more about managing a game than any other players—they call the pitches, after all—but I think it is because they don't know what else to do. By the hour, catchers are unquestionably the lowest-paid players on the team. They show up four weeks early for spring training, along with the pitchers, but, unlike us, they don't get to rest four out of five days (or, in my case, eight out of nine innings). Plus, it just takes them longer to suit up, with all the pads and guards and whatnot. My theory is that when it comes time to retire, catchers realize that baseball is all they know. They had no time to learn anything else.

"Arm feels great, Skip. Might be another thirty-five years in it."

"You're a funny guy, Adcock."

"Thank you, sir."

"Not sure that's a compliment. I wonder sometimes about you."

"If this is about my other job, sir, I promise that it never interferes with my playing—"

"Let's keep it that way."

As a representative of Bay Dogs management, Skipper is required to condemn players' side businesses as violations of their contracts. I've always wondered how he really feels. From what I hear, he's kept himself out of trouble. He would appear to have no vested interest in stamping me out. But he's never expressed any support, either.

"Adcock, what I'm sitting here wondering is this: didn't you ever want to be a closer?"

"Excuse me?" This was the last question I was expecting to hear, but my answer comes quickly: "I'm a setup man, sir. I have always been a setup man, and I'd like to think I'm a good one."

"And I'm glad to have you. Plenty of times I've thanked God you were out there warming up when the other team had some left-handed gorilla waiting on deck. But I worry that maybe we've taken advantage of you. Denied you a promotion, as they say in the world of suits and ties."

"I don't think so, Skip. Besides, we've got a closer. Big Bob's got that role nailed down."

"What would you say if I told you Bob Schneider was on his way out?"

"I would say I'm surprised."

"Really?"

"Well, Schneider's not the brightest bulb in the box, but he throws hard, and he never complains. Plus, this is only his second year in the bigs, so he comes cheap, if you're into that sort of thing."

"What if I told you he hurt his thumb again?"

"Same way?"

"Yep."

Big Bob Schneider has a notorious—and, in terms of his pitching career, dangerous—addiction to video games. His thumbs are plagued by cramps. Last fall, his first in the major leagues, he landed on the fifteen-day disabled list with a sprained palm. Most of us had never heard of such an injury.

"Dipshit was jerking off on the PlayStation," Skipper explains. "What are they up to now, PS Four? Seems like I buy one of those things every year for my grandsons. Anyway, the trainers think he might have torn a ligament this time."

"Did they do an MRI?"

Skipper holds my eyes. "They did."

"And?"

"The results were not good."

"Ah, shit . . ."

"So you see I've got to promote someone fast."

"What about Garcia?"

Malachy Garcia is one of our long-relief men—someone to call if the starter gets in trouble before the sixth inning. A side-armer in the mold of Dennis Eckersley, Garcia throws only two pitches, a fastball and a slider, but they operate more like six pitches, because of the different arm angles he uses. He comes from San Pedro de Macorís, a village in the Dominican Republic that has produced more professional baseball players per capita than any other spot on earth.

"Garcia is an option," Skipper says, "but I want to be fair about this. You have been with the club longer. The opportunity should be yours if you want it."

"I appreciate the consideration, Skip, but I think I'm happy where I am."

"What if I said it has been decided already, and you are the new closer?"

"That would be your prerogative, sir."

"Maybe so, but the fact is, this is my choice. If I say you're the closer, then you're the closer."

"That's what it means."

"And if I say you're not, then you're not."

"Right."

Skipper stares at me hard, his pale eyes so still they're shaking.

"So am I the closer?" I say.

"Damn it, yes! And you should be happy about it. Closer is a big deal. The front office will want to talk to you, take some new promo photos, that sort of thing. You ever been on the side of a public bus before?"

"I don't think so."

"Well, get ready. It's going to be loud."

10

Skipper was right, of course: closer is a big deal. Outside his office, a young front-office employee in a jacket and tie is already waiting for me. He has a goatee, and the edge of some kind of a dragon tattoo is visible above his collar.

"Mr. Adcock? I'm Buzzy from Marketing. Do you think I could have a few minutes of your time?"

Tattooed Buzzy takes me upstairs to the club level, where the team has its front office. One of the rooms up there has been turned into a kind of photo studio, with lots of bright lights and two armchairs set in front of a navy-blue backdrop.

"This won't take half an hour," the kid tells me as he leads me to one of the chairs. "I'm just going to ask you a few questions to get you talking. It doesn't matter if it makes sense; our guys will cut it up anyway."

He goes behind the camera and pushes a few buttons. The lights come on even brighter, and I have to squint.

"Just act natural," Buzzy says.

I take off my cap and smooth down my hair. "Like this?"

"Fine. Now I'm going to start asking the questions, and I want you to answer them in complete sentences. Like, if I ask you where you're from, you say, I'm from . . . and then where you're from. Got it?"

"I know what a complete sentence is."

"Sure you do. So tell me, what is your name?"

"My name is Johnny Adcock."

"And where are you from?"

"I'm from Los Angeles, California."

"I bet you were a Dodgers fan growing up."

"I was a Dodgers fan growing up."

Buzzy gives the obligatory boos and hisses. I wait for the next question.

"So why did you become a pitcher?"

"I became a pitcher—"

I stop. Why did I become a pitcher? There's the line I usually give, Dad's bit about left-handed relievers never being out of work. And that's part of it. But there is more.

"I guess it's because I hate waiting around," I say. "All the other positions are about waiting. But the pitcher has the ball. Nothing happens until he moves. Everyone waits for him."

The kid frowns.

"Do you have anything else, any other reasons? Like maybe something your grandfather taught you on his farm or something?"

I wind up. Lean back. Kick my leg and deliver.

"Well, Buzzy, my dad always said if I wanted to make some easy money I should be a left-handed pitcher. . . ."

"Ha! That's great! Now could you say it again with more energy? You looked a little sad just then."

"I don't think so."

"Pretty please? And then I'll let you go?"

"I'm not that kind of guy. Sorry."

I put on my cap and walk out, sure I've thrown a monkey wrench into Buzzy's works—and feeling satisfied, too. Let him collar fucking Modigliani if he wants that kind of interview. What does my childhood have to do with winning ballgames? This is precisely the reason why I resisted this "opportunity" so long. You want an answer, Skip? There it is: I don't do interviews unless I am asking the questions.

11

I'll give Buzzy one thing: he works fast. The game starts at 1:05 p.m., and it turns out to be a pitchers' duel. Our starter, Ben Osmond, has a perfect game going until the Padres string together a couple of singles in the fifth. Our lineup scatters a handful of hits over the first few innings, but the only run of the game comes in the seventh, when Chichi Ordoñez, our leadoff man, reaches on an error and then steals second. The next guy grounds out to first, moving Ordoñez over to third. Finally, Modigliani lifts a long fly to center, which is caught but allows Ordoñez to tag up and score. One run, no hits: classic Bay Dogs baseball.

In the bottom of the eighth, with the score still 1–0, Sutcliffe sends me out to warm up. In San José the home team's bullpen is in foul territory behind third base. When you go to warm up, you take someone with you to guard the bullpen catcher from foul balls. On my way up the dugout steps, I tap Díaz on the shoulder.

"Grab a glove," I say.

"Me?"

"Warm-up time."

As I toss the ball back and forth with the bullpen catcher—who is a coach, by the way, not a player—I see Díaz losing himself in the action on the diamond. He is watching every pitch, every checked swing, every pickoff attempt, as though it is game seven of the World Series. I used to be that way. Right now all I can think about is Frankie Herrera. Poor guy signed with the Bay Dogs organization out of high school, spent the better part of a decade in the minors. Years of traveling by bus, sleeping in shitty motels, cashing laughable paychecks. Then he finally makes the big-league club, and a year later he's dead. He must have been grateful for a taste of the limelight, but it also seems cruel.

I force myself to perform the usual warm-up routine, starting easy and gradually increasing the speed on the fastball, finally tipping the glove to signal an off-speed pitch or two. When I'm loose enough, I stop and slip my left arm into a jacket. Our guys go down in order, and suddenly it is time to go to work.

I have not pitched a ninth inning all season. Have not pitched one in four years, to be exact. I give my jacket to Díaz and jog out to the mound. They are doing the kiss-cam thing on the Jumbotron, where they scan the crowd for likely couples and shame them into making out. It occurs to me that Frankie and his wife might have started out this way. Give or take a few garments, it is basically the same routine.

I am due to face the bottom of the Padres' order in the ninth: the shortstop, the catcher, and the pitcher's slot. Everyone assumes they will pinch-hit for the pitcher, and they have some bruisers on their bench—hoary old guys who can still swing the bat even if they can hardly walk to first base. Pinch-hitters are the only players in the league who work less than me.

I toss my eight warm-up pitches while the crowd howls at the PDA on the Jumbotron. The background music is classy: "Feel Like Making Love" by Bad Company.

Then the music stops, and I hear my own voice come over the public-address system:

"My name is Johnny Adcock. I'm from Los Angeles, California."

I turn around and see my face three stories tall on the center-field screen.

"The pitcher has the ball. . . . I hate waiting around. . . . I'm not that kind of guy. . . ."

The tape rewinds and repeats the last phrase three more times, with a scratched-record sound effect between each: "I'm not that kind of guy. [*Zweep!*] I'm not that kind of guy. [*Zweep!*] I'm not that kind of guy. . . ."

The crowd is silent, unsure how to react. To be honest, I am not sure myself. It appears that Buzzy from Marketing is trying to present me as a kind of rebel. On the face of it, the quote makes no sense: the definition of a closer is someone who waits around—i.e., till the ninth inning—but I can admit that it sounds vaguely badass.

Then the screen goes black and the music starts: "Kashmir" by Led Zep. As the volume swells, a yellow-and-black "SJ" appears on the screen, pulsing in time with the punishing beat. The announcer comes on: "Now pitching for your San José Bay Dogs . . . John-ny Ad-cock!"

I am startled to find the crowd cheering for me. My name is nothing new to them. Promoting me to closer is like giving your children their old toys for Christmas. But Buzzy from Marketing knows his business. Christmas is not about toys, it's about wrapping paper.

The ump calls for the batter, and the Padres' shortstop steps into the box. He is right-handed—yes, a righty!—and is one of these guys with an "open stance," which means he points his left foot toward third base, showing me the letters on his chest. I am sure it is a psychological trick invented by batting instructors—something to take the guy's mind off the real business of swinging the bat. I find it hard to believe that such a dumb-looking stance is actually good for your swing. He looks like a goddamn penguin.

Anyway, this silly penguin drives my first pitch into the gap in left-center for a stand-up double.

Ahem. Who hates waiting around? Who is not that kind of guy?

The crowd is now silent.

I have no one to blame. Modigliani called for a fastball low and inside. It was exactly what I had been thinking, and that is what I threw. It was not a bad pitch, either. It would have hit the mark if the bat had not gotten in the way.

I circle the mound, pick up the rosin bag, bounce it a couple times in my hand. I look over at second base, where the runner is chatting with Ordoñez, our shortstop. Ordoñez toes the ground with his cleat.

The Padres' catcher steps in. He is a switch hitter, so he bats righty against me. I throw out of the stretch, checking the runner twice before delivering. The batter fouls off a decent fastball. I get a new ball, rub it between my palms. Modigliani calls for a slider, but I shake him off. Marcus would be proud. I keep shaking my head until he calls my pitch: a fastball, low and inside. Best pitch for avoiding the sacrifice bunt.

But the batter's not bunting. He turns and smacks it through the left side of the infield, past Ordoñez's outstretched glove. The left fielder charges in, scoops it up, and fires home, but the runner, who was going on contact, easily beats the throw.

In the meantime, the gimpy catcher takes an extra base. Once again, I have a runner on second with no outs.

Sutcliffe comes out to talk to me.

"You look nervous," he says. "Everything okay?"

"Why'd you shake off the slider?" Modigliani asks. It is just the three of us in the huddle, but I can see whose side he's on. "The slider was the thing," he says. "I called for the slider, asshole."

"Easy, buddy," Sutcliffe says. He taps Modigliani on his chest pad. "You do your job, and Adcock does his. Are we straight?"

"Straight," I say.

Modigliani has no choice but to lower his mask and trot back.

As predicted, the Padres send up a pinch-hitter, Jim Rambus. Rambus was once an everyday player, a first baseman for St. Louis and Philadelphia. When his knees gave out, he moved to the American League and did a couple of DH gigs. Now he is back in the NL, and this is widely believed to be his last lap. He never hit for average, but in his prime he was good for thirty homers a year—along with four times as many strike-outs. The key with a guy like Rambus is to prevent him from getting the bat on the ball. He does not make contact very often, but when he does, it travels.

I start by pushing him back with three straight fastballs on the hands. Lucky for me, he fouls two back, putting me up in the count, one ball and two strikes. At this point, the crowd wakes up. In the field boxes behind the plate, a few patriots stand up and start clapping. Modigliani calls for the logical next step in our strategy: a pitch on the outside corner. I shake him off. He tries all my pitches—fastball, changeup, slider—asking for each of them outside. Finally, he gives in. He sets up on the inside corner, left knee hidden behind the batter.

I don't know exactly what happens next, whether it is an honest slip or what, but I plant the pitch square in the big man's back. He drops his bat, flexes his still-massive shoulders, shakes his head. As he trots to first, I think I see him smile.

And that's it for me. Skipper walks slowly from the dugout. He steps carefully over the foul line. The organ plays something cheerful—no "Kashmir" now.

"Maybe you were right," Skipper says as I hand him the ball.

"Yeah," I say, "I don't know what happened."

"Sure you don't," he says.

Skipper raises his right hand, and Malachy Garcia races in from the bullpen.

12

So my career as a side-of-the-bus man is over before it starts. After the game, I am surprised to find that even though I never wanted to be the closer, the failure stings. It was a humiliating performance, and I wasn't lying to Skipper: I don't know what happened. Just because I don't want to be the closer doesn't mean I like giving up runs.

I have been in this position before. I never wanted to be a husband until I ruined my marriage. Okay, maybe "ruined" is too strong a word. The official line is that Ginny and I married too early. We have come to accept this explanation for the sake of simplicity (and also because it comes with a ready-made lesson for our daughter), but what actually happened is much more complicated. We met in college at Cal State Fullerton. Our age certainly contributed to our demise as a couple, but maybe more important was the fact that Ginny never graduated. After I got my signing bonus from the Bay Dogs, she decided it was senseless to keep dragging herself to lectures and labs. She had been majoring in leisure studies, which is a ridiculous name for a major but was actually the most efficient path to achieving her ambition of running a nature camp for needy children. It was hard to escape the name, though: if she was going for a degree in leisure, why not just drop out and start practicing? My signing bonus made that possible. We bought a small house near her parents in Culver City, and Ginny stopped taking the pill. It had always given her headaches, and, really, what was the point? Her mother had gone through menopause at forty and warned Ginny and her sisters not to wait to have children. So, when she missed her first period three months later (I was by that point playing rookie ball in the Arizona League, flying her in once a month to take the edge off), we decided to go for it. We got married after a day game in Vegas, and when the season was over, I returned home a married man.

I became resentful nearly right away. Here I was, twenty-two years old, locked down for life. During the season, it had been exciting having a steady girl. We met in hotel rooms, hotel bars, rental cars. The foreign players on the team especially envied my situation—their girls could never get visas to visit them in the States. I felt lucky. But when I got home to Culver City, it felt like something else: Ginny and her mother had painted the second bedroom yellow (we were not going to find out the sex of the child) and dolled it up with furnishings—bassinets and changing tables and musical mobiles and diaper cans and wet-wipe warmers—that I knew existed but thought I would not own until much later in life.

Of course, when Izzy was born, I loved the hell out of her. But I was always on the road. Every time I saw her, she was another couple months older. She had a new word, a new tooth, a new friend at playgroup. Ginny changed quickly, too. At first she embraced the mom thing like nothing else, becoming the leader of Izzy's playgroup, hatching plans with some of the other moms for a line of sexy lace nursing bras. But Ginny is just as restless as me, and none of it stuck. By the time Isabel turned one, Ginny was talking about going back to school, but we had no one to watch the baby. Ginny's mom was still working full-time, and we couldn't afford a nanny. (I was earning a minor-league salary, the bonus money spent long ago on the house and the conjugal visits.) I asked her to wait a bit longer. Frustrated and angry, she began drinking to pass the time. Even worse than the drinking, she began to think of me as the cause of her stalled ambition. I couldn't defend myself, because I was playing ball seven nights a week on the other side of the country. I had moved up to double-A, playing home games in Richmond, Virginia. For a player aged twenty-three and a half, double-A was not bad. I could see a path to the majors in a year or two. But I was not allowed to feel any pride. My phone, my e-mail, my voice mail—all were filled to capacity with bile from my wife, three time zones away, drunk, with a screaming baby in the background. It started to affect my concentration on the mound. The pitching coach suggested that I "mute" her. ("Worked for me in the Marine Corps," he said, "and it was my fucking life on the line there, not a game in the double-A standings.") I took his advice and stopped returning Ginny's calls. At first the volume of messages increased, but then it slackened off. My pitching improved, and by the end of the summer I had been called up to triple-A—the last step before the big leagues.

I finished out the season with the triple-A Riverside Iguanas, posting an earned-run average in the low twos and putting together a twenty-five-inning scoreless streak (just luck, really). I started listening to the buzz, heard talk of trades in which I was mentioned in the same breath as major-league players I had watched on TV. I came home a conquering hero, dick swinging like an elephant's trunk.

And my key did not open the front door.

Since then I have learned that very few marriages survive the minor leagues. What Ginny and I went through—rather, what I put us through—is second only to military deployments in the number of divorces it provokes. The combination of uncertainty and estrangement is tough on even the strongest bonds. For the tenuous union between Ginny and me, it was death.

I made the big-league club midway through the next season, bouncing back and forth between Riverside and San José several times (just as I described to Díaz). The following spring, I made the opening-day pitching staff, and I have never looked back.

Never about baseball, that is. I have tried to be as clear-eyed as possible about my marriage. I try never to forget that I probably would have stalled out in Virginia if I had not blocked out my wife. She was desperate, raising a baby by herself, feeling trapped and isolated. She needed me, but I was on the other side of the country with my own set of problems. Ultimately, I made a choice. Part of me still cannot believe I did it, because there was no guarantee I would regain my confidence on the mound. I might just as easily have lost both my wife and my career. I consider myself lucky that one of the two panned out.

So, yeah, I realize that I will probably regret blowing my chance to be the closer. But in the decade since my divorce, I have learned not to put all my eggs in one basket, even if doing so means a broken heart. And a second job hunting down blackmailers.

The beat writers want a word with me after the game. Besides the usual shit about how it felt to blow the game, they want me to expand on the comments in Buzzy's interview montage.

"Hey, Johnny—what does that mean, you hate waiting around?"

"It means I've got to get out of here, guys."

"Sure, Johnny, but give us a sentence at least. What does it mean that you're not that kind of guy?"

"Whatever I meant when I said those words, it's not what

they mean now. You know how it is, fellas, they cut and paste like scrapbookers up there."

"I can't use that, Johnny. Gimme something else."

"How about this: Johnny Adcock says he's glad to be a setup man."

I grab my coat, unplug my phone from the charger. There is a missed call from Marcus.

"Really, guys. Tomorrow."

"Fine, Johnny, okay . . ." The reporters' attention fizzles away from me like a fuse. "Hey," I hear one of them say, "where is that new kid, the backup catcher? I have been meaning to get some color on him. . . ."

13

The next morning, three days after Frankie Herrera's death, his funeral is held in a dark and dour Catholic church in Los Gatos, a tony suburb in the foothills southwest of San José. A house here runs about two million dollars. I'm pretty sure Los Gatos was chosen because it's the home of the Eberhardts, the family that owns the Bay Dogs. Frankie Herrera had no family in the Bay Area—his people are all in southern California—but if he did, Los Gatos is the last place I'd expect to find them.

The widow Herrera is in the front pew, flanked by her twin sons. She's wearing a tight-fitting black skirt suit and a veil. The pew also contains an older couple I assume are her parents, or maybe her in-laws. The Bay Dogs contingent fills most of the other seats. All the players are in attendance, along with the coaches, front-office staff, and various members of the Eberhardt family. Rumor has it that the Eberhardt fortune dates back to the gold rush, but I have always thought ladies' footwear is a more likely bet. The current scion is Richard L. Eberhardt, a spoiled but ultimately benign middle-aged child—a Californian Prince Charles. Mr. Eberhardt sits next to his latest wife, a twenty-eight-year-old blonde named (I kid you not) Laura Ashley. From the looks of it, they've been busy: Ms. Ashley is sporting a baby bump.

Because Frankie hadn't been with the team that long, the eulogy is given by a player who knew him in the minor leagues, a young outfielder named White.

"Frank Herrera was many guys all at once," White says. "He was a ballplayer first of all, but he was also a husband, a father, and a businessman."

A couple of the guys in my pew snicker at the word "businessman," even though the speaker hadn't meant it to be funny. I want to reach over and clock them. Silence is an underrated virtue, but there are a few instances where it is absolutely essential. A funeral, for example. I know very little about Frankie's life outside baseball, but what I do know suggests he was a selfless and energetic member of his community, both here and in Mexico. He didn't have to build a baseball field in Sonora. Plenty of athletes make millions and give nothing back.

The outfielder continues, "After games, on the road, in the middle of the night, Frankie was always there to listen. His friends would do anything for him. And he had friends in every city, it seemed like. Anyone who knew him understood that Frankie loved bringing people together."

Another snicker from the assholes in my pew. Look, I get it: "bringing people together" could mean that Frankie enjoyed female companionship. I understand that you can't say that in front of the guy's wife, but still I wish these guys had the decency to shut their mouths.

After a perfectly competent rendition of "Eagle's Wings" by the church organist, the mourners form a line to pay their respects. The casket is closed—a smart move, given the scene I saw on Highway 92—and propped on a cart before the altar. One by one, we pass before Frankie's remains. The widow and the twins stand off to the side, receiving condolences. The Latin players make a big show of kneeling and crossing themselves, muttering prayers in Spanish even before they reach the front of the line. When my turn comes, I put my left hand on the casket and bow my head. A few seconds later, I straighten up and walk over to the widow.

"I'm so sorry," I say. "We're all going to miss him." I lean in to give her a hug—the polite kind, where you pat the other person's back and leave room for the Holy Spirit. But as I'm patting, I feel something between my legs. For a minute I think it's one of the twins horsing around, but then I realize it's the widow's hand. She's cupping my balls. Or maybe grabbing them. I can't tell if it's a gesture of flirtation or aggression. I lean back. The look on her face offers no clues. Her wide, dark eyes are intent; her mouth is tight and small. The expression could mean "Let's fuck" as easily as "I own you." Sometimes the two go hand in hand. Or balls in hand, as the case may be. I would never sleep with her, but I'm tempted. Six years and two babies since she made that film, and she hasn't lost a drop of the juice. But even if she's coming on to me—it's a funeral, what does she expect?

"Any progress?" she whispers.

"Stay tuned," I say. "It's early days."

This is not the answer she was hoping to hear. She squeezes my nuts.

"What the—?"

"Work faster," she says.

I understand she's upset, so I repeat my promise to do everything I can, adding (because she has me by the balls) that I will work as quickly as possible, but that, like her late husband, I am a professional ballplayer with a busy schedule.

With her other hand, she reaches up and strokes my cheek.

"Oh, Adcock," she whispers, "I know you won't let us down." She gives my balls one last tug, then lets them swing free.

The team has chartered a bus to take us home from the funeral—home being the ballpark, where batting practice awaits. I'm slouched in a rear seat, reading the paper, when the phone rings.

"You need to get your ass down here," Marcus says.

"I'm on the bus," I say, "but I've got my bike at the park. Let me see if I can sneak away for a few minutes."

"No—I'm not at the restaurant."

"Where are you?"

"L.A."

"L.A.?"

"Yeah, I found Bam Bam."

"No shit, that was fast. How is he?"

"He'd be a lot better if he wasn't dead."

"How do you know he's dead?"

Marcus snorts. "How do I know? Because I just fucking shot him, that's how."

14

After my shaky debut as a closer, Skipper doesn't owe me any favors. But when was the last time you needed a favor from someone who actually owed you one?

"My daughter is sick," I say.

Skipper is halfway through his customary pregame plate of linguine. Today is Wednesday, which means clam sauce. I wince as he slurps the greasy noodles, pausing every so often to chew a rubbery morsel of gray mollusk.

"I'm gonna call bullshit here, Adcock."

"Skip, I promise—"

"Spare me. We both know it."

Skipper slurps. "But I'll tell you what," he says, "let's make a deal. We go to L.A. the day after tomorrow."

"Right. But you know, I keep thinking about Herrera, wondering if he got to say goodbye to his kids—"

"I talk, then maybe you talk. Got it?"

I nod.

"How about this. How about I let you go—I can repeat that disgraceful lie about your daughter if you like, or I can come up with something better—and then you rejoin the club when we get to L.A."

"What's the catch?"

"The catch is that when you come back you quit this pussy-footing and man up to the role I gave you."

"You mean being the closer?"

"Don't be an idiot, Adcock! What the hell were you doing out there? You may have fooled the frigging Padres, but you didn't fool me. I know you were trying to throw the game. And let me remind you, that is a capital offense."

Skip played for the Reds in the mid-eighties, when Pete Rose was player-manager. He took the lessons of Charlie Hustle very seriously—the bad as well as the good.

"I wasn't sandbagging out there, Skip. It was bad luck."

"Bad luck, my ass. You don't want to be our closer, fine. But here's news for you, Johnny: we don't always get to do what we want."

"I know that, Skip. I wasn't trying to fail."

Skipper finishes the noodles. He tears a hunk of garlic bread from the half-baguette the kitchen provides with his meal. He uses this like a sponge to mop up the oil on his plate.

"This is the deal I'm offering you," he says. "Take it or leave it, but there are plenty of arms in the minors perfectly willing to do what they're told."

15

Half past midnight, my plane touches down at LAX. I turn my phone back on and see that I have a text from Bethany. Two words: *Call me.*

Her voice is garbled, which worries me until I remember that she swims two-a-days on Wednesdays. She is back in the pool, talking to me on her waterproof throat mike. She says that because of the poor sound quality—it is an early-stage prototype from a company she has funded—she uses the apparatus only on calls where she is expected to speak very little, like board meetings. The fact that she takes my call suggests her news must be important.

"Hello, Johnny? [*Gowmp! Gowmp!*] Johnny, can you hear me?"

"Roger that, deep-sea diver."

"Johnny [*Grrrrimp!*], I went to the San Mateo coroner. [*Krrrz-gowmp!*] Can you hear me?"

I try to speak as slowly as I can: "The name, Bethany—tell me the girl's name. That is all I need."

"Yeah, that's the thing, Johnny. She has lots of names. They ran the prints [*Grrrgle grrrgle*], and this girl is known as Luisa Valdez, Alejandra Sol, and one more [*Gowmp!*] that I can't remember right now. I will e-mail it to you when I get home."

"Don't e-mail anything! Do you hear me? Something has happened."

"Where are you?"

"I'm in L.A."

"Why L.A.? [*Gowmp!*]"

"Marcus is here."

"But you have a game."

"It's okay. Skipper knows. Listen, Bethany, I want you to go home and stay there. As a favor to me."

"What happened, Johnny? [*Grrrrkle!*] Tell me what happened."

"Nothing—a guy down here was killed. A pornographer. Nobody important."

"Do you know who [*Gowmp!*] killed him?"

"I have some idea. So are you going home after this?"

"Yes [*Grrkle grrkle*], yes, Daddy."

"You know I don't like it when you call me that."

"Sorry. You should come [*Gowmp! Gowmp!*] and punish me."

"I have to go," I say. "Thanks for going to the morgue."

"No problem [*Splash!*]. It was fun!"

Either she ends the call or her submarine Bluetooth finally gives up. At any rate, I text her a proper thank-you (no specifics, just in case) and grab my bag from the overhead bin.

Three names. A girl with three names is nothing but trouble. You can quote me on that.

Marcus is waiting curbside, leaning against the front fender of a 1972 Cadillac Eldorado coupe, brown paint and a brown vinyl canopy. The hood alone is longer than any other car in sight. I have never been a car guy, but there is a special place in my heart for the Eldo. One of my buddies in high school had one—a gift from his father, who taught auto shop at our high school. It got about six miles to the gallon, but you could lie down flat in the back seat. My buddy and I couldn't understand why the girls didn't flock to him. It was like a bedroom on wheels. We even loaded the ashtrays with condoms.

Before I can ask where he got the car, Marcus tells me it's not his. "Belongs to a friend," he says.

"Does she know you have her car?"

"You think I'm a car thief?"

"Just be careful when you open the doors—they swing wide."

Marcus heads north on Sepulveda into silent, foggy Westchester and begins to tell his story.

"It was like Bam Bam wanted me to find him," he says. "I show up at his office Tuesday morning at ten-thirty, but nobody's there. I go around to the back—but before I do, I take a little something from my girl's glove box, you know what I'm saying, and stuff it down in my pants. Not that I ever thought I would have to use it."

He looks me square in the face and I can see he's pissed. Yeah, I'd be angry, too.

"I go around back, and there's nobody there, neither."

"This his porn company's office?"

"Yeah, Two Lives Video in North Hollywood. Then, all of a sudden, I hear a motorcycle, and this fat dude riding a Kawasaki crotch rocket turns the corner and stops right in front of me. Sure enough, he lifts off his helmet and I see it is Bam Bam, and of course he's surprised to see me. I sense right away that he's coked up or something. He's all smiles and hugs and my-nigga this and my-nigga that. I'm making up some shit about how I was in the neighborhood and heard he was making videos, and he says, 'Oh yeah, come in and see!' So I'm, like, 'Great,' and he unlocks the back door and leads me into his office. It's a plain sort of room, blinds over the windows, lots of flat-screen TVs hanging on the walls. He flips the light switch and all the TVs turn on at once. Each one is playing a different scene. Bam Bam is smiling ear to ear, just all the gladness you can stand, and he says, 'I almost don't miss base-ball.' So we start laughing about old times while these folks are slanging bone on the TVs. I say, 'Hey, Bam Bam, you ever heard of this girl name of Maria Herrera?' And as soon as I say the name, this motherfucker reaches into his jacket and pulls out a fucking nine."

"Like as a joke?"

"I wish. His face is set, man. No more smiles. He lifts up the gun and just kind of admires it for a second. He must have been high. Then he pulls back the slide—"

The Cadillac swerves a little. Marcus has been cool to this point—much cooler than I expected him to be—but this part of the story is hard to tell.

"What did you do?"

"What could I do?"

"Karate?"

"Fuck karate, man! I shot him in the head."

We ride in silence for a moment, then Marcus says, "You realize you owe me."

"I know. Big-time."

"Bigger than big-time. You told me to come down here and find the motherfucker. To find him, not to spray his brains against the wall."

"I know, I'm sorry."

"You are going to make it up to me."

"I will. I promise."

Another few minutes of silence as we roll north. We are not far from the neighborhood in Culver City where Ginny and I had that first house. She doesn't live there anymore; she sold the house years ago and moved to Santa Monica. She said the schools were better in Santa Monica, but then she put Izzy in private school. I never asked why. This is one of the battles I have chosen not to fight.

"Did anyone see you go into Bam Bam's office?"

"I don't think so."

"And did you pick up the casings?"

"Of course. I ditched his gun, too."

"Was anyone in the office when you left?"

"Don't you think I would have told you that?"

"Calm down, Marcus. It's over with, and I said I was sorry. I'm just trying to figure out who might find the body."

"Nobody going to find shit."

I raise an eyebrow. "Why's that?"

"Because I took him with me."

"You what? Where?"

Marcus flips his head back slightly, quickly—the motion he used on those rare occasions when he accepted the catcher's sign. "In the trunk," he says.

16

My professional opinion is that Marcus is too shaky to drive. I reach over and steady the wheel. "Move over," I say. And, just like we used to do in high school, I slip over Marcus's knees into the driver's seat. He slides along the warm Naugahyde to shotgun.

"Did you wrap him up in something?" I say. "A tarp, maybe?"

"No time for that."

"Sounds like I owe your girl a detailing."

Marcus snorts.

We're in West L.A., near the interchange of the 10 and 405. "You know this neighborhood?" I ask Marcus.

"No. You?"

"A little."

I get off at National and turn right. Aside from a few bums loitering in front of a twenty-four-hour Ralphs supermarket, this part of Babylon is fast asleep.

"Look for a church," I say.

"A what?"

"You look right, I'll look left."

"What kind of church you want?"

"Doesn't matter." I pause, reconsider: "Catholic is best."

Five minutes later, Marcus hollers. He reads the shingle out front: "Our Lady of Sorrows Catholic Church. Says they welcome all worshippers."

"Perfect." I haul the Eldo into the dark parking lot and coast around to the back. Behind the church there's a little entrance for the rectory, a mailbox, and a porch light that has been put out for the night. I maneuver the car against the fence at the rear of the lot—far enough from the rectory that the priest won't hear the idling V-8. I put the car in park and cut the lights.

"Give me a hand?" I ask. Marcus leaps out onto the blacktop. We move around to the rear of the Cadillac. I put the key in the trunk and turn the lock; the lid swings up.

I know it's a cliché, but I am surprised by how peaceful Bam Bam looks in death. His eyes are shut—lips, too—and a single dime-sized hole mars his forehead. It looks like he's been rocking a well-kept goatee, sort of a Latin Satan look, but his cheeks now sport a healthy five-o'clock shadow. His head is cocked toward one meaty shoulder. Bam Bam was never a slim character, but I estimate he has put on nearly a hundred pounds since his playing days.

"You got him in here by yourself?" I ask Marcus.

"Guess I was pumped," he says.

"Guess so." I reach in and touch Bam Bam's tattooed wrist. The flesh is cold to the touch. "You want head or feet?"

"Seriously? Feet."

"Okay, count of three."

The body is as stiff as a bundle of two-by-fours, which means my uneven grip on Bam Bam's head and shoulders is good enough. I take care not to let the fingers of my left hand slip too far inside the cavity where the skull was blown out. The brain is cold, too, and firmer than I expected. It will be a long time before I scoop the seeds out of a cantaloupe, that's for sure.

I catch Marcus's eye and nod toward the back door of the

rectory. My plan is a kind of morbid ding-dong ditch—or a twist on Lazarus, if you prefer. We'll drop the body, ring the bell, and speed off in the Caddy. It's not the most graceful plan, but it's the best I can do under the circumstances.

We are standing in front of the door, getting ready to drop the load, when the porch light comes on. I look at Marcus. His eyes go wide, and he breaks for the car, dropping Bam Bam's feet. I drop the other end and follow. Behind me, I hear the door open.

"Hey!" a man's voice says. "What's going on here? What the hell is this?"

I run to the rear of the Cadillac and slam the trunk shut. After I slide into the driver's seat, I look back at the rectory. The door hangs wide open, but the priest—at least I assume he's the priest—is no longer there. I experience a moment of terror as I consider that he might have run around behind us, maybe to get a look at our plates. But then he appears in the doorway: a short, balding man. Thin through the shoulders. From this distance, maybe twenty-five feet, he looks Asian. Then I see he's got a shotgun. He's peeking at the breech, checking the shells.

I throw the transmission in gear and floor it. The parking lot is gravel—that or some seriously decomposed asphalt—and the wheels of the Cadillac spin before catching. The car lurches forward.

"Come back here!" the priest yells. "What do you think this is, Skid Row?"

He fires a shot, but he must have aimed wide, because nothing breaks and the car continues down the driveway. Without checking traffic, I swing a hard left back toward the freeway and narrowly avoid colliding with an oncoming semi truck. Walgreens, it says on the side. Good to know the world will have Q-tips and ChapSticks when they wake up tomorrow.

There's another loud noise as I escape down National Boulevard, maybe another shot from God. Maybe nothing. I don't look back. When we've driven ten minutes, I pull into the deserted parking lot of a medical-office plaza. I idle the car, look at Marcus. "Do you think he saw the plates?" I ask. I feel awful for what we've already done to this girl's car. An APB would be the icing on the cake.

"Hold on," Marcus says. He opens the glove box and removes a Phillips-head screwdriver. "Ain't the real plates, anyway."

"What do you mean?"

"I took some before I picked you up at the airport."

"Took some from where?"

"I don't know—a dump truck or some shit. There's a city yard near my girl's place."

Sure enough, when Marcus returns with the plates, I see that the first digit is an "E" inside an octagon, the symbol for a tax-exempt California government vehicle.

"A dump truck?"

"Or a cherry picker—some big truck. It was dark."

Oh, it was dark, all right. I want to puke. When did my life become so dicey? To this point I've had a comfortable run in the investigation game—cheating spouses, paternity threats, nothing bloody or life-threatening. Now I'm disposing of bodies in the dead of night. To quote my new favorite preacher: "What the hell is this?" Meanwhile, in my real life I've been chugging along for a decade-plus as a setup man—a very comfortable groove, if I say so myself—and now, suddenly, I'm promoted to closer. Why me? I'm not sure I like either of these developments. I feel like a rookie, and as any big-leaguer will tell you, that's about the worst feeling there is.

17

Marcus tells me to head for Hollywood, where he says we can spend the night. "Natsumi loves ballplayers," he says. "Just act cool."

Half an hour later, we're turning onto a quiet, tree-lined street off Fountain, near Hollywood High. I pull the Cadillac into the driveway, leaving it behind a pair of old Volkswagen Beetles, one on blocks. Natsumi's place is a single-story house in the Spanish style, with a tile roof and security bars on the arched windows.

"What about the trunk?" I say. "I read about this cleanser you can use. It contains bacteria that actually digest blood."

"Tomorrow," Marcus says.

Marcus can stay up most nights, but once he hits the wall, he's done. He gives a ten-minute warning, and if he hasn't found suitable bedding in that time, he will sleep where he falls. Aside from the silver hair, this may be the only way he shows his age.

"Hey, baby," he says when the door opens. Like the windows, the door is arched and short, as though the house were built for a family of Hollywood dwarves.

"Y'all later than I thought," says an African American woman in a white shift nightie. She is middle-aged but well preserved, dark-skinned, and on the thin side, with prominent cheekbones and a dazzling smile. "This your friend?"

"Johnny Adcock, meet Natsumi."

I put out my hand. "It's a pleasure," I say. "Thanks for letting Marcus borrow your car. Sorry we're so late—my flight was delayed. Fog, you know."

"Um-hm. I ain't been in the Bay Area for years, but Marcus is always saying he gonna drag me back up there. Ain't you, Marcus?"

"It's late, baby. You got a place where Johnny can crash?"

Natsumi whisks us inside and shuts the door. It takes me a minute to adjust my eyes to low light. The living-room walls are covered with framed posters of Natsumi in boxing regalia— padded headgear, gloves clenched before a snarl. One of the posters is a reproduction of a magazine cover: *Boxing News,* it's called. Natsumi is the cover girl. She's alone in a boxing ring, holding a metallic belt the size of a car's floor mat. If her hairdo is any indication, the photo is at least twenty years old.

"What position you play, Johnny?" she asks me.

"I'm a relief pitcher."

"Course you are. Marcus say you got a little business on the side, too."

"That's right. Just a little something, that's about the size of it."

I look over at my friend and see that he's found the only chair in the room—a cheap-looking plastic folding number in the corner—and is already nodding off.

"You used to box?" I say. "My dad was a boxer."

"Was he, now?"

"Just amateur, but he was serious about it."

"That's the only way to do it. Can't use your fists no other way if you want to live."

"I guess not. Hey, listen, Natsumi, can I ask you something?"

With Marcus gone for the night—thank you, Marcus, you have done your duty for today and many days to come—I decide to air out a question that has been bothering me since I spoke with Bethany.

"Sure, what you want to know?"

"I'm going to go out on a limb here and assume that 'Natsumi' wasn't the name your parents gave you."

It takes her a minute to see I'm not teasing, but then she loosens up. "That's right," she says. "My daddy never even heard of soy sauce." She walks over to the magazine cover and points to the name at the bottom: Linda Jones. "That was me," she says.

"So what makes a woman want to change her name?"

She smiles broadly. "Oh, there's lots of things."

"Give me an example."

"Well, if you getting married, that's one. Same if you getting unmarried. Or if you trying to hide from somebody."

"Yeah, what about that? Since you changed your name, do people look you up less? I know you're not hiding from anyone, but if you were, do you think it would have worked?"

"I wondered that myself. I think the answer is no."

"It didn't hide you?"

"Right. 'Cause I still got lots of people showing up at my door. And not just people who know me from boxing. I'm talking about folks I known my whole life, folks from Oakland and Hollywood and everywhere I been in between. Lord knows how they found me. Seems a person can't stay hidden these days. I think it's the computers."

"Could be."

I am both satisfied and worried by Natsumi's answer, because it is the same conclusion I have reached on my own. This girl, Frankie's passenger, should have known that another name (or another couple of names) would not hide her. Not with fingerprints, DNA, facial recognition. Even if she only knew this stuff from cop shows, she would understand that it was pointless to change her name if her goal was to disappear.

"You know, Johnny Adcock, I wasn't trying to hide from nobody. You want to know the real reason I changed my name to Natsumi?"

"What's that?"

She grins. "Because it sounded pretty."

18

I wake up in Natsumi's spare bedroom. The clock says it is six-thirty in the morning. There is blood crusted along my cuticles and under my fingernails, but my first thought is not to scrub it off but to lie there and do nothing. I have not had a day off in three weeks. I lie inert for another five minutes, because that is what you do on a day off, or so I recall. Finally, I get up and take a shower, helping myself to a towel from the bathroom closet. Afterward I find I'm still the only one up, so I turn on the TV. On the morning news, a reporter with plastic hair speaks earnestly into the camera:

"We are here at the Cathedral of Our Lady of the Angels in downtown L.A., where a crowd of the faithful is gathering. Earlier this morning the archbishop announced via Twitter a major development in his yearlong crusade against crime. Diocese officials are reporting that a body was found at the parish of Our Lady of Sorrows in West Los Angeles this morning, an apparent murder victim. The deceased has been identified as Javier Rodriguez, a Puerto Rican native who went on to play baseball for several major-league teams before embarking on a second career in hard-core pornography. The archbishop's Tweet went as follows, and I quote, 'Welcome back, Javier Rodriguez, from the dominion of Satan. You will always have a home with the Lord. Praise be to God.' A touching story of redemption, here at the Cathedral of Our Lady of the Angels. Now back to you in the studio . . ."

This is even better than I had hoped. I expected that the parish priest would fall in love with Bam Bam, but I had no idea he'd share the news with his boss. And no mention of the fleeing car. Just goes to show that, although you cannot rely on the kindness of strangers, you should not rely on the absence of kindness, either.

I make some coffee and wait for Marcus to wake up. I'm hoping the news about Bam Bam's redemption will settle his nerves. That and whatever art Natsumi practices in her bedroom. I feel bad about putting him in this situation. We have been in some tight scrapes before, but never this bad. Now we're in the shit, as they say. Marcus has shot and killed a man, and I helped dump the body. To be honest, I'm less worried about the law than I am about whoever Bam Bam was running with. I doubt they make an exception for self-defense.

I grab the paper from the front porch and pull out the sports section. The Dodgers lost by one to the Rockies, and I notice that my friend and former roommate George Luck took the L. I played with Luck at Fullerton, where he was drafted by the Dodgers after his junior year. By the time I made triple-A, George was already established in the bigs. In fact, it was George who took me in after Ginny locked me out, when I had nowhere else to go. I remember calling him from a gas station in Culver City, telling him what had happened. The Dodgers were on the road, but he told me where to get a key to his place in Manhattan Beach. I only stayed three weeks, but it was a kindness I will never forget. We texted last week about grabbing a drink after one of the games in this series, but with the Herrera case heating up like this, I am not sure I will have time—unless George is up for more than a beer.

Marcus comes out of the bedroom, rubbing his face with one of his enormous palms. He was one of those pitchers who seemed to be able to wrap their fingers around a baseball twice. Imagine Jimi Hendrix as a pitcher, or Kareem Abdul-Jabbar. The hand is so large, Marcus doesn't see me when he enters the kitchen.

"Good news," I say.

Marcus jumps. He drops the hand, and I see he's got a shiner on his left eye.

"What happened to you?"

"I told Natsumi about the car."

"I thought you said she was cool?"

"She is, but the car was supposed to be a wedding present."

"For whose wedding?"

Marcus looks at me.

"Oh," I say. "I didn't know."

"Course not. I never told nobody."

"I can see how that would be a problem."

"You better leave."

We shake hands, and I pull him in for a hug.

"Good luck," I say.

"You too, Adcock. See you up north."

19

I call a taxi, and the dispatcher says it will be an hour. I think of that old sailors' line: "Water, water, every where, nor any drop to drink." In L.A. there are more cars than human beings—but none for me. When my cab finally arrives, it is a bright-yellow Ford driven by a fifty-something man in a beard. He has a hard-luck complexion but truly stunning blue eyes, to match the Dodgers cap on his head. As I settle into the back seat, I watch his face in the rearview. I wonder how many times those eyes have saved his ass. Or gotten him some.

He catches me looking but thinks I am admiring his cap.

"Dodger fan?" he says.

"Used to be."

"Nah," the man says, "once a fan, always a fan."

I want to point out that, though this is an attractive notion, it is not technically true. A Dodger fan who becomes a member of the San José Bay Dogs, for example, cannot remain a Dodger fan. I have never read my contract all the way through, but I am sure this is covered under Conflicts of Interest, right next to the discouraging words about side businesses. The fans take these rivalries seriously. In California, baseball is a proxy for the very real political tension between north and south. The talk of splitting into two states only crops up seriously every ten years or so, but the Bay Dogs and Dodgers (and Giants, A's, Padres, and Angels) go at it every summer. Five years ago, I might have come clean with the taxi driver and told him who signed my checks. But that was before opening day 2011, when a gang of Dodger fans cornered a fan in a Giants jersey and beat him within an inch of his life. The guy was in a coma for a year and only recently remembered the names of his three kids.

"I need to go to Santa Monica," I say, "Fourteenth and Carlyle—you know where that is?"

"Sure do."

For the rest of the ride—and it is a long, hot forty-five minutes on surface streets—the driver checks his rearview compulsively every couple of minutes, as though he expects me to open the door and leap out without warning. Eventually, we are stopped at a light on the corner of Fourteenth and Montana, in the dappled shade of a magnolia, and the guy lets on: "You're a ballplayer, aren't you?"

I reach for the door handle.

"Don't tell me," he says, "it's on the tip of my tongue . . . Mets?"

"No, sorry."

"Red Sox?"

"No. Hey, the light is green."

He keeps eyeing me in the rearview.

"You know what?" I say. "Just let me out here." On the right is a supermarket that sells eight brands of fig preserves but not a single kind of potato chips. I know this because I have been there, looking for chips.

"Here?" he says.

"Yeah. How much do I owe you?"

I give him the fare plus a twenty, hoping he will drive away fast. I know it's silly—baseball is just a game, right? Maybe I'm just shaken up from last night. At any rate, I roll my suitcase the rest of the way.

Three blocks later, I am standing in front of my ex-wife's house. Here's a riddle: what do you call a home you paid for but do not own? The manicured lawn and flagstone path, the whimsical window treatments and mature fruit trees, the navy-blue BMW in the driveway, which you also paid for (and also do not own). The multicolored porcelain house numbers painted by your daughter and baked at the pottery shop down the street. I remember that, once upon a time, a football player named O. J. Simpson stood in front of a similar house—not so far from here, actually, just a few miles up San Vicente—and what he saw so enraged him that he broke in, dragged his ex outside, and cut her head off. I can think of half a dozen guys who might have been O. J. Simpson if they'd had one more drink on a given night, or if they had struck out just once more, or if that last pitch had been two centimeters to the left. . . .

It is the most common rant you hear on the bus: *My ex wants more money. My ex won't let me see the kids. My ex is getting remarried, and the guy's a total prick.* Let me tell you something: what these guys are struggling with has nothing to do with money, or kids, or even the ex-wife. I'm not making excuses for the crimes of O. J. Simpson—I use him as an example only because everyone knows his name—but the real object of his rage that night was not his wife and her lover but his own failure. He failed at something billions of human beings have managed for centuries, that thing called marriage. The man was one of the five or ten best running backs of all time, and somehow he could not do something an eighty-pound villager in Bangladesh has no trouble with. How does that compute? That is a lot to take for a man so revered that he is known by a single common noun.

The solution, of course, is simple: you have to let it go. Sometimes people fail at simple things, even world-class athletes.

Back in the days of Matt Young (the object of my father's scorn, you remember, the southpaw who bounced home a run on TV), money might have been an issue between players and their exes, but really, these days, there is plenty to go around. Anyone who disagrees is not being honest with himself. Besides, wouldn't you rather give money to your wife, who might share it with your kids, than to some business manager you hardly know, who will probably send it up his nose?

So, yeah, I am standing in front of the house I bought but don't own. Our financial arrangement is maddeningly simple—maddening to my lawyer, that is, who never tires of reminding me it does not have to be this way. What I do is this: I take my salary, minus taxes and the agent's commission, and I divide it into thirds, because there are three of us: Ginny, Isabel, and me. Two-thirds of my net income is wired directly to Ginny, and she is free to spend it however she sees fit. Presumably she spends half on Isabel, not only for clothes and food but also saving for her college education. Just in case she does not do these things, I have another account where I lay away half of my third—one-sixth of my net income—as a rainy-day fund for my daughter. I do this because I would never forgive myself if I should one day tear my rotator cuff and Isabel was destitute because I put too much trust in a woman who once locked me out of my own house.

Not this house, mind you. This one is Ginny's through and through. I have never thought of it otherwise. I think it is important to move houses after a divorce, and I give this advice to anyone who asks. Unfortunately, plenty of people do.

I ring the bell before I realize that Ginny never replied to the text I sent her from the taxi, the heads-up that I was stopping by. It is nine-thirty in the morning. Isabel will be at school. It occurs to me that Ginny might not be home.

But then I hear steps behind the door, the chunking of the lock, and there she is.

"Johnny?"

"Hi, Ginny. May I come in?"

She is barefoot, nails unpainted, wearing black yoga pants that flare a bit at the ankle. Her faded tank top reads MID-NIGHT MADNESS 5K above a stick-figure drawing of runners breaking a finish tape. I gather that she is coming rather than going: the fair, freckled skin of her face and solar plexus shine with perspiration. Her hair is gathered, twisted above her head. It is the color of the sweaters she buys for Isabel to give me for Christmas. Undyed organic wool. Brown, with more than a few strands of gray.

"I just got your text," she says. "I was at the gym. I thought you were coming later."

"Sorry. I was expecting more traffic."

"Well, come in. Izzy's at school."

"I know."

"Let me change my shirt at least."

Ginny has always been a proficient perspirer. The first time we met, at a summer orientation in Fullerton for student athletes, she was in a similar condition. The orientation started at 8 a.m., but Ginny had managed to squeeze in a jog before-hand. She might have gone back to the dorm to shower, but that would have made her late. Her mind works like this—always prioritizing and living with the consequences. She was at Fullerton on a soccer scholarship, but as a freshman, she was relegated to the bench. Hence the extra workouts. When we got together, I learned that she became instantly sweaty from all kinds of physical exertion, even without clothing.

She said her sweating embarrassed her. I always took it as a compliment.

"Why don't you make some coffee," she says.

"Sure. Take your time."

Ginny goes upstairs, and I show myself into the kitchen. It is my favorite room in her house, full of warm light, always clean and well stocked. A single man's kitchen is never a comfortable place, no matter how many times we see George Clooney or Matthew McConaughey whip up dinner while his lady friend moons over a glass of Cabernet. A stained-glass mobile hangs over the sink, catching light and throwing it around the room like a baby with a paintbrush. Like me, Ginny has a fancy espresso machine, but I decide to make the coffee by hand. I find some filters in the pantry, grind some beans. When Ginny walks in fifteen minutes later, I hand her a mug I can take credit for.

She is wearing a pair of white shorts and a black sleeveless sweater. Her hair is still wet from the shower.

"You look good," I say.

"Thanks." She takes the coffee and raises it to her nose but does not drink. "I thought you weren't coming into town until tomorrow."

She no longer follows my games, but I let her know at the beginning of the season all the dates I am going to be in L.A.

"The team comes tomorrow," I say.

"Did you get fired?"

"I have a contract, Ginny."

"You know what I mean. Did they let you go?"

From her tone of voice, I can tell that she is trying to be sympathetic—just trying it on, in case she is right. But sympathy does not come easily to her.

"Actually, I got promoted. They want me to be the closer."

"Good for you, that's great."

"You think so?"

Ginny may not look it, with her country-club clothes and Santa Monica lifestyle, but she is smarter about baseball than half the professional players I know. Her dad was a high-school coach, a southern California legend. Ginny spent a good portion of her girlhood in the aluminum bleachers at Culver City High, absorbing all there is to know about baseball—along with a fondness for ballplayers, which served me well for a while.

"It will be good for your career," she says. "Pitchers don't go from closer to nothing. If you fail at this, they will kick you back to setup before they let you go. And that's especially true because—"

"Because I'm such a great guy?"

"I was going to say because you're left-handed."

"That's encouraging, thanks."

"You're not going to fail, Johnny. That is not what I meant."

"It's okay, I already have."

She raises an eyebrow.

"Tuesday, at home against the Padres, I started the ninth and gave up a double, then a single, then hit a pinch-hitter in the back."

"Ouch. And they're sticking with you?"

"They say I'm the closer whether I want it or not, end of story."

Ginny sips her coffee. "Never heard that one."

"It's complicated. Skipper doesn't have a lot of options."

"And he gave you a day off to think things over?"

"Something like that, yeah."

Ginny does not know about my other life. I have thought about telling her on several occasions, but, as the father of her child and the source of her livelihood, I decided it would only worry her. If I were Ginny, I would not want to know. Usually this doesn't bother me too much—I don't want to know her secrets, either—but today I feel guilty. Three people are dead. Bam Bam's associates, whoever they are, could find her. She and Izzy aren't living under assumed names. Why would they? I might tell Ginny that my second career has entered a new, more perilous phase, but I'd have to start by explaining that I have a second career. Wouldn't it be easier just to wrap up this case and leave her in blissful ignorance?

"Are you coming to the game tomorrow night?" I ask. I always reserve two tickets when we play the Dodgers, even though I can't remember the last time she used them.

"We'll see. Izzy has a play rehearsal."

So it goes, that our daughter, spawn of two jocks, has zero interest in sports. She prefers to spend her time learning how to be Woman with Newspaper in her school's production of *Stuart Little.*

"Well, if your plans change . . ."

The chance is so small it is not even worth considering. And Ginny's mind is on to something else already.

"Simon said something interesting the other day—can I tell you?"

Simon Fine was Ginny's therapist during our divorce. Later, he became her second husband. A year after that, Simon revealed he was gay. Ginny declined therapy during her second divorce, but she and Simon still talk. I guess some people just stick to your fur.

"He asked if I would lock the bathroom door when I took a shower if he was in the house."

"What did you say?"

"I said yes, I think I would. But here's the thing. Just now, while I was upstairs taking a shower, I realized I didn't lock the door."

"Should I be flattered?"

"I don't know how you should feel. I just thought I should tell you."

I think I know what Ginny's getting at. I would not have locked the door, either. I might even have left it cracked.

"Izzy will be sorry she missed you."

"Tell her I'll see her tonight. Meantime, can I ask a favor?"

"What's that?"

"Do you still have Simon's Porsche?"

20

My ex's second husband was a Germanophile, which should have been a sign. Another is the license plate on his Porsche: ERREGEN, a German word meaning "arouse." The car is a model 911, vintage 1977. After a few tense moments, it turns over and purrs like an emphysemic cat. I promise Ginny that I will bring it back by dinnertime.

I need some time to piece together the events of the last few days. Top of the list is figuring out the connection between Bam Bam and Herrera's wife. Unless Bam Bam was brainwashed like Frank Sinatra in *The Manchurian Candidate* and had no idea what he was doing, he was ready to kill Marcus for asking questions about Maria. I don't get it. I saw her film—it wasn't bad, but it wasn't shocking, either, except maybe for the identity of the actors.

I get out my phone and call Maria. She answers on the first ring. "Hello, Adcock."

"Listen, Mrs. Herrera, you may be in danger."

There is a long pause as she waits for me to explain. Then she says, "That's it? That's all you have to say?"

To protect Marcus, I can't be specific, but I felt compelled to give her some kind of warning. "Something has happened," I say. "I can't give details without compromising the investigation, but you need to be careful. This might be a good time to take a trip, for example."

"My husband died less than a week ago. I'm not about to hop on a plane to Cancún!"

"Of course not. I could put you in touch with a security company. You and the kids could get a bodyguard."

"That won't be necessary."

"Mrs. Herrera—"

"I have my family, Mr. Adcock. They're all the security I need."

"Promise me you'll call the police if you notice anything suspicious. At least do that."

She says nothing.

I placed the call with the best of intentions, but after hanging up I feel guilty, and also somehow diminished. This is no time to brood, however. Phone in hand, I look up Two Lives Video in North Hollywood. Forty minutes later, I'm parking the Porsche behind the building. I stroll around front to case the place. Amazingly, the police have not been here yet. Maybe Bam Bam didn't register the business in his name. I wouldn't be surprised. Through the blinds I can see that the office is empty. I'm guessing the receptionist started looking for another job when she heard about Bam Bam on TV. Pornography is like gymnastics in more ways than one: a girl needs to break in while she's young or she will miss her chance forever.

Back in the alley, I try the rear door. Every off season for the last ten years, I have resolved to learn lock picking, but every year something comes up, and I arrive at spring training just as ignorant as the year before. I must say, it's a real handicap in this line of work to be stymied by something as low-tech as a lock. Then it occurs to me that maybe Simon Fine has tools. I pop the trunk of the Porsche and find . . . the engine. Fucking Germans. I walk around the front of the car, pop the other trunk—the frunk?—and discover a tire iron nestled next to the spare. I shoulder the rod like a bat. It makes noise, but in fewer swings than it takes to strike out, I've got the springs of Bam Bam's security door bouncing down the alley.

Bam Bam's office is just as Marcus described: half a dozen flat-screen TVs suspended from the ceiling, a couple of desks littered with greasy debris from Taco Bell and Jack in the Crack. One wall bears the evidence of Bam Bam's demise, an ugly splatter painting of brown blood. A dark stain on the carpet and a long smear from there to the door answer one of the questions that have been nagging me—namely, how Marcus managed to carry all three hundred pounds of Bam Bam Rodriguez from here to the Caddy. Forensically, this is a *Sesame Street* case. A police detective could figure it out in thirty seconds; an actor playing a police detective would require only slightly more time. The good news is that, without any witnesses, it will be nearly impossible to pin the deed on Marcus. Common sense suggests he wiped his prints off the door. I'll assume Natsumi's little pistol wasn't of the licensed-and-registered variety. I make a note to ask Marcus about the gun, but for the moment I'm reasonably satisfied that, although this job was regrettable, it was safely done.

As I scrutinize the room more carefully, it occurs to me that, except for the blood on the wall, you might not find evidence of a murder here if you weren't looking for it. Such is the state of disarray in Bam Bam's lair. Next to the desk is a seedy couch stained from God knows how many casting sessions. You know those TV shows where they shine black lights to reveal hidden stains and spills on upholstery? This thing would glow like a float in Disneyland's electric parade. Next to the couch is a mini-fridge filled not with rotten leftovers but with drug paraphernalia—coke spoons, empty baggies, glass pipes, a butane torch—the makings of a healthy after-school snack. I am not sure what I'm looking for, but there are some conspicuous absences. I discover that the video monitors are not connected to anything—the cords all lead to the desk, where two squares in the dust suggest there were once a couple of computers. I recall that Bam Bam showed videos to Marcus on these monitors. Someone besides me has been here since the murder. Someone with a key.

Before I leave, I run my finger quickly along Bam Bam's bookshelves. Beside the titles you might expect to find in an operation like this—*HTML for Dummies, Professional Lighting for Home Video Shoots,* a Xeroxed volume called *The Pussy Pages, 2011 Edition*—there are some odd inclusions: for example, half a dozen investment prospectuses. The white plastic binders have spine labels like "AG Partners Blank Check Corporation" and "California Restaurant Finance, LLC." I only know what these are because Bethany sometimes has them in her bag. They contain financial statements and business plans prepared by entrepreneurs looking for money. They're generally as dry as dirt, but as clues go, they are the best I'm going to get. I choose the newest-looking binder, one proposing a chain of low-cost OB/GYN clinics. I slip it under my arm. After wiping down the doorknobs one last time, I am back in the arousalmobile, one binder richer but no more enlightened than I was an hour ago.

On my way back toward Santa Monica, I get a call from George Luck.

"Hey, George."

"Johnny?" He seems surprised to hear my voice, even though he is the one who called me. "Are you hiding your phone? I was expecting voice mail."

It takes me a minute to understand that he thinks I am in San José. I look at my watch. It is almost noon. The game up there is about to start. How soon the vacationer forgets his office.

"Yeah, I came down to L.A. a day early. Family trouble."

"I'm sorry to hear that. Listen, if you could sneak away for even half an hour, I would really appreciate it. I have a favor to ask you."

"How about now? When do you have to be downtown?"

"It's a seven-thirty start, but I pitched last night."

"I saw that. Sorry about the loss."

"What could I do? Two runs a game, that's what they're giving me this year. Two point one, something like that."

"Rough. But that's Dodger baseball, right?"

"Unfortunately."

"Are you still in Manhattan Beach?"

"Yeah, same place. You remember how to get here?"

My watch says it is two o'clock in the afternoon when I park the Porsche on the concrete incline next to Luck's house. Thanks to traffic and a couple of nonnegotiable pit stops—gasoline, In-N-Out Burger—the trip took longer than I expected. George is waiting for me, and I see right away that he is on edge. He sticks his head out the door and looks left and right like he is expecting someone else.

"I got here as fast as I could," I say.

"Come in, quickly—"

He grabs my shoulder and pulls me inside.

"Easy, buddy. That's my career you're yanking."

He slams the door behind us. He is breathing hard, almost hyperventilating. His eyes are puffy, raccoonish, like he has not slept in days.

"What's the matter with you, George? You feeling all right?"

"Was anyone following your car?"

"No."

"Are you sure?"

"George—relax. I'm sure."

He gives it a good effort, breathing deeply, closing his eyes. George has never been a handsome man. Ginny used to call him Skellington, on account of his gangly limbs and dead-white complexion. He has a long, arched nose, a pointy chin, and sandy hair that settles over his forehead like feathers. Also a nice smile, if you're lucky enough to see it. Normally, his expression is about as blank as vanilla ice cream. He is a control pitcher, a guy who makes his living staying cool. I almost don't recognize him strung out like this.

"What do you keep looking at?" I say.

"The Mexicans."

"What Mexicans?"

"The guys who— You are sure you didn't see anybody out there?"

"Sit down, George."

His house is small, compared with what he could afford these days. It's a two-story town house on a side street, facing away from the beach. I lead him to the cream leather sectional sofa, make him sit on one end. His eyes are still glued to the door.

I order him to tell me everything.

"I have a girl," he says. "A Mexican girl. We've been together two years."

"That's great, man. I had no idea you were seeing someone."

"Nobody knows."

"There is nothing wrong with having a girlfriend, George."

"Yeah, I know. But the thing is . . ." He pauses, puffs out his lips. "The thing is, I pay her."

"I pay my ex. What's the big deal?"

"This isn't a joke, Johnny. She's a hooker."

"You're dating a hooker?"

"Not exactly. No, wait—yes, I'm dating a hooker. Her name is Ana Velásquez. She's from Sinaloa, real nice family. They are mango farmers. We're in love."

"How did you meet her?" I ask.

"We were introduced by a mutual friend."

"Anybody I know?"

Luck lowers his eyes. "No, no . . ."

"So now you have friends who deal in— Never mind. Let me guess, you tried to stop paying, and her pimp came calling?"

George shakes his head. "I don't expect you to understand this," he says, "but I prefer to pay. It is less complicated this way. On any given day I know exactly where we stand."

Now I remember that Luck used to bring a manicure kit on the road. No doubt, if I were to walk into his bedroom right now, I would find his closet organized by color.

"The guy who's following you isn't her pimp?"

For the second time, I see him recoil at the word "pimp." I begin to see how deep this girl has sunk her hooks.

"First of all, I don't recognize the guy following me. And second, Ana doesn't have a pimp. A man named Miguel takes care of her and the other girls who live in her house. He's like an older brother to them."

"A brother, huh? I am sure he takes good care of his sisters."

"Actually, he does. You can ask Ana, he does. He pays the girls their salary, pays for a house in Redondo Beach, gives them clothes, jewelry, everything."

"Green cards?"

"Well, no."

"But the guy on your tail isn't him."

"No."

"Does the pim— I mean, does Miguel know anything about this?"

"That's the thing. I haven't been able to reach him. I have called about a hundred times."

"And the girl, has she seen him?"

"I haven't told her that I'm being followed. She is out of town this week. I am going to tell her when she gets back."

"I think I know what's going on here."

"You do?"

"It's king of the hill. Your guy Miguel has been replaced."

"By 'replaced,' you mean—"

"Gone. Ana has a new boss."

"Somebody just came in and killed him?"

"Don't act surprised, Luck. He wasn't running a lemonade stand."

"I know." Luck hangs his head like Charlie Brown. I am sure that on some level he already knew. "What does he want from me?" he asks.

"Money. It is time to renegotiate your girl's contract."

"Fine, as long as he doesn't hurt her . . ."

I take a deep breath. I see what my role in this drama is supposed to be.

"Let me look into it," I say. "Give me a couple of days."

I don't normally take two cases at once, but for Luck I will make an exception. Poor guy. When you are mourning your girlfriend's pimp—that's rock bottom by anyone's standards.

21

After Luck leaves for the stadium, I go back to the car and watch his house. To pass the time, I tune in the pregame program on the Dodgers' AM station. The host is a guy named Jesse Ursino, a former reliever who played for half the clubs in the National League before realizing what everyone in baseball knew all along—that he was better with his mouth than his arm.

"Our caller, Joseph, wants to know how we think the death of Frankie Herrera, the Bay Dogs' backup catcher, is going to affect the race in the NL West. Did I get that correct?"

"That's right, Jesse."

"Well, off the top of my head, I'd have to say that it won't affect the race at all. I can't think of a time when a team's backup catcher made any difference at all."

"Yeah, that's a good point, Jesse, but it's not quite what I'm getting at. I know that tragedies like this can damage a team's morale—"

"And you played for how many major-league teams?"

"Uh . . ."

"Joseph? Are you there?"

"None, Jesse. I never played for a major-league team. In fact, I haven't played baseball since grade school."

"Right. So you have this psychological insight about the inner workings of a major-league clubhouse how?"

"I was just . . . I think I read it somewhere."

"A scholar, folks. We have a scholar on the line."

Ursino was always a dick. The most famous incident was at the start of the 1988 season, the year Kirk Gibson hit that epic home run off Eckersley in Game 1 of the World Series. Ursino and Gibson were both new to the Dodgers, and in spring training, Ursino thought it would be funny to smear black shoe polish inside Gibson's cap. Gibby flew off in a rage, castigating Ursino and basically setting the no-nonsense tone for the rest of the year. The usual moral of this story says that Gibson's ethic prevailed; he went on to be the National League MVP. An alternative moral is that assholes have their uses.

"You know, Jesse, it wouldn't hurt you to treat the deceased with a little more respect."

"What is this, the AARP info line? We're talking baseball here, Joseph."

"Frankie Herrera was a model citizen. He was involved in youth programs in Mexico, for example."

"Why should I care about youth in Mexico?"

"Aren't you Mexican?"

"Father was Italian, mother was Puerto Rican and Irish. Where's Mexico in that?"

"Forget it, Jesse, just forget it."

"You bet I'll forget it—next caller!"

Around this time, I hear a noise in the alley. I jump out of the car to take a look around. Behind Luck's house, a young Latino man in Dickies and a plain white T-shirt has fallen on his ass, surrounded by recyclables: empty soda cans, bottles, newspapers, magazines. An overturned blue trash can rests by his side. At first I think he's a canner—but, then, nobody stealing cans out of trash bins would bother to hustle like this.

When he sees me, he picks himself up and tears off, flat-bottom sneakers clapping the asphalt like pimp slaps.

I believe we have found our man.

He turns right on Twelfth Place, heading toward the beach. When I round the corner, I see that he is already halfway down the block, almost to Ocean. The streets here are narrow and steep, and the sidewalk is grooved perpendicular to the road for traction. I gallop down the concrete incline as fast as I can in long, knee-crushing strides. There are coaches who swear that pitching is a lower-body phenomenon—that the torque of the hips provides the force that propels the ball, and the arm is just a little whip at the end. Could be. For my own sake, I hope they're wrong.

At Ocean, the punk turns south for one block, then cuts left, away from the beach. I follow, almost losing my footing in the sandy intersection. He runs behind a public bus, and for a minute I fear I have lost him—that he has paid his buck fifty or whatever and given me the slip. But when the bus pulls away, I see him disappearing through the front door of a Mexican restaurant called El Dingo. I push my way into the restaurant, filled at that hour with lunchers from the nearby office buildings, men and women in pressed khakis with magnetic badges clipped to their belts and blouses.

"Where is he?" I say to the room.

The diners go silent, the cowards, before a chunky gal in an asymmetrical coral dress points to the kitchen door and says, "He went that way."

I nod my thanks and charge on. The kitchen is bright, hot, and steamy. It smells strongly of beans and cumin. One of the cooks' cell phones is playing a *norteño* love song, something about a heart as big as the moon. Everyone stops what they are doing. Peppers burn on the grill. Fajitas sizzle in cast-iron skillets.

"Who the hell are you?" says a bald man in a stained white apron. Like everyone else in the kitchen, he is Latino, but he is not my guy.

"Give him up," I say, "or I'll close you down. I'm the health inspector."

There is a crash behind the dishwasher—one of those tall rack-load jobs—and our guy squirts out into the room. I reach to grab him, but the floor is wet, and I am standing in the only spot in the room not covered by a black rubber mat. I go down hard. Out of the corner of my eye, I see the suspect climb out the window onto the roof of the next building.

"He's not the fucking health inspector," the pudgy cook says in Spanish. *"Look at him."*

I look at the bastard and say, in Spanish, *"Maybe I'm not the health inspector, maybe I'm from Immigration. You want to try me?"*

This silences the room. Can someone please tell me why it is always such a shock to Latin dudes when I speak Spanish? The language is only spoken by—what?—half a billion people worldwide? If they are looking for a secret code, they would do better to learn Lithuanian.

"Tell me who he is," I say.

Nobody says a word for a minute, and then one of the line cooks, a skinny kid with a fuzzy lip and enormous, satellite-dish ears, says, *"I saw him once at Redondo Beach Pier. He's a gangster."*

"I don't believe you."

"He is! Drugs, guns, girls—business."

"A businessman, huh?"

"Yeah."

I scrape myself up off the kitchen floor. My ass is wet and my left ankle hurts. I hobble through the swinging door into the dining room and walk straight to the exit, avoiding eye contact. Years ago I would have said something to the people in the room, made a joke, something to save face. Now I know better. More often than not, the best strategy is to get the hell out, fast.

I walk up the main drag a few blocks, heading back toward Luck's street. I am not sure if I believe the cook's assessment of our little friend. He may have stolen George's girl from her last pimp, but drugs and guns are something else entirely. Something like 95 percent of the drug trade is controlled by a handful of Mexican syndicates. Same with guns, which run north to south, opposite the stream of drugs. Both are economies of scale. The flesh trade does not work that way. Pimping is still a mom-and-pop business. Each girl needs to be turned out individually, broken like a horse, and that takes time. You cannot simply land an unmarked 737 on an airstrip in Colombia and fill it up with hookers.

I turn onto Luck's street and walk downhill, slowly this time. My ankle might be fine, or not—it is hard to tell. There are no nerve endings in cartilage.

I find the Porsche where I left it, the radio still blaring. Jesse Ursino raises his voice with the caller: "The root problem—are you listening?—the root problem is not that the McCourts got divorced. It is that they were married in the first place! Marriage is a time bomb, people! Major League Baseball should never allow married couples to own teams. Owners should be bachelors, widows, or faceless corporations, period."

I can't help smiling. Jesse has always had a talent for stating what everyone is thinking but would never say.

I reach in to open the little toy door of the Porsche, and then something catches my eye. A flash of white in front of Luck's house. One look and I recognize our guy. In broad daylight, he is trying to jimmy the screen off one of George's front windows.

Rather than risk another high-speed footrace, I duck behind the car and observe him for a minute. He manages to pry the screen off, placing it neatly next to the wall. Next he reaches into his back pocket and takes out an object like a double-A battery with a black wire hanging off one end. It looks like one of those microphones they clip on your shirt for TV interviews. He places the device in the lower right corner of the window, fiddles with it a moment, then moves to the left side and places another. When he is satisfied, he replaces the screen and stands back. For at least ten seconds he just stands there, admiring his work. Then he walks off.

I turn off the radio, lock the Porsche, and walk over to Luck's front door. I have decided that I will knock, just in case any neighbors are watching, and then check the window. I walk up the steps, open the screen door, and reach for the knocker. There is something stuck under it—a tiny envelope of thick, expensive paper, like the reply card in a wedding invitation. Inside the envelope is a business card with a headshot of a pretty Latina. There's a phone number, but no explanation. I assume it's a gift from an overzealous realtor and am about to toss it away when I recognize the name under the digits: Alejandra Sol. This is one of the names Bethany gave me—an alias of the dead girl in Frankie's car. I look more closely. The back of the card is a full-color photo of the same woman in a bikini. Her body is turned away from the camera, and she is looking back over one shoulder. She has glossy dark hair and a gleam in her eye that tells you she's selling much more than condos.

I raise the knocker and give it a few good whacks for appearance. I take another look at the card. It might be a coincidence. "Alejandra" is a common name. Two of my colleagues on the Bay Dogs' pitching staff have girlfriends named Alejandra. And "Sol" is pretty common, too; there was a guy who played for Milwaukee named Pedro Sol. He could never hit my changeup, bless his little heart.

But what if it's not a coincidence? What if this is the same girl who died with Frankie Herrera? It seems impossible. Even the most frequent-flying whore couldn't serve johns in L.A. and San José at the same time. But if there was a network of girls, up and down the state, marketed to certain clients . . .

Or what if she marketed herself exclusively to professional baseball players? Why not? We certainly have the money, and we're fairly discreet. Not to mention lonely.

I am coming down Luck's front stairs, head full of theories, when I run into the little pimp. He looks surprised to see me here, which I can hardly believe, because what kind of moron returns three times to a location he knows is being watched? I reach back, ball up my right fist, and aim for his nose. My dad taught me to punch like boxer, with dexterity in both hands. Knowing how to hit with the right arm became a real asset later, as soon as it became clear that the left was going to be my meal ticket. When I connect with the kid's face, there is the familiar crunch, and he doubles over. Blood trickles through his fingers.

I know I should beat his ass on principle. The little shit made me run halfway across Manhattan Beach. He deserves worse that what I've given him. But I am unarmed, and I do not feel strongly enough about teaching him a lesson to risk further injury. Here's another boxing lesson from Dad: just knock out your opponent, don't kill him. You don't get extra points for beating on a corpse.

"What was that for?" the kid says. His voice is surprisingly low, a growl seasoned by nicotine. I notice grays mixed into his buzz and realize he is not a kid after all. He just acts like one.

"Where's Miguel?" I say.

"What do you care, bro? This is business."

"Some business," I say. "Planting microphones in people's windows—what kind of business is that?"

"They ain't microphones. They're like . . . firecrackers. I flip the remote, the glass breaks, that's it. I wasn't going to burn the house down or nothing."

He has managed to get his nose to stop bleeding, so I pop it again.

"Hey! What do you want from me? I'll take the pyros down, just leave me alone."

"First you leave my buddy alone."

"Fine, bro, but he ain't who you think he is."

"You mean his girl? I know all about her." I pull out the business card and wave it in front of the punk's face.

He spits a wad of blood and snot on the concrete. "Look, I'm just paid to send a message, that's all."

"And what's this message? That the price has gone up?"

"Yeah, that's what happens when you have new management." He tips his head back, pinches the bridge of his damaged nose. "You're not going to clock me no more, right?"

"Leave my friend alone. He is happy with the girl he's got, and he's not interested in paying more."

"Fine. My boss won't be happy, but fine."

"Who's your boss?"

The pimpito shakes his head. "You don't want to get mixed up in this."

I raise my fist. He winces.

"Tell me his name," I say.

"You want to die? Because that's what is going to happen. If my boss knew what I told you already, both of us would be dead, like tonight."

"Glad I'm not the only one in danger."

"Tell your friend he can keep his ho. Same price. But don't ask no more questions—not you or him."

I keep watch as the little shit struts to the window, pops off the screen, and puts the little remote-controlled firecrackers back in the pocket of his Dickies.

"Get the fuck out of here!" I yell after him.

He walks away slowly in a kind of impotent defiance, his two hands in the air with middle fingers extended and crossed like six-guns. The irony is that he has big hands, bigger than mine. With a little discipline, he might have had a career.

22

Though I was hoping the unlocked bathroom door meant I would be invited for dinner, it turns out to be just another of Ginny's half-wrought gestures, full of sound and fury and signifying nothing. At six o'clock I am back in the house in Santa Monica, Simon's pocket rocket returned to the garage.

"Can I take Izzy out to dinner?" I ask.

"Please, Mom," our daughter begs. "I haven't seen Dad since the All-Star break!"

"You know it's not easy to see your father during the season."

"But, Mom, he's standing right here."

I am standing, to be precise, in my ex-wife's haunted living room. The house actually has two living rooms—or parlors, I guess you'd call them—to the left and right of the entry hall. We are in the left parlor, which Ginny has decorated with a Day of the Dead theme. One wall is completely covered with painted papier-mâché skulls, or *calaveras,* that Ginny bought in bulk from a Mexican artist on the Venice boardwalk. Each skull is about the size of a baby's head, and if that was not eerie enough, some of them are painted with commercial logos and other symbols of contemporary life. Not surprisingly (since the skulls were purchased in Los Angeles), there is one with the San José Bay Dogs logo, the interlocking yellow-and-black "SJ," on its sparkling black dome. That one has blood running from its eyes.

"Fine," Ginny says, "but don't go far. And no driving—the headlights don't work in the Porsche."

"We'll walk," I say.

There is a trattoria on Montana where I eat occasionally after visits with Izzy—other afternoons that might have led to dinner invitations but did not.

We set off into the Santa Monica night. Izzy is pumped, adrenalized. For her it is a treat of epic proportions to be out for dinner with her peripatetic father. I hope this never changes, but I cannot see how it won't. Because I travel for a living, I have bought myself a little more of her adulation than other fathers enjoy. If I were living at home, or even divorced but readily accessible, she would be over me by now.

Then there's the investigation thing, the other side of my professional life. I used to feel dirty—doing what I do, solving the kinds of problems I solve, and then spending time with my daughter. How else could you feel after spending a four-game series flying back and forth between Miami and Santo Domingo, tailing the left fielder's wife, only to discover that the left fielder is banging his thirteen-year-old cousin? How do you then spend a weekend with your own thirteen-year-old without feeling that some part of you has been tainted by association with these predators? How do you not feel contagious?

Short of re-engineering the male endocrine system, there is little I can do. It should not surprise anyone that the hormonal imbalances that cause a thirty-year-old man to seduce and deflower his teenage cousin are the same ones that allow him to turn around on a baseball thrown ninety-five miles per hour and drive it 450 feet—and to do this once every four games,

115

on average, for ten years straight. That's a valuable endocrine abnormality, a multi-million-dollar freak show.

And also a business opportunity. Just ask Alejandra Sol.

"I thought we could go to Angelo Mio," I tell Izzy. "You like the pasta there, right?"

"When I was like ten."

"Is pasta just for kids?"

"Dad, pasta is all carbs."

"I know that. I went to college."

"I'm carb-neutral."

"What does that mean, anyway?"

"It means you have to offset every serving of carbs with something else. You can choose between protein, fat, and vegetables."

"And you don't choose fat very often."

She looks to make sure I'm not joking. "No, I don't."

"So why don't you have a salad with your pasta?"

"How about I order my own salad," she counters, "but we split a pasta?"

"Izzy, I weigh two hundred pounds. Have a heart."

"Fine, I'll get the kids' size."

"Why, because you're a kid?"

"Dad!"

"I'm just saying, when was the last time you ordered off the kids' menu?"

"At Angelo?"

"Anywhere."

She stops and thinks about this—God, could I love her any more?—and finally says, "I still get a Happy Meal sometimes at McDonald's."

"Wait a minute—you won't eat a full plate of pasta, but you will eat a burger from McDonald's?"

"I take off the bun. It's called a Skinny Mac—my friend Jenna invented it."

I hold my tongue the rest of the way to the restaurant, while Izzy tells me about a boy named Kurt, the current heartthrob of her eighth-grade class.

"I don't even think he's handsome. He's too hairy. Jenna said he started shaving in sixth grade."

"Sixth grade, really? You should stay away from him."

Izzy bites her lip. This was not the answer she was hoping for. I can see her recalculating behind those wide brown eyes.

"Are you sure?" she says.

"Of course I'm sure. The sooner hair grows on the face, the sooner it falls off the head. And I wouldn't want you to have a bald husband."

"I'm not going to marry him! We're just—"

She stops. Too late.

"You're just what?"

"I haven't even kissed him, Dad." Suddenly it looks like she is going to cry.

"Relax, honey. I was just joking."

"No, you're right. He's too mature."

I start to say that was not my point, but then I realize it was. Isabel is still a girl—and I say this objectively, not just as a protective father. She got her period last winter, when she visited me in San José, but I only know because of the way she pranced self-importantly to the bathroom every hour, clutching a bright-pink LeSportsac in one hand. Her body has barely begun to change. She grows taller all the time, but she looks like an eight-year-old on stilts.

"Listen, Izzy, I'm sure Kurt's a nice guy. I shouldn't pass judgment until I meet him."

"You sound like Mom. She's always saying things like 'You

shouldn't pass judgment.' But only after I start passing judg-ment. If I just talked about how nice he was, how gentlemanly and all that, she would tell me I wasn't being careful enough. There's not much in between, you know?"

"Unfortunately, life is like that."

We take a table in the window, and I persuade Izzy to order a normal-sized plate of spaghetti marinara. The tomatoes in the sauce, I argue, cancel out the noodles. I order eggplant par-migiana, and I promise to supplement her tomatoes with some of my eggplant if she feels tempted to eat more pasta. We have to keep the equation in balance, I say. I sense that she appreci-ates the effort.

"Tell me about the new play," I say. "Is Kurt in drama with you?"

"No, he plays water polo."

I cringe. At my high school, the water-polo team worked out in the mornings before class, and then wandered around bleary-eyed all day. A sport that explains bloodshot eyes at 8 a.m. is attractive to a certain type of guy. We used to joke that they traveled to road games in the Mystery Machine.

"Tell me, does he . . ." I pinch together my thumb and fore-finger and raise them to my lips.

"Does he get high? Probably, although he says he doesn't. Jenna says his brother has a prescription."

What kind of world is this, I wonder, where kids score their pot from a sibling with a medical condition?

"You have every right to be skeptical," I say. "When I was in high school, people bought their pot from water-polo players."

"Did you?"

"Sometimes. But I was stupid."

"In health they told us that pot rots your brain. The boys were all laughing and saying they didn't care."

"You should care."

"But pot doesn't rot your brain. Does it?"

"No one knows. They haven't studied it much."

"Come on, Dad."

"Is my brain rotten?"

"That's what I'm asking you."

I have to think about this. Did smoking pot in high school rot my brain? Hard to say. What difference would it make if I lost a few IQ points? I didn't exactly choose a heady profession.

"I got lucky, Izzy. Suppose I topped out at triple-A. Then where would I be? It would be a shame if a couple dozen bong hits in high school made the difference between selling sporting goods and curing cancer."

Who knows what young Isabel Adcock may decide to be? If she chooses law or physics or diplomacy, she may need those mental edges, the ones that weed sands off.

"I stand by my first advice," I say. "Be wary of Kurt."

Izzy sighs. "I know you're right. But I still want him to ask me out."

"I thought you said he wasn't good-looking."

"Yeah, he's pretty much a god."

"They always are."

"Was Mom like that?"

"Your mom is a beautiful woman, but she wasn't dangerous like this Kurt kid, if that's what you're asking."

"Were you dangerous for her?"

I realize this is the question she's been meaning to ask all along. Screw Kurt. Maybe there is no Kurt.

"Yes," I say, "but neither of us knew it until much later."

"That's not fair," my daughter says, and I know she means to be generous, to say that it isn't fair for me to accuse myself of a crime I could not have foreseen. But it is fair. One way or another, justice is always done. Just ask Frankie Herrera. I don't expect Izzy to understand. I didn't understand it myself for a long time.

"Yeah, it's too bad," I say lamely. "But if your mom and I hadn't done what we did, I wouldn't be sitting here with you."

"She says that, too."

"She does?"

Izzy catches my eye. "Among other things."

23

Another day, another one-run game. This time we were losing the whole way, which means that yours truly, the Bay Dogs' new closer, did not pitch. I text Luck and tell him to meet me in the players' parking lot at eleven-thirty. He texts back, *Why? What happened?* But I'm not going to give him the news over the phone. I don't care how normal he thinks it is to be dating a prostitute. That kind of information should never be encoded into waves and sent around. Someone may be listening—the FBI, the NSA. Also, it's just bad mojo, hanging your dirty laundry from a telephone wire.

Luck is late—probably lingering in the clubhouse to bask in the warmth of a victory. It is a tough year to be a Dodger. Even with one of the highest payrolls in the majors, the Dodgers are ten games out of first place. The local media are furious, disgusted. But a chill still moves up my spine as I stand outside the stadium. As a kid, I used to come to this very spot, a chain-link enclosure beyond the left-field bleachers, and stand around after Sunday matinees with my friends, waiting to ask the players for autographs as they emerged from the clubhouse: Valenzuela, Guerrero, Scioscia, Sax. We used to say how great it would be when we got driver's licenses and later curfews and could come here after night games. Of course, by the time we got our licenses, we were more interested in stalking high-school girls than professional baseball players. Now, twenty years later, I have finally made it back. The same orange "76" ball is rotating above the gas station at the edge of the economy lot. The stadium lights have been cut to half-power to save a few bucks while the janitors sweep beneath the seats. This is my favorite time at the ballpark—any ballpark—and it doesn't matter if I have won or lost the game. Either way, the pressure is off. For a little while, you can pretend it is all still magic.

My phone buzzes and I see a message from Bethany. Attached is a photo of the dead girl from the morgue in San Mateo. It's not a pretty sight: her face is smashed on one side, cheekbone caved, skin lacerated. I can't tell for sure if I'm looking at Alejandra Sol.

At eleven-forty-five, George Luck comes out. He is wearing his usual polo shirt tucked into Levi's 501 jeans. Braided belt, boat shoes—you couldn't pick him out of a lineup of suburban dads. You would never guess he pays for sex. Or maybe you would. The pervert is never actually the guy with the scraggly white beard. Just look at our politicians.

"Hey," Luck says, "sorry I'm late. Skip had words for us."

"No kidding. I would have thought he'd be happy with the W."

"You would think so. It was reverse psychology. He said we won disgracefully, that we were a disgrace to the franchise, something like that."

The Dodgers' new skipper had made his name managing clubs in the American League, where keeping score requires all your fingers, and sometimes your toes.

"How does he figure?"

"We scored two runs. Again."

"Last I checked, it only takes one to win."

Luck's Benz coupe is last year's model, but it still smells new.

"I have some good news," I say. "I talked to Ana's new boss, and he has agreed to honor your deal."

"What deal?"

"The deal. Your financial arrangement."

"Oh." Luck's face falls. "No word on Miguel? Did I tell you he is actually Ana's uncle? Sorry if I wasn't clear about that."

"For Christ's sake, Luck. You asked me to find out who was tailing you, and I did. Your tail was a little shit who was going to blow out your front window."

"That's it?"

"You don't like your windows?"

Luck is antsy, tapping the steering wheel with his thumbs. "Miguel still hasn't picked up his phone," he says. "I tried him all morning."

"Well, I am sorry." I pause there. I don't want to say more, but I get the impression Luck is not connecting the dots here.

"You like sushi?" he says.

"Sure."

We drive through a warehouse district east of town, taking a hard right onto an unlit street where trash is stacked on the curbs for a.m. pickup. There are few cars and zero pedestrians. My alarms start to go off, but then I remember who I'm with. I can smell the sanitizer gel Luck spread on his hands before he left the clubhouse. You know the expression "Danger is his middle name"? Luck's middle name is probably "Checklist." Or maybe "Insurance." Danger avoids him like vampires avoid light.

He parks in front of a concrete loading dock where well-dressed professionals are sitting at bistro tables. Ties are loosened; hair is down. Even though it is after midnight, you get the feeling these people just got here. Fresh, frosty Sapporos sweat on the tabletops. The steel doors behind the dock have been rolled open. Warm yellow light fans out across the alley.

"Funny little place," Luck says as we get out of the Benz. "You know that Japanese infielder we had last year? He told me about it. Those guys have a sixth sense."

It is true: Japanese players could find good sushi in Lubbock, Texas. It's like the embassy gives them a guide.

We get a table inside. My chair is made of stacked corrugated cardboard. It feels like a hay bale, but it holds. Luck orders green tea, miso soup (he does not drink). I tell the waitress I'll have the same. I want to maintain a clear head. I have a theory about the Frankie Herrera case that I want to test out.

"You ever heard the name Luisa Valdez?" I ask Luck.

"No." He snaps apart his chopsticks. I can't tell if he's evading me.

"How about Alejandra Sol?"

Now Luck sets down his chopsticks. "What is this, an inquisition? I asked you to get me out of trouble, not to make things worse. Aren't you supposed to provide relief?"

"To a point."

"Where did you get 'Alejandra Sol'? That's Ana's name!"

"Her what?"

"Her working name, stage name, whatever. It's the name on her cards."

"Does her card look like that?"

I pull the card I found on his door from my pocket and hand it to Luck.

"Where did you get that?" he says.

"George," I say, "I have some bad news. Ana is going to be out of town longer than she thought."

24

Thank God for green tea. Turns out I need all my mental faculties and then some to persuade George Luck not to desert the Dodgers and fly up to the San Mateo County Coroner's Office. He swears there is no way the dead girl could be Ana. Why would she be in a car with another man—let alone another ballplayer? They had a deal. They were exclusive. And besides the deal—she loved him! Why would she sneak around with Frankie Herrera? It was not her in the car, he insists, and viewing the body would surely confirm this.

"You can't just leave," I say. "You'll get fined by the club and maybe the league."

"You left for a couple of days."

"That's different. I had permission."

"I don't care, let them fine me. I have to see the body. You said your girlfriend can get us in?"

"Wait." I pull out my phone, thumb through the gallery, and hand it to Luck. "I want you to know," I say, "that I hope this is not her."

Luck's face clenches up like a fist, and it looks like he is going to cry.

"This wasn't supposed to happen, Adcock. Me and Ana, we had a deal!"

"I'm sorry, George."

I ask Luck to drop me at the team hotel. He nods but says nothing. I want to tell him that the silver lining is that we are closer to cracking the Frankie Herrera case. But I have a feeling it won't cheer him up to know that he and Herrera were sleeping with the same prostitute.

"I'm sure she was a lovely girl, George."

"I won't ever love again."

"You don't know that."

"I do. She was the one."

"But, George, she was a hooker—"

"I'm not normal." Luck looks at me and his eyes are wet. "You don't understand. There's nothing wrong with you."

"Of course there is," I say. "And you are normal, George. A little peculiar, but normal."

"No, I'm really not. But it's kind of you to say so."

25

Luck leaves me at the door of the Bonaventure Hotel in downtown L.A. Since they opened the Staples Center down the street, there seems to be at least one professional sports team staying in the hotel at all times—baseball, basketball, hockey, whatever. A few of us have talked about forming an investment group and buying the place, closing it down to the public. The talk always stalls over the issue of groupies. They would still be allowed in, right? Dennis Rodman once famously said that life in the NBA was 50 percent sex. He was dating Madonna at the time, so you can adjust his figures however you like. But at the risk of stating the obvious, the fact is that sex is a big part of professional sports. How could it not be? We are men living out our boyhood fantasies. Once you have stepped to the plate with two outs in the bottom of the ninth, runners at second and third, your team down by one (does this sound familiar, gentlemen?)—once you have actually lived that fantasy, what's next? The league and the players' association like to paint a picture of baseball players as hardworking family men, and that is true for some percentage of us. But the vast majority of ballplayers couldn't make a marriage work if they were coming home every night on the six-thirty train. A hundred days a year on the road? Forget it. Those "behind the scenes" ESPN documentaries made a big deal out of players packing suitcases, kissing their children, a big teary montage. Those films are moving, but they aren't entirely truthful. The wives know the score. They know what they are getting into. It is a pretty nice bargain, if you think about it: a big home in some sunny spring-training city, large enough so your mom and your sisters can come and stay as long as they like. Five-figure deposits appearing in your bank account every couple of weeks. A bunch of kids to play with if you're into that, and if not, a staff of nannies to watch the little brats. Really, it is the best possible widowhood you can imagine. There might even be a pool boy or a yoga instructor to take the edge off the loneliness.

The problem from the players' perspective is the sketchiness of it all, the sneaking around, the threat of disease and paternity suits. Hence the plan for the Bonaventure. We would close it down to the public, screen the staff and the, um, *staff,* and *voilà*—no team visiting Los Angeles would stay anywhere else. And L.A. would be just the beginning: there could be one of these in every big-league town. Sam Malone be damned, this is my retirement plan. Or should be.

I walk through the brightly lit lobby past a gaggle of young women in Bay Dogs jerseys. I know even without seeing the number on their backs that they are "Diggies"—Modigliani fans.

"Is he a Bay Dog?" I hear a girl whisper as I walk by.

"No, he's too old," her friend answers.

I am waiting for the elevator when I hear my name. I turn to find Skipper sitting alone at a table in the lobby restaurant.

"Come here, Adcock," he says. "I need to talk to you."

"Late dinner?" It is nearly two o'clock in the morning. Skipper is twirling spaghetti marinara around his fork. "My daughter says you shouldn't eat pasta," I say. "She says carbs make you fat."

"I always thought it was fat that makes you fat," he says. He takes one more mouthful of spaghetti and pushes the bowl away. "But I am willing to be wrong."

"What's on your mind, Skip?"

"GM called and woke me up." He exhales loudly, thrums his fingers on the tabletop. "Used to be that front office business was conducted during business hours. That's why they call them business hours. But now all the GMs are twelve years old, and they sit up at night with their computers, talking to each other through the computers, and they treat this whole sport like it's a video game."

"Like fantasy baseball, you mean?"

"It's a fantasy, all right. Do you see where I'm going with this?"

"You're trying to tell me I've been traded."

The manager's blue eyes shiver. "Not yet," he says. "But there's a deal on the table that sends you and Big Bob to San Diego."

"For who?"

"For Richard Millman."

Millman is fourth or fifth on the all-time saves list, and among active players, he is number one. But his fastball has lost its edge, and his off-speed stuff is no longer beguiling batters like it once did. Everyone knows the Padres have been trying to unload him.

"Are the Pods going to pay part of his salary?"

A word of explanation here. Sometimes a club will be so desperate to get rid of a player that they offer to keep paying him while he plays for another team. Sometimes in these cases there are clubhouse issues nobody talks about. One time, a guy I knew got traded because he took the GM's daughter on a date and then didn't call her. But I have heard no rumors about Richard Millman.

"Millman has another year on his contract," Skipper says. "Naturally, we don't want to pay the whole thing if we don't have to." He takes a deep breath, lets it leak out of the sides of his mouth. "Used to be," he says, "that when a guy played for your club you had to pay him."

"Times have changed," I say.

"That's for sure." Skipper reaches for his spaghetti. He takes a stab, then thinks better of it and pushes the plate away again. "I mean, this guy . . ." He stops. I know who he means.

I should clarify, our GM is not twelve years old. But he can't be more than twice that. He is a scrawny, undernourished young man who probably could not swing a thirty-ounce bat. But he is smart and shrewd. He signed Modigliani as a minor-league free agent after the Tigers organization let him go. The Tigers said that the twenty-five-year-old catcher was too old for them, that his knees were already turning forty. Now that Modigliani is an All-Star, Detroit's GM claims Modigliani was not healing from knee surgery when they ditched him, but everyone knows what really happened. The Tigers were just impatient. Because, you see, their GM is also a Red Bull–slurping teenager.

"I would be sad to go," I say.

"I know you would, Adcock. And I'd be sad to lose you. Less adult supervision in the clubhouse, for starters."

"Thanks, Skip. That means a lot."

This gets a smile out of the old manager. "You know," he says, "if you don't want to go to San Diego, you could always just retire."

The thought has already crossed my mind. I always imagined I would retire a Bay Dog, same as I started. These days it is rare to spend your whole career with a single club. You probably can't name ten players who have done it. Chipper Jones in Atlanta. The holy trinity of Jeter, Rivera, and Posada in New

York. Varitek in Boston. Jimmy Rollins in Philly. Who else is there?

Thirteen years with San José. It was never my favorite marriage, but it was the one that stuck.

"What if I'm not ready to retire?"

Skipper nods. "It's a hard decision. Me, I knew my time was up when I started looking forward to meals. When I first came up, I would eat anything—pizza, cheesesteaks, the quicker the better. I hated to spend time eating. Then, one day, I was sitting on the bench halfway through a game, and I realized I had spent the last two innings dreaming about what I was going to have for dinner. I quit as soon as the season ended."

I am not sure if Skipper has seen me zoning out, but his story strikes a nerve. I have basically had the moment he describes—seeing the rookie Jerry Díaz staring wide-eyed at the game in progress, noticing his dumb wonder and how far I had come from anything like that. But I never thought to quit. Does that make me a bad man?

"I don't know, Skip. I tend to think my body has more baseball in it."

"Might be," he says. From the way he picks at his pasta, I can tell he is skeptical.

Privately, I consider the risks of pushing on: I might die tomorrow in a burning wreck alongside a girl who is neither my wife nor my daughter, who has three names, and who is dating a starting pitcher on a rival club. It might happen—it happened to Frankie Herrera—and would anyone care in that case whether the charred body in the car was a Bay Dog or a Padre?

26

As I wait for the elevator, I return to thinking about Frankie Herrera. My stomach sours. I feel like a surgeon who has cut into a patient to remove a section of cancerous intestine only to discover, once the guy is laid open, that all the other organs are diseased, too. I've read that in a case like that the doctor just sews up the patient and calls a priest.

On the eighth floor, I root in my pockets for the keycard, trying to remember the room number the clubhouse guys gave me at the ballpark. I try a few doors until I get a green light.

Even before I'm inside, I know something is wrong with the room. For one thing, the lights are all on, and the air is thick and wet, like Atlanta in August. The mirror on the closet door is fogged. It might be Bethany. She has surprised me on the road before. Then I see the rest of the room: the drawers have been pulled out of the bureau, the mattresses upended and slashed. I roll open the closet door. Inside, my suitcase has thrown up: clothes and toiletries everywhere, strewn across the carpet like flood debris.

I reach into my pocket to make sure Herrera's phone is still there. I've had hotel rooms searched before; you can't be too careful. When I'm working a case, I never travel with anything I can't replace at Target. Anything that can fit in my pocket stays there. Anything else of value—and even items of questionable value, like the investment binder I took from Bam Bam's office—I leave at the ballpark with my playing gear. That stuff follows me at a distance, hauled to the next park by the clubhouse crew.

I go into the bathroom and turn off the faucet, then sit on the bed and calmly dial Security.

"This is John Adcock," I say. "I'm going to need another room."

While I wait, I scroll through Herrera's texts, looking for a clue. The threatening notes all came from a blocked number. I decide to give the thing to Bethany first chance I get. She'll know what to do.

Five minutes later, a young man in a police-style brush cut arrives at the door. He is wearing black cargo pants and a black polo shirt with the hotel's logo on one breast. A walkie-talkie dangles from his hip. "Mr. Adcock?" His eyes grow wide as he looks into the room. He says, "Holy shit," and then, regaining himself, he thanks me for calling. "Normally when the phone rings on third shift it's some old lady who can't figure out how to turn off the TV. But this—whew—this is an actual burglary!"

"Glad to make your night more interesting," I say. "But this wasn't a burglary."

"With all due respect, Mr. Adcock," the kid says, "I think I know more about crime than you do."

"Let's hope not."

I go to the closet and begin scooping my clothes back into the suitcase. Behind me, the kid fumbles with his walkie-talkie and tells the scratchy voice on the other end that Mr. Adcock needs a fresh setup, and that an upgrade would be good. The voice agrees, and the kid replaces the radio on his belt.

"Mr. Adcock, sir, I'll be right back. I have some forms you need to fill out for the report."

"Fine."

A few minutes later, I finish packing and wheel the bag into the hall. I tell myself I wasn't tired anyway. I'll go downstairs and have a drink while they fix up the new room. If Skipper's still there, I can tell him this trade has me all worked up. Which isn't exactly a lie.

Then I stop. Halfway down the hall, I see two well-muscled men in black polo shirts. They have just stepped off the elevator and are now running full-tilt toward me. Twenty-five yards between us. Now twenty. Now fifteen. Years ago, I would have stopped and tried to piece this out: Who are these guys? Are they with the kid from the security desk? Maybe one of them was the voice in the walkie-talkie? Now I know there is a time to be Sherlock Holmes, and there's a time to be Dr. Richard Kimble. This is the latter. I turn around, dig for the stairwell, and slam the metal door behind me. I begin leaping down the stairs, taking three and four at a time. I descend maybe twelve stories. When I exit, I am in the hotel's parking garage. The air is stale and hot, like the exhaust from a clothes dryer. I look around. I am alone for the moment. I duck behind a red Ford pickup and lift myself onto the running board so my feet are hidden from view. In the driver's-side window, the red LED of the truck's alarm pulses like a slow heartbeat.

The stairwell door slams open. "Where the fuck is he?" one guy says.

"Fuck if I know," says the other.

They make a few halfhearted laps around the lot, bending down to look under a few cars, but it is clear they were not prepared to do any real work to find me.

"How many levels of parking they got in here?"

"I don't know. Four? Five?"

"Mother*fucker*!"

I want to peek and get a good look at them—see if I recognize a face—but before I can stick my neck out, they've gone up the ramp to the next level.

I stay behind the red Ford a couple more minutes, just in case. The guys on my tail don't seem like geniuses, but you never know. They may have crept back down the ramp to wait for me. I advise young pitchers never to underestimate the enemy. Just because a hitter has sixteen-inch biceps and the bat looks like a twig on his shoulder, do not assume he is a moron. They say Barry Bonds knew what pitch you were going to throw before the catcher even gave the sign. There are 150 pitchers in the National League, and Bonds knew every one of them by heart. He was a student first of all, and then a monster.

But neither of these assholes is Barry Bonds. When five minutes have passed, I stand up. My knees pop like knuckles, and I am reminded what a luxury it is to be a pitcher. Skipper is right: had I been stuck behind the plate, I would not be agonizing over whether to call it quits; that call would have been made for me, probably five years ago.

As I turn for the stairs, I nearly trip over a beer can standing in the middle of an empty parking space. The can is unopened, which is strange, but it gives me an idea. I scoop it up, and when I get to the stairwell, I turn around to face the red Ford. I put the can in my left hand and call up the ramp, "Hey, assholes! Hey, you pieces of shit! I'm down here!"

I wait.

Four sneakers appear at the top of the ramp—new Jordans, red with white lace covers. They stop for a minute, then start pussyfooting down.

"Hey!" I yell again. "I have something for you."

I square up and throw a fastball through the windshield of the Ford. The garage explodes with noise—first the glass, then the ruckus of the truck's alarm.

Through the wired-glass window in the stairwell door, I watch my pursuers come down the ramp. Squinting at the noise, they stand dumbfounded before the Ford. One guy puts his hands to his ears. The other retreats back up the ramp halfway to the next level. They shout into each other's ears. One of them must have realized that security guards—real security guards—would be arriving soon, because now they start shedding their fake uniforms. One is down to his wifebeater and the other bare-chested when I decide I have seen enough. I make my way upstairs.

"And how would you like to take care of the room charges, Mr. Washington?"

The woman at the desk is a blue-eyed blonde with skin so fair you can see the veins in her temples, the kind of girl you might injure by staring too hard.

"I'm going to be using points," I explain. "It's a company account—Sushi Makasu."

It has become clear that Johnny Adcock is unlikely to get any sleep tonight, at least as long as he still has Frankie Herrera's phone. Luckily, he has friends with loyalty points. When Marcus opened his restaurant, I put in a hundred G's on the condition that I be allowed to use his name in a pinch. He said it was a raw deal but he knew it was worth more to me than a lifetime of free rail drinks. I maintain that I have been a responsible identity thief.

The blonde keeps looking up from the keyboard as she types, smiling nervously. I doubt she recognizes me as a ballplayer. Why would I be booking a room on my own dime when the rest of the team is upstairs asleep?

Well, not exactly my dime, but still.

"Okay, Mr. Washington, I have a suite for you on the twelfth floor."

She slides the little envelope containing the keycard across the counter. Then she takes a business card from the drawer, turns it over, and writes something with a blue ballpoint pen.

"And here is my personal number if you have any trouble."

"Trouble?"

Her eyes flash, and she mouths, "Call me."

This is almost how it would be if we owned this hotel. No need to whisper, but the same idea.

I take the card, remind myself that what I need right now is a good night's sleep.

"Is there anything else I can help you with tonight, Mr. Washington?"

"Actually, there is one thing. While I was parking my car, I saw a red Ford pickup that looked like it had been vandalized." I pat my pockets absently, as though searching for my parking ticket. "It was level P4, I think. You might want to send someone down there."

"My goodness. Yes, of course . . ."

She looks genuinely concerned, as surprised as the guard boy who responded to my call. *This is an actual problem,* she must be thinking. *Normally this shift is all champagne and blow jobs in the twelfth-floor suite. . . .*

I look at her card in the elevator. Her name is Brita, like the water filter. I think about Natsumi's observation that there are a million different reasons to change your name, none of which have to do with escaping. This girl's name conveys freshness, purpose, and hygiene. I am impressed. If the hotel job doesn't work out, this Brita may have a future in advertising.

27

First thing in the morning I call Bil, the clubhouse manager, and tell him something came up at home and I will get my own ride to the stadium.

"One of those mornings, Johnny?"

I hear him wink through the phone. Perhaps because he lives with his mother (or more likely because he's a ringer for George on *Seinfeld*), Bil's sex life is a completely vicarious experience. It's not hard to imagine clubhouse managers living out their baseball fantasies through the guys on the team, but Bil is doing more than that.

"What's that, Bil? I'm not sure I know what you mean."

"Come on," he says, "I know you got some lady up there with big knockers, and you just pulled out, right before I called, and your rod is still wet—"

"I called you, Bil."

"Am I wrong about the girl?"

I turn and watch Brita, in the nude, cut a Belgian waffle into squares along the ridges. Her breasts are lovely, but they're small. So, technically, Bil is wrong.

"Just tell Skip I'll be there in time."

"Sure you will, Adcock."

"Bil?"

"Yeah, fine. I'll tell him."

I hang up and then thumb out a message to Bethany: *Would you call these big knockers?* I raise the phone like I'm looking for a better signal and surreptitiously snap a photo of my grazing guest. I hit Send.

Say what you will about Bethany—she's no chump. She knows what I do on the road. Her only condition is that I tell her everything when I get home. It is like filing an expense report. Photos like this one are my receipts.

"Are you working today?" I ask Brita.

"No," she says, "are you?"

After she fell asleep last night, I checked her wallet. Real name Brittany Wells, twenty-two years old, resident of Granada Hills. Wears corrective lenses.

"I have to go to a funeral," I say. "You want to come? I need a date."

"For a funeral?"

"That's right. Want to go?"

She takes a small piece of waffle, puts it in her mouth, and chews it thoroughly.

"I would love to be your date," she says, "but I have nothing to wear. I can't go to a funeral in my uniform. People look at you strange when you're wearing a uniform."

"Tell me about it," I say. "How about when the stores open I buy you a dress?"

My phone shivers. *Not bad,* Bethany has replied, *but not knockers. Maybe before her kids sucked the life out of them?*

"Do you have kids?" I ask Brita.

She smiles. "That's a funny thing to ask."

"Do you?"

"Why? Do you want to give me some?"

"I want to give you a dress."

"Do you have something against kids? You're supposed to be a teacher."

"Who told you that?"

"You did, last night."

"Oh, right. No, I have nothing against kids. I actually have a daughter—" I am about to say *She's not that much younger than you,* but I stop. Has it come to that? Not yet. But it will soon.

"To answer your question, yes, I have a baby boy. His name is Dustin, and before you guilt me for spending the night with you, I'll have you know that he's staying with his grandma this week."

"I would never give you grief. Not for that."

She looks at me suspiciously. She wants to believe me, I can see it in her eyes, but she can't understand why I'm not going to criticize her parenting.

"Lucky kid," I say. "Does he like baseball?"

She grins. "He's just a baby!"

"Well. Tell him to think about pitching. Relief pitching. Lots of money in that, I hear."

She rolls her eyes and says, "Sure, sure," like I just gave her a tip on a penny stock, but here's the thing: She will remember this conversation. She will remember the time she was working at the Bonaventure Hotel and spent the night with a man who didn't cut her down when she told him about her son. He bought her a dress, maybe, and gave her this crazy idea about Dustin and baseball. It doesn't take much, folks: a drop of human kindness, the acknowledgment that we are people, unique and imperfect. In an inhospitable world, sometimes that is all it takes.

28

The funeral for Javier "Bam Bam" Rodriguez is exactly what you'd expect to honor a slugger turned porn king. The air smells of rum, roses, and Drakkar Noir. The walls of the Catholic church in Van Nuys are covered in a mosaic of gold-tinted mirrored tiles, like a shrine to Our Lady of the Disco. The pews hold a mix of Bam Bam's family and associates, and it is hard to tell the two groups apart. I cannot rest my eyes without tumbling over half a dozen bulging, surgically enhanced chests. These people are like another species: *Homo pectoralis,* a rare creature capable of performing 350 push-ups while nursing twins.

Brita sees someone she knows, and her friend's planar physique suggests she is either an adolescent *H. pectoralis* or a good old-fashioned *Homo sapiens.* My date excuses herself, leaving me with Bam Bam's widow. I barely recognize her. Mrs. Bam Bam has lifted, peeled, and dermabrasioned her face to an eerie high gloss—think Rip Hamilton, the basketball player, in his see-through plastic mask, plus permanent makeup. As she greets me I consider the maintenance it must involve, the hours with the rotary buffer, wax on, wax off, wax on, wax off. . . .

"Thanks for comeen, Johnny," she says. "This would have men a lot to Javier."

"It's lucky we were in town. I am truly sorry for your loss."

Mrs. Rodriguez raises one overplucked brow as far as Botox will allow. "He was no a good man, my husban', but I love heem anyway."

"We all did," I say. I want to add that she's right, that he was not a good man, but this is one of those moments when the truth does not need to be underlined. Mrs. Bam Bam nods serenely, and I realize Bam Bam had a good woman, too, however grotesque. Probably better than he deserved.

The service is heavy on testimony. After a few well-worn prayers, half a dozen brothers and uncles step to the mike to deliver their eulogies. They talk about how Bam Bam started shaving when he was ten years old. How he lost his virginity at eleven. Got his girlfriend pregnant at thirteen. A young woman who says she worked for Bam Bam yanks down her tube top and shakes her hard, shiny breasts at the congregation. "He paid for these!" she says. A few people laugh, but it makes me uncomfortable. I wonder when it became fashionable to embarrass the deceased at a funeral. I suppose laughter can help ease the pressure of grieving, but I don't see a lot of tension as I look around the room. These people seem awfully loose to me. It makes sense: who but the pathologically loose could be counted on to perform sex acts under television lights?

I am scanning the pews, thinking I am alone in my discomfort, when I see a familiar face: a young Latino dressed in a dark suit, black dress shirt, and an ivory tie. He looks so different from the last time I saw him that it takes me a minute to realize who he is: Luck's new pimp, the firecracker whiz. The left side of his face looks odd, until I realize he is wearing makeup—foundation—to cover the bruises I gave him.

After the service, I follow him to the restroom. He goes into a stall and comes out a minute later, rubbing his nose with one finger, like a chipmunk with a toothbrush.

"Hey there," I say. "Remember me?"

He looks up quick, sees me leaning against the hand dryer.

"I thought we was good," he says behind wild eyes.

"We are. I just have a couple more questions."

He winces and wiggles his shoulders, as though shaking something off his back. "Questions? I just came up here to pay respects to my man, then I got to get back to the South Bay, you know what I'm saying?"

"Bam Bam and I were teammates. What's your connection?"

The guy pinches his nose like he is holding it in place, like it might run off his face. "Same shit," he says. "Teammates."

"I want to talk about Alejandra Sol," I say.

He smiles. "I knew it. All right, homes, I didn't come here to do business, but we can talk—"

"She's dead."

"Wait—who's dead?"

I pull out my phone and show him the photo from Bethany.

The kid crosses himself but displays no emotion. "Who did it?"

"You tell me."

"I ain't heard from her in like a week." He looks at his feet. He's almost wistful. "You told your friend yet? Homeboy is going to be messed up. He fucking loved that ho."

"There was someone else in the car with her. A married man and a father. You see where I'm going with this?"

"Look, I don't know shit about shit. The boss needed a girl up north, and Ana had to go—" He winces at the slip. "I mean Alejandra."

"Which is it?"

"Same thing, man. Alejandra Sol is, like, a flavor. You ask for Alejandra, and you get a girl like her. Maybe not the girl in the picture, but she looks similar. Dark hair, dark eyes, all that. Nice big tits."

On the one hand, this is excellent news. It seems to explain why the dead girl had so many names. On the other hand, it sucks. It suggests that Luck's girl may have been just one of dozens of girls calling themselves Alejandra Sol. Something tells me that tracking them all down would be a fool's errand, like catching bees with a butterfly net. If I want to get to the bottom of this case, I'm going to have to aim higher.

Before I know what I'm doing, I grab the pimpito by the collar and cut his legs out with a swipe of my foot. He drops to his knees, and I smash his face against the front of the sink, then raise it up so he can see me.

"Who's your boss?" I say.

"Didn't I tell you to forget it? You don't want to know."

"Tell me his name."

"I never met the motherfucker!"

"Why should I believe you?"

He spits a wad of blood and phlegm onto the cold tile floor. "Because it's the truth. I told you about the girls—what more do you want from me? That's all I know!"

I want to bash him again, but I suspect he's not lying. If he has half a brain in his head, he can see that fate is working against him. Twice now he has run into me for no reason but bad luck.

"Fine," I say. "Stand up."

And just as I am starting to feel good about what I've done, this little bit of mercy I've extended to an undeserving soul, my reward arrives in the form of two hombres so thick around the neck that their ties reach only halfway down their chests. They see the blood on the sink and the state of the pimpito's face. It doesn't take a GED to figure out what's going on.

The next thing I know, I've taken a punch in the gut. My

breath escapes with a sickening groan. I double over. Then I notice their footwear: two pairs of new Jordans, red with white lace covers.

"Where's the binder?" the one who hit me says.

"What binder?" I croak.

"The white binder, player. It don't belong to you. We know you took it."

So these are Bam Bam's thugs—and they're not after Herrera's phone. I'm confused. It doesn't make sense that they would care about the binder—or anything in that office—now that Bam Bam is on the permanent DL. Makes me wish I actually read the damned thing before I stashed it with my equipment.

I look up in time to see the pimpito disappear out the bathroom door. The thug closer to the door steps back and barricades it with his ass.

"You got three seconds," he says.

"Sorry, guys," I say. "I know what you're looking for, but I don't have it anymore."

A blow to the neck from a heavily tattooed fist. I drop flat on the filthy restroom floor. My nose cracks. Blood is running between the shitty little Chiclet tiles. I roll my body over my left arm. They kick my spine, the right side of my rib cage.

There's pounding at the door, and the thugs look at each other. "We better go," the smart one concludes. Between eyelids already swelling shut, I watch these two animals straighten their ties in the mirror. Then one of them walks over to me, stares down at my pathetic heap of a self, and says, "How about it, player? Was it worth it?" Pure genius. The guy could write an ethics textbook. He gives me another kick in the neck—not too hard this time, but it does the trick.

Lights out, Adcock.

29

I wake up in a hospital bed, surrounded by puke-green institutional curtains. A familiar voice is speaking on the phone nearby.

"I said fifty-one percent of equity." Long pause. "Yes, I know my first offer was higher, but that's what happens when you make me wait." Another pause. "No, Terrence, this is not a surprise. I warned you."

I lift my head. "Bethany?"

"Let me call you back." Bethany tosses the phone into her purse. Her face is stern. "She may have small tits," she says, "but you owe that girl your life."

"Who, Brita?"

"Is that her name?"

"Yeah, like the—" I cough.

"Like the water filters. Cute. Anyway, write her a thank-you note. I'll remind you."

Bethany leans over, kisses my forehead with surprising tenderness, and starts slipping pillows behind my back so I can sit up.

"Brita called you?"

"She checked your phone and saw all the calls to my number. I have to admit, Johnny, I was touched."

"How long was I out?"

"She found you on the men's room floor. By the way, why don't you ever ask me to funerals?"

"And then she brought me to the hospital."

"She called 911."

Shit.

"She was surprised to learn that your name was not Marcus Washington, but on the whole she rose to the occasion."

"Does she know?"

"That you play baseball? No, but it's funny, one of the paramedics recognized your name and asked if you were *the* Johnny Adcock of the San José Bay Dogs."

"What did she say?"

"She must have said no, because she asked me if a bay dog was a breed of retriever."

"Does the team know?"

"Oh, thanks for reminding me: you've been traded to San Diego."

"What?"

Bethany produces my phone from her jacket pocket.

"Your agent called an hour ago."

30

The news stings, even though I expected it. My agent answers the phone breathless, as always. "They waived the physical," he brags. It's a win only an agent could appreciate. Todd Ratkiss is a forty-year-old man-child, a redheaded Jew on his third marriage. The most recent Mrs. Ratkiss was a rental-car clerk he met at the airport in Cabo. I hate going out to dinner with Todd, because I'm always afraid he is going to propose to the waitress.

"That's fine," I say. "But I'm not worried about a physical." It is the supremest irony imaginable, given my condition.

"You are not a young man anymore, John. All kinds of things can happen at your age. Things you don't even feel. Hairline fractures, bone spurs, shredded ligaments, sports hernias."

He stops, perhaps sensing, in that way agents have, that I am hiding something from him, something (to use his legal term) "material."

Or maybe Bethany just told him what happened.

"Hey!" he yells. "You should be thanking me! I saved you from waivers!"

"Nobody mentioned waivers."

"Not to you. But it was there, Johnny. Like an angel's voice."

He whispers through the phone, "Way-vers . . . Way-vers . . . *Waivers!*"

Waivers is when a baseball team puts its old sofa out on the curb. When a player is waived, all the other teams get a chance to claim him. If more than one club is interested, the team with the worst record has dibs. In my case, all roads lead to the Padres, owners of the worst record in the National League.

"But back to the physical," Todd says.

"Thanks to you, I have an extra fifty milliliters of urine to play around with."

"Haven't I always tried to get you something extra?" Todd tells me that I need to report to the Padres' stadium, Petco Park, by five-thirty this evening. Although my left arm is more or less unhurt, the rest of my body is a shit show: the swelling under my eyes makes Joe Torre look like Miss America.

"So you're welcome. And, Johnny," Ratkiss adds, "try not to fuck this up if you want to keep playing."

"What do you mean, *if*?"

"I'm just saying, you're coming up on your expiration date."

"You're one to talk, Todd. You probably couldn't get the ball over the plate, and we're the same age."

"This isn't about me," he says, suddenly cool. "I get fifteen percent if you play and zip if you don't. That should tell you where I'm coming from."

"I know where you're coming from."

The conversation ends sour, which was never my intention. Todd is a decent guy and a dedicated agent. I'm just upset that everyone seems to think I should retire. I wonder if I have been limping and everyone notices it but me, like a dog who needs to be put down. Doubtful, but sometimes even Johnny Adcock, the great detective, fails to see the obvious.

31

Unlike the tenderfoots I work with, Bethany has zero patience for injuries. She and her ultra-endurance friends don't even trade aphorisms like "You gotta play through the pain." For them, it goes without saying that if you can walk you can run. And if you can go a mile you can go ten. Medically speaking, it is probably not the soundest strategy, but I know a few pampered infielders who could learn a thing or two about duty from these masochists.

Lucky for me, this mind-set means that Bethany has no qualms about helping me escape medical supervision. She strips me out of my gown and helps me into a new charcoal Zegna suit. She calls it a get-well present, and it fits like a glove.

We take her rental car to her hotel in Westwood, where she leads me to an air-conditioned suite on the tenth floor. She tells me that she is scheduled to give a talk about venture investing to a business-school class at UCLA. The professor is a friend who told her to stop by next time she was in town.

"A student is picking me up downstairs," she says. "I'll be gone two hours. Three, tops. Can I trust you to stay put?" The plan is that I will wait here until Bethany gets back from her lecture, and then she will drive me down to San Diego in her rental car so I can report for work. But she knows I won't wait around. And I know better than to lie. So I say nothing.

We look at each other in silence for a minute.

"You know," I say, "there is one place the doctors forgot to check. Would you mind taking a look? I think it might be broken."

I drop the Italian suit trousers to my ankles.

Bethany decides UCLA can wait.

Twenty minutes later, she ties up her hair, pulls the pencil skirt down over her spectacular ass, and repeats the question: "Will you be good, Johnny? Or do I need to call someone to watch your door?"

"You would do that?"

She smiles. "No one watches their own boyfriend's door these days."

It is the first time she has ever used the word "boyfriend" with me, and I have to admit it gives my heart a little jolt. It casts the indomitable Bethany in a strangely juvenile light, so that I catch a glimpse of Bethany Pham at age fourteen, sitting by her parents' phone, praying for the courage to dial that cute boy from geometry. She may be human after all.

Or maybe not. But she was once fourteen.

"Just do me a favor," she says. "Don't do anything stupid. You've been beaten up enough for one day."

I rub my aching ribs. "You think?"

"This isn't even your full-time job, John. And fishing you out of trouble isn't mine."

"I know. Hey—do you still have that guy?"

"I have lots of guys."

"Sorry—the hacker. The one who can pull information from anonymous e-mails, find out where they're from? That guy."

She nods. "Sure. And the best thing about him is that he's hung like a freaking ox."

"That's great. Here—" I throw her Frank Herrera's phone. I found it as we were leaving the hospital, still in the pocket of my bloody jacket. "I need to know who sent the last text message. And, Bethie, please don't let anyone know you have that thing."

She gives me a peck on the forehead and says she'll see me in a few hours. After she leaves, I open the curtains. The hotel has a view of the Westwood veterans' cemetery, row upon row of uniform white markers, punctuated by sycamores and live oaks. In the distance, the freeway winds into the hills, a river of windshields shimmering in the heat.

Bethany has a point: I am in no shape to continue this investigation, not the way it's going. I'm not an accountant or an insurance adjustor; I don't sit behind a desk to earn my keep. I have a professional obligation to maintain my body in working order. God help me if the Padres call on me to pitch tonight, but I'll deal with that when the time comes. I could always fake the flu.

The phone rings, and I see that it's Marcus. "You're not going to believe what happened to me," I say.

He laughs. "Richard Millman? I was traded a couple times, but never for a washed-up closer. My sympathies, kid. You must be hurting."

"I am, but it has nothing to do with Richard Millman. I got the crap beat out of me yesterday at Bam Bam's funeral."

"Damn. You know why?"

"I took something from Bam Bam's office, and now I've been rolled twice for it."

A short pause, then: "You went to his office?"

"I had to go back and make sure you didn't leave anything behind. You were pretty rattled."

"Rattled? The fuck I was!"

"Anyway—I took a binder, some kind of investment prospectus. I stashed it with my gear in the visitors' clubhouse at Dodger Stadium. Problem is, I'm no longer a Bay Dog, so I'm probably locked out."

Marcus isn't worried. "The clubhouse guys will pack it up."

"I hope so."

"Did you tell Herrera's wife about the chick in his car?"

"Jesus Christ, you wouldn't believe the story on that girl. Turns out there's a whole operation going on. Another buddy of mine was screwing the same girl. Looks like a ring of prostitutes aimed at ballplayers. I'm thinking Bam Bam was involved."

"With the hos?"

"Sure. He sent the video to Frankie because he was shaking down his johns. Or something like that. What do you think?"

"Could be," Marcus says. There isn't any doubt in his voice, but I get the feeling he's humoring me. I agree that it seems unlikely a small-time operator like Bam Bam Rodriguez would have been running girls as well as porn, but why else would Luck's pimp have attended his funeral? Bam Bam Rodriguez was a juiced-up power hitter prone to flattery, dirty jokes, and swinging at the first pitch. I know the type all too well. It doesn't fit that he could have managed an operation like this. How would he have laundered the money, for instance? The guy couldn't even keep his desk clean.

"You okay to play tonight?" Marcus asks.

"Not sure. My arm is fine, but the rest of me is jacked."

"Well, if you need anything."

"Thanks, but you've done more than enough."

After we hang up, I stand and lift my arms above my head. It feels like knives are slotted between my ribs. Buddies who have undergone reconstructive surgery tell me this is how rehab begins, with pain so unbelievable you're reminded that what you're doing (rebuilding an elbow with tendons from the

153

leg, for example) is not supposed to be done. The human body has natural limits. Our profession ignores those limits, and this is our reward.

In this era of piss tests and mandatory suspensions, you have to be careful with your remedies for pain. Something as benign as a muscle-relaxing ointment can trigger hormones that will land you on unpaid leave for fifty or a hundred games. Fortunately, the little cocktail I have in mind is as old as the hills, and as far as I know still legal. It has many names: Scope-a-Dope, Advil Shooters, or my favorite, Champion's Tea. I go to the bathroom and grab a handful of ibuprofen from Bethany's kit. On the counter, the hotel has set out an assortment of toiletries. I grab a travel-sized bottle of mouthwash, crack the seal, and drop the pills on my tongue. Mix, swish, and swallow. Who needs HGH?

32

I am crawling south on the San Diego Freeway behind the wheel of Bethany's rental car, in what must be the slowest getaway since O.J. and Al Cowlings. I flip the radio to AM and find—what else?—Jesse Ursino's call-in program. As usual, Jesse manages to be both reasonable and reactive, but this time the topic hits close to home:

". . . and what's with these who-cares trades? I mean, it used to be that when a club swung a deal the night before the trade deadline, it was an impact move. I'm thinking of the Dodgers snagging Manny Ramirez in '08, or the Rangers and Cliff Lee in 2010. Now what do we have? Richard Millman to the Bay Dogs for Johnny Adcock? I'm sorry, but Johnny Who? I played with the guy, and I consider him a friend, but for Christ's sake, a left-handed setup man is not going to make the difference between playing in October and going home."

Just goes to show, you never know who your friends are until you hear it on AM radio.

Asshole.

I grab my phone and dial the number Ursino barks to the listeners before every commercial break. Two rings and I am speaking with a screener who sounds about two hundred pounds overweight, wheezing like a whale with a congested blowhole. "*Talking Trash with Jesse Ursino,* please state your name and location."

"This is Johnny Adcock. Let me speak to Jesse."

You can hear the guy sit up. "You're kidding, right?"

"If you don't believe me, tell him it's Sparkle Dick."

Ursino is famous for the incident with Kirk Gibson, but he staged plenty of other pranks, too, including one on yours truly. Unlike Gibby and the shoe polish, this one never entered baseball lore. Only a member of the late-nineties Bay Dogs would get the reference.

There is a full minute of silence before Jesse Ursino comes on the line. "Fucking Sparkle Dick Adcock, is that you?"

"Since when am I your friend?" It comes off more aggressive than I intended, but I decide not to worry about it. After all, this is the man who put glitter glue in my athletic supporter.

"Hold on," Jesse says, "let me patch you in."

There is a pop on the line, and the fat assistant asks me to turn off my radio. I do as I am told.

Through the phone now, I hear the show's theme music, followed by Jesse's voice: "Welcome back to *Talking Trash.* Would you believe that during the commercial break none other than the who-cares man himself, Johnny Effing Adcock, picked up his phone and called the Trashman? Yes, it turns out Adcock was cruising through the airspace in his automobile and heard our program. Seems we hit a nerve. Can't imagine why that would be. . . . Johnny, are you there, my man?"

"I'm here, Jesse. Thanks for having me on."

"So tell me, how are you feeling post-trade?"

"I haven't joined the Padres yet, but I know I'm going to miss my teammates in San José. And the whole Bay Dogs organization, the Eberhardt family, the front office, everyone."

"You've spent your whole career in San José, correct?"

"That's right. Thirteen years."

"You don't see that much anymore."

"You would know."

"Hey! Okay, yes, it's true. The Trashman did make the rounds a little bit. But as I always say, baseball is a business, not a hobby. We sell our services to the highest bidder."

"That's one way to look at it."

"Are you saying you would have preferred to remain with San José? I would have thought you'd want to move closer to your family. They're still in SoCal, no?"

"I don't talk about my family with the press."

"Oh, right . . ."

I hear the rare twinge of regret in Ursino's voice. He knows he fucked up. Any other player, sure, but he knows what I do in my spare time. In fact, he knows too well: six years ago, just before he retired, I helped him find his teenage daughter. She was a rebellious girl who got mixed up with drugs and disappeared with some questionable friends. All Ursino knew was that she was heading south. Thanks to my network of contacts in Central and South America—yet another reason to be grateful for Latin American baseball—I located her at a resort in Costa Rica and had her home within a week.

"Anyway, the Padres—not exactly a trade up. fifteen games out of first place with sixty to play. Mathematically, their season is not over, but for all intents and purposes . . ."

"I don't want to talk about the pennant race, Jesse. I want to talk about Frankie Herrera."

"Herrera, folks, was the Bay Dogs catcher killed in a car crash last week."

"That's him. I wanted to say for the record that Frankie Herrera was a good man."

"I never said he wasn't."

"You suggested earlier this week that the callers were making too much of his charity work in Mexico."

"Did I?"

"You did."

"We can review the tape, but I have no recollection of saying anything like that. I never knew Frankie Herrera, and I certainly had nothing against him personally."

"You should be careful what you say on the radio, is all I'm saying."

"Thank you for the warning, Johnny Adcock. The Trashman will certainly mind his P's and Q's. But now it's time to pause for a station identification. You're listening to K—"

The show goes to a commercial break, and Ursino clicks over to a private line.

"You there, Sparkle Dick?"

"Yeah, sure. I don't know why I called in. It was a bad idea."

"I'm glad you did, because I've got a piece of news that may interest you. It concerns our friend Frankie Herrera, as a matter of fact."

"What's that?"

"Turns out he was something of an actor, if you know what I'm saying. I haven't seen the clip personally, but ESPN is about to break the news that there is a video on the Web of Herrera and another dude tag-teaming a chick who looks like Herrera's wife."

I take a deep breath. "They can't show that on ESPN."

"You've never seen a censor bar? Maybe they'll tip TMZ or Smoking Gun and give them the link, I don't know. Did you have any idea he was up to this?"

"Herrera isn't the first, and he won't be the last."

"I know," Ursino says, "but stories like this never get old. This is huge. We'll be talking about this for weeks, maybe more."

I hang up and throw the phone into the passenger's footwell. I am furious, but not at Jesse Ursino. Jesse can't help himself. He is paid to be an asshole. But I should have kept my mouth shut. So I was wrong about Frankie Herrera—did I really need to go on the radio and pretend I was still right? The release of the video will only make it worse: Ursino will play back the clip of me defending Herrera, juxtaposed with audio from the porno. I don't blame him. If it were my show, I'd do the same thing.

33

I take the exit for La Jolla, a tony enclave wedged between the University of California's San Diego campus and the Pacific Ocean. In that peculiar California way, La Jolla refuses to advertise its wealth. No Gangnam Style here. La Jolla is full of millionaires who wear fleece jackets to five-hundred-dollar dinners, where they order entrée salads and glasses of organic chardonnay. This bastion of restraint is where Frankie Herrera chose to settle his family. He told me it had been a tough decision: his wife's parents live in Chula Vista, a gritty strip between San Diego and the border, and Frankie knew the homeboys there would say he moved because he thought he was better than them. *Whiter* is what they meant, although Frankie told me that La Jolla is actually more Asian than white. His sons' best friend in preschool was an Indian boy named Saahil whose parents worked at UCSD and at Scripps, the medical research institute next door. Frankie said he understood why some ballplayers settled in places like Phoenix or Orlando, where you could be surrounded by the families of other professional athletes. But he did not mind being surrounded by scientists. They are quiet, he said. Nobody gets into your business.

Only as I am turning off the engine in front of the Herreras' enormous Spanish-style home, with its nonfruiting olive trees, smoke bushes, and showy fountains of raspberry bougainvillea, does it occur to me that I should have called first. But it is too late for that. Besides, it would have given Maria Herrera a chance to hide. I know she doesn't want to hear what I have to tell her, and I have no idea when the news about her video is going to break.

I pull the heavy brass knocker and let it fall. The blow echoes through the timbered door like the voice of God. I feel suddenly like an inquisitor at the door of a medieval Spanish monastery. It occurs to me that even the tastefully rich make errors in style. Laugh all you want at the hillbilly quarterback who builds a replica of the Playboy mansion on his property in Scottsdale, Arizona: a dungeon door on your fake California mission is no better. In fact, if you are Latino and have some native blood, it is worse. But I don't blame the Herreras or any of them. The root problem is not taste but wealth.

As expected, my arrival takes the widow Herrera by surprise. She answers the door wearing a pink velour track suit trimmed with shiny white stones, the kind where the butt—I know this without even seeing it—is emblazoned with some embarrassing word like "Juicy" or "Cherry" or, for the color-blind, "Pink."

"Johnny Adcock," she says. "I wasn't expecting you."

"Sorry, I should have called."

She looks at her watch. "Don't you have a game?"

"Later."

She raises an eyebrow. "What happened?"

At first I think she means the trade, but then I remember how I look. I touch my temple, the more busted-up one. It feels hot and puffy.

"No big deal," I say. "I've been treated."

She nods without any special concern, like I'm not the first injured man to show up at her door unannounced.

"Can I come in? I have something to tell you about Frankie."

She leads me through a long entry hall lined with pilasters—think Caesars Palace minus the triremes and chiming slots—ending in the kitchen. The gleaming marble island in the center is larger than my childhood bedroom. She pulls out a stool and asks if I would like some carrot juice.

"How are the twins?" I say.

"They don't understand. They think their dad is at work."

I feel bad suddenly for bringing up the twins. There is the story the boys will come to know about their dad—the star athlete, the hero, the philanthropist—and then there is the rest, which they will never be able to accept. Here I am, the bearer of that infamy, and I'm asking how they feel. *Pretty fucking bad, Adcock, what did you think?*

"Did you find him?" the widow asks, and for a moment I am stumped. *Find who?* And then I remember. The murderer, she means. She's convinced Frankie was killed. Run off the road, I guess.

"Mrs. Herrera, I have some difficult news. It turns out there was another person in the car when Frankie died."

She is silent for a moment as the information settles in, as questions present themselves.

"Now you are going to tell me it was a woman," she says.

She must see it on my face.

"I'm not surprised," she says. "Who was she?"

"She had aliases. The one she used most was Alejandra Sol."

I watch the widow's face, but there is no flash of recognition. "A girl who uses multiple names," she says. "Was she a spy or a stripper?"

"It's funny you say that. . . ."

"She was a stripper?"

"Not exactly. She was more of a—I guess you would call her a prostitute."

There, I've said it. The rest of the conversation is going to be a downhill ride. A little consoling, a little it's-not-your-fault. Maybe a hug. Then I will get into my car, drive to the ballpark, and get on with my life.

But Maria Herrera hangs tough.

"I don't believe you," she says. "Frankie never had to pay his girls."

"He had girls before?"

She snorts. "You guys always think it's a revelation."

"Us guys?"

"Ballplayers."

"You knew?"

"Not this time, not specifically. But did I know that Frankie had girls? Sure. He wasn't very careful about it." She laughs. "I wonder how many other athletes' wives got the joke when Tiger's wife found those texts on his phone."

"What was the joke?"

"You think she wasn't reading his phone for months? For years? Personally, I think he was juicing, and his wife couldn't take it anymore. Frankie never took those drugs, lucky for me, but I have girlfriends who say it's like fucking a bear. But it's the price of admission, right? If you want to live in La Jolla or Winter Park or wherever, you keep your mouth shut and spread your legs."

"For the bear."

"Like I said, Frankie never took steroids. He was gentle in bed."

"That's good to hear."

"But now you're telling me he paid for sex? No offense, Mr. Adcock, but if anybody in baseball was paying for girls, it would be long relievers."

"I'm a setup man, Mrs. Herrera."

"Same difference."

"Actually, it's not."

But the widow has no interest in debating my job description. "What else do you know about Alejandra Cruz?"

"Alejandra Sol."

"Where did she get my video?"

"I never said she had your video."

"Isn't that what I hired you for?"

"Your husband hired me, Mrs. Herrera. He was a friend of mine, a teammate, and I said I'd find out what I could." I reach up without thinking and rub my forehead too hard. The pain spreads out from my thumbprint in waves.

Maybe because she sees my grimace, the widow backs off. "I appreciate what you've done," she says. "I'm just disappointed you didn't find out more."

"There is a little more."

I weigh how much to tell her, knowing that other people's stories—George Luck's, for example—might be compromised if I go on. But this woman deserves to know. Her husband is dead. He was consorting with a hooker behind her back. She has two small children she will have to raise by herself.

"The thing is," I say, "Alejandra Sol was more than a prostitute. She was working for a group that sold foreign girls to American men."

"My husband was screwing a wetback?"

"Not exactly—"

"How do you know all this?"

"I have people."

"Who know this personally?"

164

"Let's say yes."

"Come on, Mr. Adcock. . . ."

"An old friend. He's a pitcher. And not a long reliever, either. He is a starter on a big-league club."

She sneers. "I stand corrected."

"Look, Mrs. Herrera, I know how hard this must be. But I want you to know I'm not done. With your permission, I will get to the bottom of this. I will finish it."

"Now you sound like a detective."

"What did I sound like before?"

"Honestly? You sounded like my husband."

34

In downtown San Diego, I pull into the players' lot at Petco Park—and by the way, what kind of name is that for a major-league stadium? I know the Padres' owner has bills to pay, but it's hard to maintain your dignity in a palace built on kibble.

Anyway, the guard waves me in and shows me where to leave the car. A chain-link fence rolls shut behind me. The Padres' clubhouse manager meets me at the door, shakes my hand, and shows me to my locker. I'm happy to see that my Bay Dogs equipment bags have arrived already. As soon as the clubhouse guy leaves me alone, I start digging through the bags for Bam Bam's binder, but I come up empty. I find my gloves, my (mint-condition) game bats, and a photo of a six-year-old Izzy dressed like a cat on Halloween. But the binder is not there. I don't know if I should be happy or sad about this. On the one hand, maybe now the wrecking crew will leave me alone. On the other hand, how will they know it's missing? It occurs to me that they may have put two and two together and broken into Dodger Stadium before my bags shipped out, taken what was rightfully theirs. A much more likely explanation is that Bil Chapman did his usual erratic work and just forgot to pack the binder. I'm also missing a little Buddha statue, a souvenir of the Bay Dogs' trip to Japan for exhibition games three years ago.

I call Bil.

"Johnny, my man! How's San Diego? Seen any donkey shows yet?"

"That's Tijuana, Bil."

"Same difference. What can I do for you?"

"I left a few things in the clubhouse in L.A. One is a three-ring binder, white plastic, with some investment information inside. The other is a little Buddha statue from the Japan trip. It's about two inches tall, made of dark stone."

"I have the Buddha."

"Why didn't you pack it with my stuff?"

A pause. "Let's call it a tip."

"A tip? You stole my Buddha as a tip? That's wrong in so many ways. Do you know anything at all about Buddhism?"

"I know I like that statue, and I know it'll look good on my desk. And since you're not going to be around at the end of the year, when the staff tip pool comes in, I figured it was my right."

"Your right?" I could strangle him. "What about the binder? Did you take that, too? Are you looking for investment advice now? So you can invest the tips you're not getting?"

"Sheesh. Cool your engine, Adcock. I don't have your binder. I never saw a binder. And believe me, I would have. I would never leave anything in L.A. Their clubhouse guys are rats."

"Are you sure? Did you see anyone snooping around? Maybe two guys, thick around the neck—"

"I'm sure," Bil says. "You owe me an apology."

I hang up.

An ironed jersey hangs on the bar, number 39. The Padres' usual home uniform is white with brown-and-blue trim and letters—not a bad getup—but today we are wearing reproductions of a ghastly throwback from the early eighties. Let me be clear: I was on board with the retro thing when it was about the forties and fifties. Those were tasteful styles, and especially acceptable now that baggy trousers are back in vogue. But the eighties? What is worth remembering about nut-tight pants, knee-high Ozzie Smith stirrups, and misshapen caps? Even without the recent revival, no one will ever forget the Pirates' wedding-cake hat, with those flat black sides and yellow pinstripes. A child molester would feel self-conscious in one of those.

Tonight's Padres jersey looks like it belongs to an office softball team. The sleeves are dark brown and longer than usual, sewn onto a white vest front, where the word "Padres" is spelled out in sixties-futuristic letters, like we are the baseball team from Tron. Yellow piping trims the sleeves and neck. It is a pullover, so there are no buttons or placket. It is the most hideous getup I've ever seen. Funny thing? I remember this exact uniform from my boyhood. The road version had a brown vest front and canary-yellow sleeves with matching yellow trousers. Thank God we're playing at home tonight.

Leaving the new uniform on its hanger, I change into a pair of workout shorts and head to the weight room. I sit down at the ergometer, dial in my resistance, and begin to row. The wheel hums, the plastic-wrapped cables slapping against the steel of the machine. My ribs ache from the beating, but playing baseball for twenty years is a kind of beating, too. My muscles—even those thin, smooth ones between the ribs—know that the only option is to heal, because tomorrow there will be another workout. And the day after, and the day after that, world without end, amen. The next time you take a beating, think of me. That is how I feel from the All-Star break on, from July to October, every single year. Used to be that players let themselves go during the off season. Now we are expected to stay in shape twelve months a year. This is probably good for the heart and lungs, but it gives the body no time to heal. Surgery has taken the place of rest. A friend of mine, a pitcher, recently saw a movie with his kid about robots in a martial-arts tournament. The kid loved it, but my buddy said it was eerie. Doesn't take much to imagine our pubescent GMs sitting in skyboxes controlling robots with joysticks. Jacked-up tin men might lack charisma for the postgame interviews, but think of what you could save on hotel rooms. . . .

I am twenty minutes into my workout—five kilometers of glassy lake water if you believe the erg's LCD—when I get some company. A couple of outfielders, Ray Thomas, Jr., and Floyd Witherspoon, stake out a bench. I've faced both a number of times. Thomas I own—he's something like 0-for-6 with three strikeouts, lifetime, against me. Witherspoon is the opposite: in April, on the Bay Dogs' first trip to San Diego, he burned me for a homer. I nod, they nod back, and Witherspoon lies down on the bench. For all the posturing and grab-assing that goes on in a big-league clubhouse, there are a few inviolable rules. One is that if you agree to spot a guy on the bench, you'd better pay attention. No checking your phone or the TV monitors—too much is at stake. Both lifter and spotter need to be locked in, to block out their surroundings. For this reason it's pretty easy to eavesdrop on bench-press conversations. I turn back to my erg, spin up the flywheel, and listen in.

"You still with that chick?" Thomas asks Witherspoon.

"Hell, yes." Witherspoon grunts, pushing two hundred pounds of iron off his chest. "Best damn thing I ever did."

"Tell me her name again."

"Alejandra Sol."

"Spanish pussy, huh?"

A clank as Thomas guides the bar home.

"Nigga, there's plenty of shit you don't know about me."

"Tell me this: how does your wife feel about Alejandra Sol?"

Now the two men share the kind of contagious, full-throated guffaw you might think was innocent bonhomie if you didn't know the substance of their conversation.

"For real, though," Thomas continues. "Your girl keeps it hushed up?"

"Oh, absolutely. We have a weekly schedule. The neighbors think she's the maid."

"You gave her a key to your condo?"

"It's safe. This is our thing."

"I know, I know. . . ."

Now the men shift places, and Thomas takes the bench. He's smaller than Witherspoon, and I hear the scrape of metal as they remove a few plates.

Thomas heaves his first rep with a loud exhalation. "Do they got black girls?" he huffs.

"They got all kinds. You should call. Did I tell you homeboy sent me a free sample the first time?"

"For real, free?"

"One night on the house."

"I better do this."

"You're gonna thank me."

35

At batting practice I feel like the girl who misread the party invitation and showed up underdressed. On the visitors' side of the diamond, my former teammates pace around in their handsome road grays while I wiggle my shoulders, adjust my hips, put a finger under the band of my cap—none of it feels right. I grab a bat and get in line behind the cage. I have not had a real at-bat in years, but something tells me that if I ever gave up BP, I would be called to the plate the next night. Bases loaded, two outs, the full deal.

My turn comes up and I hustle into the cage. I nod to the guy on the mound, who happens to be Chuckie Householder, the Padres manager. Householder is one of those old men who believe throwing batting practice is the secret to a long and healthy life. A small but dedicated cohort of big-league coaches subscribe to this philosophy. Clearly it's a way to avoid other types of exercise, because Householder looks like the Kool-Aid man, stubby little arms and legs coming off a big, round middle. His windup is more like a lean-back—remember Fernando Valenzuela?—and I worry that on every follow-through he is going to lose his balance and crash into the L screen. Somehow he gets the ball over the plate.

I take my cuts, nothing spectacular. One of my flies hits the warning track in right-center, the deepest part of the park, but one of my new teammates hauls it in. A long out is still an out: I repeat this to myself every night. The main reason I take BP is to remember how it feels to be the batter. *Know thy enemy,* said the wise Chinese. And because I am such a miserable hitter, it gives me a helpful sense of confidence on the mound, remembering how I struggled that afternoon in that same batter's box. Don't get me wrong, it is a false confidence—my opponent on the mound is a sixty-year-old man with type-two diabetes—but there is a whole industry built around false confidence. They call it sports psychology.

Even though I am allowed twenty swings, I leave the cage after ten. The pain on my right side has grown worse. I start to wonder if I might have a cracked rib. It's too soon to down another Champion's Tea, so I decide to visit the trainer for a mummy wrap. Going to the trainer is never an easy decision, because it means admitting you are injured, which can have contractual implications. What I need, to be perfectly honest, is a corset. Something with whalebone ribs and two rows of eyes up the back. I'm smiling about this, the thought of wearing a corset under the ridiculous future-retro Padres uniform, when I hear someone calling my name.

It is Jerry Díaz, the Bay Dogs' young backup catcher.

"Hey, Johnny, remember me?"

"I was traded yesterday, Díaz."

"Crazy," he says. "It seems like forever. How you been?"

"Been better, to tell you the truth."

The kid frowns. "I know how you feel. I got traded once in the minors."

I consider telling him, like I told Marcus, that the trade is not the reason why I feel like shit, but I decide to hold my tongue in the interest of letting this howdy-do run its course.

"So, yeah," he says, "I wanted to ask you about something."

"Shoot."

"My buddy Chris was just called up from Tucson. He's your new fifth starter."

"Yeah?" I hope my indifference isn't too obvious. "I'll have to look out for him."

Díaz reaches around and pulls a glossy business card from his back pocket. "He found this in his locker, inside a pretty little envelope. Thought it was a birthday card."

Recognizing the silhouette of a familiar Latina, I hand the card back to Díaz. "Throw it away," I say.

"Why?" he says. "Who is Alejandra Sol?"

This is the question of the day—although it seems young Díaz and I are the last to know.

"Forget about it," I say. "And even if you did call, you won't get that girl. It's a scam, a bait and switch."

He moves closer, puts his catcher's glove over his mouth like we are having a discussion on the mound that we don't want the TV cameras to see. "But, Johnny, man, I'm *lonely.* . . ."

And there you have it, ladies and gents, the reason why this is the perfect racket. On the one hand, you have the aw-shucks crowd, the Díazes and Lucks, who call the number on the card because they are curious or lonely. On the other, you have the old pros, men like Floyd Witherspoon, who know exactly what they are getting and no doubt appreciate the convenience of a calling card and the promise of a free first night.

The real problem for me is that I don't know where to put Frankie Herrera. Why would Frankie, a happily married father of two, a hero in his ancestral village, have risked everything for a romp with a working girl? George Luck is proof that you never really know about these things, but Frankie's own wife didn't believe he would pay for sex. And she knew he was no angel.

Because I feel bad for ruining Díaz's party, I offer him a bit of advice. "Why don't you hit the bar at the Hard Rock Hotel after the game? It's right next door, and I hear it's a honey pot. Take Hamilton with you—that guy is up for anything."

He brightens a little. "Will you come, too?"

"We'll see. I got into some trouble last night."

"I was going to say! The side of your face is all . . ." He winces.

"But throw that card away." I pause. Something tells me I'm wasting an opportunity. "On second thought, how would you feel about doing me a favor?"

"A favor?" He squints. "You mean with"—his voice drops to a whisper—"you mean with a *case?*"

"That's right. Any interest?"

For a moment, he says nothing. Then his face begins to shine. "Johnny, man, you won't regret this. My grandfather was a criminal defense lawyer, so I know all about being discreet. Not just that, but I also can collect evidence, find witnesses—I've been training for this my whole life."

I exhale, hope I'm not making a big mistake. I lead him away from the batting cage, into foul territory up the third-base line, where we can talk in private. "I want you to call the number," I say when we're out of earshot. "Pretend you want a girl."

"You want me to go undercover, with an alias and all that?"

"No, I want you to use your real name. Say you're a ballplayer."

He looks at me skeptically, but I know he's not going to argue. He knows this is his best chance to impress me.

"Sure, I can do that. Do you want me to . . . you know . . . do her?"

I laugh, because I hadn't thought of that part. "You're going to have to pretend that's what you have in mind or they're not going to send a girl. But when she arrives, don't touch her." I

174

look him in the eye. "This part is important. We need her trust. Tell her you'll pay for her time, but you just want to talk."

Díaz nods rapidly. "Totally, totally . . ."

"I'm serious, Díaz."

"Don't worry, Johnny. I get it."

I can see the love behind his eyes, the faith I don't deserve. I have been up and down the state for the better part of a week, and what do I have to show for it? A dead porn producer, a trashed hotel room, a couple of bruised ribs . . .

"Call me when you have a date," I say. "This is a three-game series, so you don't have a lot of time. You've got my cell number?"

"Relax." Díaz gives a toothy smile. A bit of swagger is starting to well up in him. That's a good thing. He's going to need it.

To say I'm uneasy about taking him on would be an understatement. I'm worried for his safety, but also worried he'll fuck everything up. Neither feels very good.

"Listen, Díaz," I say. "I'm not doing this right; I need to give you some background."

"Eh, just the facts," he says in what I guess is a police-detective voice.

It's going to be an adjustment working with a partner. I tell myself that I had no choice, that the case was leading me to Díaz. Without question it will be helpful to have someone fresh at my disposal, someone who can pose as a john but can't be traced back to me.

"There was someone else in Herrera's car," I say, "a prostitute named Ana Velásquez, who was calling herself Alejandra Sol—and there are more Alejandra Sols. They are being sold to baseball players. The guys behind this are violent and dangerous as hell, Diaz. We cannot fuck around."

The young catcher takes it all in. "How many players are involved?" he asks.

"I don't know. Could be just a few, could be dozens." After what I heard in the weight room, I'm pretty sure it's the latter—but there's no need to stoke Díaz's fire more than necessary.

"One more thing," I say. "Don't act like a cop."

"Yeah, okay." The kid's eyes crackle with energy. I have never felt older. He raises his mitt and whispers, "Thanks for thinking of me. You won't regret it."

Perhaps not. But at this point, what's one more regret?

36

You may think it would be easy pitching to your former team, because you know the guys so well. You know their wives' names and even what they drink in the hotel bar. Trouble is, you don't know how to pitch them. These are not hitters you have been studying all year. In fact, these are the *only* hitters you have not been studying. Which is why, when the phone rings in the bottom of the seventh, and the bullpen coach nods at me, I start to worry that this could go very, very wrong. The Dogs are sending up the meat of the order in the eighth: Ordoñez, Wood, and Modigliani. Of these, Diggy is the only lefty. There is not a doubt in my mind as I limber up, throwing casually, brushing off the rubber, what my next half-hour is going to look like. How many times have I watched Diggy hit? A couple thousand? Obviously, I am not always paying attention, but shouldn't I have noticed whether he swings at first pitches? Or how often he takes a pitch when the count is in his favor? On the flip side, he knows me inside and out. He was my catcher. He knows my setup game, knows my out pitch. He can probably tell by watching my warm-up tosses whether I have good stuff tonight (hint: take a look at my bashed-up face).

Basically, I'm fucked.

The top of the eighth unfolds according to the script: Ordoñez beats out a grounder to short, but the ump calls him out even though the first baseman's foot is pulled off the bag by the throw. Ordoñez gives some lip, and I see Skip come to the top step of the dugout, but it is halfhearted: the play might have gone the other way if we were in San José. Probably would've. Umps are people, too, sort of.

The next batter, third baseman Justin Wood, fouls off a whole box of Spaldings before drawing a walk. Out on the mound, the Padres' middle-innings guy, Freddie Ochoa, goes to the rosin bag, bounces it in his hand like he is getting ready for the next batter. He knows he is done. We all know it. He is doing this routine to give me another couple throws in the pen before Householder comes out to the mound.

As I jog in, I scour my brain for anything I may have picked up subconsciously about Modigliani. He is a prick, I know that. Maybe I can make him angry, get him to lose his cool. This late in a game, it is always risky to bust a guy inside. The ump is liable to see it as intimidation and issue a warning, or even toss you out. The eighth and ninth innings of any game are a bit like the playoffs. Tempers flare and all that. Story of my life.

Diggy smiles at me as he steps into the box. I have half a mind to plunk him in the back just for the hell of it. I will be ejected, but it might be worth it. I might even earn some respect from my new teammates.

But I do not hit him. I bust him in on the hands and he fouls off two quick strikes. He stops smiling. Then he does something that makes me realize I have been paying attention all these years after all. He steps out of the batter's box, props the bat between his knees, and crosses his arms over his chest. Then he rubs his hands in his armpits, wiggles them a little like he is scratching himself. I have seen him do this a hundred times and never noticed. But the observation works like a key, unlocking other memories about Modigliani's batting habits. For example, with two strikes against him, he can't resist the breaking ball away. How many times have I seen him fold up, chasing an outside curve? He collapses like an ironing board, knees over elbows, the bat dangling behind his back, like a drunk Barry Bonds. So that's an option. But first I test him with a fastball away—far away, like a foot outside. He does not touch it. I give him another, just to see if he's paying attention. He is. No swing.

I shake off the catcher, who wants a high fastball. (Marcus would be proud.) He cycles through the signs, finally coming around to my pitch. Like I said, I don't throw a curve, so it is going to have to be a slider—a pitch that has always been, from its inception, a poor substitute for a proper breaking ball. "Nickel curve" is what my grandfather always called it. He meant it as an insult—for example, when he lit into one of his least favorite pitchers, the mustachioed reliever Rollie Fingers. "That Fingers has nothing but a nickel curve," Grandpa would say. "Where's the frigging skill in that? Where's the art? I'll tell you where—it's on his frigging face, that's where. Frigging hair farmer. Looks like a frigging tonic salesman. . . ."

Grandpa never saw me play professional ball. That is probably a good thing.

At this point, Diggy has to know what's coming. He is a prick but not a moron. After ten years in the big leagues, he must know his weak spots. And he certainly knows my repertoire. All he has to do is add the two together. But it seems he switched off his brain with that armpit massage. I place my pitch exactly where I want it: stirrup-high, kissing the outside corner, then falling out of the strike zone. The actual break leaves something to be desired—like I said, I don't have good stuff tonight—but it turns out to be enough. The great Modigliani swings and misses.

The San Diego crowd rouses from its stupor for a round of reasonably enthusiastic applause. Householder, god of batting practice, emerges from the dugout once more.

"Well done," he says to me. "I always love to see that asshole choke."

I hand him the ball. "You and me both, Skip."

37

There are obvious post-retirement benefits to having a line of work outside baseball, but one benefit that pays off while you are still playing is that you have two potential sources of satisfaction. Take, for example, the strikeout of Modigliani. Before the phone rang in the bottom of the seventh, I had spent the hours since my discussion with Díaz despairing over my failures as an investigator. And this was not just a problem of perception: in the Frankie Herrera case, I failed twice. Not only did I fail to answer Frankie's original query (who sent the video?) but also managed to embarrass him posthumously in front of his wife. And then, in the course of all this blundering, I have discovered some kind of boutique prostitution ring, which seems to be extending its reach even without its leader.

Then: into this steaming shit sauna comes the call from Householder. Oh, right—my other job! Another chance to make good, or at least to reclaim a shred of self-respect. So I take the ball, I throw my pitches, and you know what, sometimes you get validation when you least expect it. My locker is surrounded by reporters after the game. Okay, there are two reporters, but that is two more than I normally attract. They both want to know how I pitched Modigliani. "Take us through it," they say, "tell us what was going through your head."

I say, "You know, guys, I really had no idea what I was doing. I had never pitched to him before."

"Yeah, I guess that's right," says one of reporters, an overweight white man with a boyish grin and a sparse goatee. "Not even in spring training?"

"Never. I just got up there and threw the ball."

Which is not altogether true, but it is close enough for the papers. They don't want to hear about Diggy's armpit scratching, or the depths of my despair. And even if they did, it is my right to be inarticulate. People think professional athletes don't realize how they come across in interviews—all this nonsense about "giving a hundred and ten percent," and "it is what it is," and so forth. That athletes are dunces is pretty much an unchallenged fact in our culture. But have you ever considered that it may be an act? I could have said more to these reporters, but I chose not to. It's like when reporters stop lawyers on the steps of the courthouse, and the lawyers say they have no comment. Let's be honest, if there is one thing lawyers have, it is comments. I am not saying relief pitchers are as wily as lawyers, but there is a certain logic in keeping your mouth shut.

When I get around to checking my messages, I find a text from Modigliani: *You got lucky.*

Maybe so, but what difference does it make? I thumb a reply: *You still struck out.*

The next message is from Bethany: *Call me. Have news re: porno.*

She answers the phone out of breath. She sounds sweaty.

"Hey, babe," she says. And then, muffled: "Carlos, let's take five."

I'm not the jealous type, but I have to ask: "What are you doing?"

"What do you think I'm doing? You left without a note, without saying goodbye. And you stole my rental car. . . ."

"I had a game."

Now I hear her smile. "And what a game it was!"

"You saw it?"

"I had a dinner meeting, but there was a TV in the bar."

"Did you see me and Modigliani?"

If I may add a quick aside, I wonder how many men my age, their fathers dead and gone, seek fatherly approval from their female sexual partners?

"I did," she says. "Very well played, considering you weren't your best self tonight."

"Did it show?"

"HDTV is an unforgiving medium, Johnny."

"Oh."

"So I have the report on your friend's cell phone. Would you like to hear it?"

"Yes."

"I bet you would." Affecting a terrible Chicago accent, she says, "'I've gaaat this thing, and it's fucking golden!'" She pauses to make sure I'm following. "You remember that governor, with the hair? The one who tried to sell Obama's Senate seat? I want to get the quote right."

"It's that good, huh?"

"You decide. The widow sent the video to her husband."

"That's impossible."

"The message you asked me to trace was sent from a mobile number in area code 858, registered to Maria Herrera of La Jolla."

"Are you sure?"

"Hold on, let me check." There is the rustle of sheets, and I hear her holler, "Carlos! Hey, Carlos, come back!"

A minute later, she gets back on the phone. "You still there?"

"Still here."

"You're not angry with me, are you? It's totally safe. I made him double-bag it."

Another rustle, a muffled voice.

"Carlos says it was kids' stuff. The number mask was superficial. He says you don't even need a cell phone to do this kind of thing. You can send text messages from any computer with the cloaking application installed."

"So it came either from the widow's phone or from any computer in the world. That helps a lot, Beth, thanks."

"Don't be sore, Johnny. You know you're my ace."

"I know."

"But I must say, I do enjoy having a bullpen."

38

You think you know someone. Later that night, in my hotel room near Flea-and-Tick Field, over a plate of room-service chicken, I begin to understand my mistake with Frankie Herrera. He came to me with a problem, which he described truthfully except for one major omission. Had I pressed harder on his motivation in engaging my services—*You want to protect your wife? Oh, really? From whom?*—I might have uncovered the rotten timber. And certainly when I watched the film and saw that Frankie himself had been, shall we say, involved, I should have known that there was more going on than a husband defending his wife's honor.

To be honest, I always had trouble believing Frankie was as selfless as he appeared to be. True selflessness is extremely rare in the human animal. I don't doubt that Frankie wanted to erase the record of his wife's film career—who wouldn't?—but he also wanted to protect himself. Some might call that selfish, but to me it just feels like human nature.

In fact, when you take into account that the wife was attempting to blackmail her husband, the Herrera family turns out to be quite human indeed. I see it like this: Maria Herrera was not as cool with Frankie's infidelity as she claimed to be. So she struck him with the only weapon she had—their secret porn film. Now that I think about it, I realize she was tipping me off with that comment about Tiger Woods's wife. I know I should be embarrassed I didn't catch the hint, but at this point I just want to wrap it up and move on. Tomorrow's game is a matinee, so if I am going to make another trip to La Jolla, it will have to be tonight.

I'm nearly out the door when my phone rings. It's Díaz.

"That was quick," I say.

"Dude, like I told you: I was born to do this kind of work."

"You got a date?"

"Sure did."

"Nice work," I say. "When are we meeting? Tomorrow is a day game, remember."

"Tomorrow? She'll be here in fifteen minutes."

39

The Bay Dogs' hotel is near mine, but by the time I get over there, the girl has already arrived. She sits on the edge of the bed, a petite Latina in skinny jeans, wedge heels, and a tight blouse decorated with black sequins. Her makeup is elaborate but not excessive by the standards of her profession. She steals a glance at me as I enter the room, then returns her attention to her hands, which she has folded neatly on her lap.

She's a dead ringer, I have to say, for the girl on the card.

"Want a taco?" Díaz says. From the dresser, he lifts a paper tray containing the remains of an order of carne asada.

"No, thanks. How long has she been here?"

"Not long." Switching to Spanish, he says to the girl, *"What do you think? How long has it been?"*

The girl, of course, does not answer. She's probably wondering what she's gotten herself into. I gave Díaz explicit instructions not to mention that there would be two of us.

"You were right," he says to me. "Her name isn't really Alejandra. It's Rosario."

"You told her we're not customers, right?"

He nods and shushes me with a finger to the lips. *"Tell my friend what you told me a minute ago,"* he says to the girl. *"And don't be afraid, he's one of the good guys, I promise."*

She regards me with suspicion.

"My sister Ana left home ten years ago," she says. *"I was just a girl then, eight years old. Ana said that she would come back for me when I was old enough."*

I turn to Díaz. "Does she mean our Ana?"

He nods and shushes me with a finger to the lips.

"Did you tell her Ana is dead?"

"She knew. The coroner tracked her down."

"Do you want me to keep going?" the girl says.

"I hope my friend explained that we are not hiring you to make love." My Spanish is grammatically correct, but it sounds too formal. *"However, we will pay you for your time."*

Díaz puts his hand on my shoulder.

"Go on," he instructs the girl.

"Ana finally came back last year to recruit girls for her boss. She chose six girls from the group of twenty who applied. We all felt lucky to be chosen, so we did not object when Ana told us we were going to see a doctor before we went to California. She said the clients did not want girls with diseases, and also she wanted to make sure we would not become pregnant. She took us to a house in Tijuana. Every hour Ana led one of us into the back room. It was a small room with a window onto the yard. There was a vanity mirror with a pink wooden frame hanging on the wall, so I guessed it had been a bedroom at one time. Other than the mirror, there was no furniture except a folding bed on wheels, like in a hospital, and a tray with some surgical instruments drying on paper towels."

I am astounded. I haven't seen him play much baseball, but Díaz is a natural at this. There are aspects of investigative work that I will never do well; interviewing witnesses is one of them. But Díaz earned this girl's trust in less time than it took me to walk six blocks across town.

"When I entered the room," she continues, "the doctor was using a sponge to wipe blood off the bed's plastic cover. He told me to take off my pants and get up on the bed. Then he put my feet in the stirrups, and he moved a lamp between my legs. I asked what he was doing, and he said it was a simple operation—hardly an operation at all. He reached into his apron and took out a plastic bag. He held it up so I could see. Inside was a little wire in the shape of a 'T.' 'This goes into your womb to prevent pregnancy,' he said. 'When you get married, you can have a doctor take it out.' I was frightened, because I did not want him to put anything inside me. I was still a virgin, and I was afraid it would hurt. Ana smiled and said I had nothing to worry about. She said millions of women all around the world have these wires in their wombs. I asked her, 'Will I be able to have children after the wire is taken out?' She said yes, I would. Then she left the room to comfort one of the girls, who was just waking up from her operation."

I interrupt: "They put you to sleep?"

"The doctor put a mask over my face. Next thing I knew I was waking up, and I saw out the window that it was night. Several hours must have passed. Two or three hours at least. Ana asked if I felt any pain in my pelvis, and I said no. She said that was good. She said, 'You may have some pain later, but it will go away.'"

For a long couple of minutes, we sit in silence. Through the wall, I hear a TV playing the theme to *SportsCenter*. The girl stares at her hands. Díaz and I are both choked up by her story, but we pretend not to notice each other.

When I've gathered myself, I say, "Rosario, did you know what kind of business Ana's boss was running in America?"

"We knew exactly what Ana did. Lots of girls from my village do it. You can make a lot of money that way."

"Did your sister make a lot of money?"

"Oh yes. She sent my mother five hundred dollars a month. We *built a concrete house with Ana's money. She also paid for my brother to go to school. She paid for everything—fees, uniforms, books, the whole thing."* As Rosario lists the projects financed by her sister's remittances, her eyes shine for the first and only time in our interview. *"Ana's dream was to attend university in the U.S.,"* she explains. *"And you know what? She almost made it."*

40

It is nearly one in the morning by the time I leave the hotel garage for the drive to La Jolla. Sorry, Maria: next time you are thinking of blackmailing your spouse, consider that it may cut into your sleep. At this hour, the freeways are empty except for long-haul truckers and drunken sailors weaving behind the wheels of their Mustangs. As I travel north into the suburbs, the billboards for Latin radio stations and Hooters franchises give way to warnings about immigrants crossing the road. Yellow diamond-shaped highway signs show a family in silhouette, black paper dolls joined at the hands, mom-dad-sister-brother-and-baby, the last pulled through the air like a doll. Somewhere in the dark hills, these people are crouching, waiting for a break in traffic. Or so Caltrans would have us believe.

I exit into the hushed and leafy womb of La Jolla, park a few blocks away from the Herreras' home, and walk the rest of the way. The neighborhood is so quiet at this hour, you can hear the waves at the foot of the cliffs half a mile off. Salt and iodine and peace: the recipe for expensive coastal real estate. I step up to the Herreras' dungeon door, lift the knocker, and let it fall. A minute passes with no answer. It appears that someone is home; lights are burning in the living room and in the rear hall. I knock again. Still no answer.

I consider throwing in the towel and coming back tomorrow. The thought of letting this case go on even one day more is so distasteful that I pull out my phone and dial Maria. It goes straight to voice mail. I hang up.

I am scrolling through a few text messages—Jerry Díaz wrote twice, asking for an update—when I hear footsteps behind me. Before I know what is happening, a gloved hand closes over my mouth. A kick takes out my knees. I'm down, eye-level with a pair of black boots. I struggle to lift my head but get only as far as a pair of dark polyester slacks before I'm shoved back down, nose to the terra-cotta tiles.

"Wait," I mumble, "I'm a friend of the Herreras!"

Out of the corner of my eye, I see a second pair of boots. A man's voice says the Spanish word for "truck." Again I manage to raise my head, and this time I see a face—or really just eyes, because my assailant is wearing a black ski mask. "Please," I try to mumble, but the man shoves his fist in my mouth.

"Tie him up," he grunts to his partner.

The second guy ties a blindfold over my eyes and stuffs another into my mouth. He binds my wrists behind my back with a plastic zip-tie. Another tie goes around my ankles. I am tied up like a rodeo calf. The first man throws me over his shoulder. He is wearing cologne, something cheap and overwhelming. I hear the door of a van slide open, and then I am dumped, knees first, onto the molded steel floor. I scramble like a hobbled crustacean, bashing my head against the wall of the van. The door slams shut. Muffled voices outside. Then the van bobs on its shocks as the men get in. A seat belt clicks. Up close more cologne, some heavy breathing. I feel a needle pinch my shoulder. These are not the same guys who beat me up at Bam Bam's funeral. They might be rent-a-cops—maybe this is like Bel Air, with a private security force—but what kind of rent-a-cop wears a ski mask? My last thought before I black out is that I ought to tell Ginny that if she and Izzy ever feel unsafe in Santa Monica, they should move to La Jolla. Goddamn safest place I have ever been. Safe like a police state.

41

I wake up in a dark, windowless room. The blindfold has been removed, but not the gag. My hands and feet remain bound. I am lying on a bare mattress in the corner. A little light comes in under the door. I see the shadows of feet, hear rapid Spanish and occasional laughing.

My shoulder is sore from the injection, but it's my right shoulder. Once again the gods of baseball are looking out for me in their sadistic way. My first inclination is to grunt, or howl, or whatever I can manage, to get the attention of my captors. But this, I realize, would be a poor decision. I have no idea where I am, who they are, or why I am being held. Best-case scenario, I am still in La Jolla. Who knows, maybe the security force has a guardhouse? Worst case—my imagi-nation spirals down—worst case, I am in a Mexican prison, I have lost a year of my life, and my ex-wife and daughter have given me up for dead. Then I remember the soreness in my shoulder. So much for the lost year. Before I have time to test any more hypotheses, the door opens halfway and a head appears: a Latino about my age with a handlebar mustache. When he sees that my eyes are open, he jumps back, slams the door.

"*He's awake,*" I hear him say in Spanish.

Another voice says quickly, *"Already? Damn. That shit is supposed to last, like, much longer."*

I feel a surge of pride. That's right, I think, your drugs can't hold me down.

"Call the boss," the first guy says.

"I am already!"

The foot shadows move away from the door, and I am not able to hear the substance of the phone call. The guard gives a series of sharp military affirmations: *"Sí. Claro. Pronto."*

Slowly, the door opens. My captors have donned black ski masks. It seems beside the point, since I have already seen one of them, but I understand the psychological value of a uniform, to me and to them.

"Get up," barks the guard on the left in heavily accented English. He is holding a strip of cloth, which I correctly assume is my blindfold. "Now is time," he says. "You see the boss."

"I speak Spanish," I manage to say through the gag.

The guy with the blindfold laughs. *"Oh yeah? Fine, we will speak Spanish."* He turns to his partner. *"Who is this asshole, anyway?"*

"A pitcher," he replies.

I see the first guy's eyebrows twitch. *"No shit? Anybody I've heard of?"*

"He's a reliever," explains the partner. He yanks the blindfold tight against the back of my head.

"Ah. Righty or lefty, do you know?"

"Lefty, I think."

"A closer?"

"More like a LOOGY."

"What's a loogie?"

He spells it out: *"L-O-O-G-Y. It stands for 'lefty one-out guy.' They bring him in to face one batter, lefty on lefty, that kind of thing."*

"What does the 'Y' stand for?"

"No idea. Some shit in English."

The partner grunts and hauls me to my feet, puts his hand on my back, gives a little push. He is surprised when I start to fall forward; my feet are still tied up.

"Oh, fuck," he says. "Sorry about that."

He crouches down and I hear the click of a box cutter, then a snap as he cuts the zip-tie.

"No bullshit, you hear me, pitcher?"

I nod.

They lead me out of the room—right, then left, then right, then left. I lose track after a while. At some point I judge from the street noise and the chill in the air that we are outside, but I can't be sure.

Meanwhile, the conversation continues.

"My cousin, he was in the minor leagues for two years. He was a pitcher."

"Really? I didn't know. Is that Jesús?"

"No, his brother Felipe. He was supposed to be a starter, but they put him in the bullpen, so he quit."

"Just like that?"

"I know, huh? Me, I would prefer the bullpen. You don't have to work hardly at all."

There is a conspicuous pause, and I can tell the guards are tempted to untie the gag and get my two cents on this point. Who better to judge once and for all the foolishness of Cousin Felipe than a major-league reliever?

Fact is, every pitcher wants to be a starter. The only possible exceptions are closers, but most of those guys are batshit crazy to begin with, bomb-squad types with an inflated sense of their own importance. That movie *The Hurt Locker* could have been about closers. Seriously, they could have used the same script but set it in a bullpen. Any reasonable guy understands that the bullpen is the second tier. But pitchers go back and forth between the rotation and the pen all the time. Cousin Felipe could have waited it out, worked on his game. The guy's real failing was not his arm but his perseverance. The minor leagues is about more than just physical development. You learn resilience, too. Like how to hit through a slump, or how to come back fully charged after blowing a save the night before. If you don't learn how to deal with setbacks, you ought to quit. Baseball is no place for the easily discouraged.

Anyway, that's what I would have said, had they asked.

After twenty minutes of walking around like this—in circles, I am sure now—my blindfold begins to slip. I can see up and out from the right eye. For the most part, all I can make out are mildewing acoustic ceiling tiles, but eventually we step outside and I see a billboard for a Latin radio station: *"XRAZA 103.5-FM, El Estación Más Emocionante en Todo Baja California!"* There are photos of the late Tejana singer Selena and a couple other stars I recognize but can't name.

We go back inside. Evidently the men are satisfied that I have been turned around enough, because now we stop in front of a door—I see the top of the frame, white paint peeling away from the wall. One of them knocks. A voice on the other side asks for the password.

"Alejandra Sol," says the one on my right.

42

The widow Herrera is dressed in dark jeans and a short denim jacket. Her hair is blown out straight, makeup freshly applied. She is calm and clearly in charge, a Noriega in jeggings. Behind her, against the concrete-block wall, a couple of guards in black paramilitary attire stand at attention, clutching shoulder-slung Uzis over their hearts.

I am on my knees on the concrete floor, wrists bound behind my back. My gag has been removed, but so far I have said nothing. It occurs to me that I ought to do so, because this may be my last chance. To paraphrase the United Negro College Fund, your last minute on earth is a terrible thing to waste.

"I know you sent Frankie the video," I say.

The widow holds a nine-millimeter pistol at arm's length, peers down the barrel, and pulls back the slide to load the chamber. "What's that?" she says.

"You're not the first wife to take action, and you won't be the last. I see it all the time, and I don't judge. He was cheating, and it broke your heart. You said it didn't bother you, but it did. Look, Mrs. Herrera, your husband was the one who hired me, but he's gone now. I see no reason not to tell you that I understand why you did it."

"I appreciate the compassion, Adcock, but you're wrong. I didn't send that video. I couldn't care less who saw that thing. I thought I was clear about that."

"I have it on good authority that the message was sent from your phone."

"You ought to question your authority, because I didn't do it."

I expected her to deny it—when I imagined this conversation occurring in her kitchen in La Jolla. My plan was going to be to lay out my evidence, including the call records dredged up by Bethany's guy, and declare the case closed. The widow could accept my conclusion or not. But circumstances have changed. I'm no longer in a take-it-or-leave-it situation. Time for a change in strategy.

"You were trying to scare Frankie into breaking off his affair. When he didn't do it, you had him killed. Excuse me—you had both of them killed. Two birds, one stone."

"You think I killed my husband because he refused to be blackmailed? If that's your conclusion, you're not much of an investigator. You're not going to believe this, but I looked forward to meeting you, Adcock. When Frankie told me he hired you, I thought, here's someone I should know. With your contacts, we could have saturated baseball, then moved on to basketball, football, maybe international soccer. In this business, you can't stand still. There's always somebody trying to knock you off the hill." She pauses to make sure I follow. Apparently, she doesn't like the look on my face, because she says very quickly, "You know what I'm talking about, don't you?"

"If you're referring to the prostitutes, then of course I know. Everybody in baseball knows."

She laughs. "You didn't know! I can see it on your face. That's amazing. Well, Frankie was a man of his word. He said he wasn't going to tell you. He said we might need to use you someday, and he didn't want you to think he was corrupt. I always assumed he was kidding."

She's proud her husband's integrity has outlived him—ironic, given Frankie's deceitfulness in other aspects of his life. Strange what we will cherish about the deceased.

"It was Frankie's idea?"

"His and mine both. He was in the minors a long time, you know. There was never any guarantee he was going to get called up. I told him he needed something else, something to fall back on."

My mind races. Bam Bam wasn't behind the operation; it was the Herreras. Maria worked the girls, and Frankie worked the sales. This explains the innuendo in the eulogy at Frankie's funeral. I can see it now, Frankie strolling up next to an acquaintance at batting practice, somebody on the opposing team, talking about this girl he's seeing. She's hot as hell, fucks like a champ. He takes out his phone and shows the guy a picture—or maybe a video? Then he says the best part is that she's discreet, that his wife will never know. When the guy expresses interest, Frankie gives him a card with a photo and a phone number. The number rings the local pimp, somebody like Ana's "Uncle Miguel," who hooks the guy up with a girl. It's all squeaky clean from Frankie's point of view: as far as the new customer knows, Herrera is not the owner, just a very satisfied client. I bet he made most of his sales that way. And after a while, the sales made themselves by word of mouth, as I witnessed in the Padres' weight room. It could have gone on like this forever—a happy family business, Maria and Frankie working side by side—until Luck's girl drove a wedge between them.

"But then Frankie made the big leagues," I say. "Why did you continue to risk it?"

"With his knees? He had one more season, two tops. A family needs to plan for the future, Mr. Adcock."

"Tell me about Ana Velásquez."

The widow raises her brows. "Ana was the first girl we hired. She was fresh off the boat, but she was smart, anybody could see that. She was always telling me she wanted to go to college. I told her she had a talent for business, and I left her in charge when I flew out to meet Frankie on the road. I even paid for some accounting classes at Mesa. Best investment I ever made, I must say. She was the one who realized that there was only so much money in the girls. It was her idea to tape them with the johns."

"You taped them?"

"Sure, you tape the player in bed with the girl, and then threaten to send it to his wife. Suddenly the fee we charge goes up. Sometimes way up."

"Clever."

"Yeah, Ana was clever," Maria says. "I saw a lot of myself in her."

"Sounds like she saw it that way, too."

"When the twins were six months old, I found out about her and Frankie. They had been meeting behind my back for almost a year, whenever he was in town and even sometimes on the road. I had set it up so perfectly for them. When I went down to Mexico on recruiting trips, she was already in the house. All she had to do was climb into our bed. But what could I do, fire her?"

"Even better," I say. "Hire someone to run her off a mountain."

The widow has been almost wistful to this point, but now she returns to the moment. Her eyes turn sharp, and she says, "I didn't kill Ana Velásquez, and I certainly didn't kill my husband. I know what it's like to grow up without a father. I

would never wish that on anyone, least of all my own children."
With this, she raises the pistol to arm's length and cocks the
hammer with her thumb. She is very comfortable handling a
gun. "Do you have children, Adcock?"

"I have a daughter. She's thirteen."

"That's too bad. I wish I didn't have to do this, but you've
given me no choice."

"Wait. You came to my apartment to say Frankie was killed.
You asked me to find out who did it. If you shoot me now,
you'll never get your answer."

"And you have the answer? I find that hard to believe."

"It's your choice. But if you want me to talk, you'll have to
put down that gun."

43

The widow lowers the gun but maintains the game face. "You have one minute."

"You mentioned the secret blackmail tapes of the johns. Did you set up those shoots yourself, or did you hire someone to do it for you?"

"We used a guy in L.A.," she says, "somebody Frankie knew from baseball."

"Bam Bam Rodriguez?"

"That's him. You think he killed Frankie?"

In essence, yes, that's what I think. I don't know what sort of agreement he had with the Herreras, but what if he got greedy and wanted a bigger piece of the action? What if this led him to blackmail Frankie? If anyone knew about that video, it would have been Bam Bam. And it explains his bizarre behavior when Marcus came calling. Bam Bam must have thought the gig was up—that Frankie had figured out who was behind the blackmail and sent some muscle to set things straight.

"Put it this way," I say, "there was bad blood between your husband and Bam Bam."

"And you know this how?" The widow's tone is dismissive, almost condescending.

"I can't tell you that."

In one swift motion, the gun is leveled at my head. "Is this really the time to be protecting your sources, Adcock? I'll give you one more chance to explain yourself. After that . . ." She swivels to the right and squeezes off a shot. The slug bores a hole in the cinder-block wall behind my head. A plume of dust rises toward the fluorescent tube lights. Behind the widow, the guards raise their Uzis a little higher.

"The source is a friend of mine," I say. "A ballplayer."

"The same one who tipped you on Ana? The starting pitcher?"

"He is a pitcher, but he's not the same guy."

Just then the door opens, and a guard in a Kevlar vest strides into the room. He goes to the widow's side and whispers something in her ear.

She raises an eyebrow. "Here?"

"Yes," the guard says in Spanish. *"He brought some black girls. Very cheap, he says."*

"Fine," she says to the guard. *"Bring them in."*

Once more she lowers the nine. "It's your lucky day," she says. "You get to see how this works. Not that it will do you any good, but I'm sure you don't want to die confused."

A moment later, the door reopens, and the guard appears with the guests: two black girls in miniskirts and fuck-me pumps, and a tall black gentleman in red snakeskin boots, leather jeans, and a bolo tie.

It is Marcus.

"Everyone out," the widow tells the guards. *"Leave one man to guard the girls. The rest of you go. We will negotiate alone."*

"What about the pitcher?" someone says.

"The pitcher stays."

Boots squeak as the guards leave the room. The door slams shut.

"So," the widow says to Marcus, her voice airy now, almost flirtatious. Gone is the grieving wife, the devoted mother, the long-suffering minor-league spouse, and all the other avatars she cycled through in our conversation. This is the business-woman, the negotiator. "I don't think we've met."

Marcus nods but does not extend his hand.

"Do you have a name?" the widow asks.

"My name don't matter."

"Fine," the widow says. "I respect your caution."

"I got two ladies here that didn't come cheap," he says.

Marcus does not acknowledge my presence, does not even look at me, which when you think about it should have raised the widow's suspicions. (Marcus: *I've got these hos to sell you, but I'm not going to tell you my name—oh, hey, there's a beaten-up white boy on the floor—so, anyway, how much you going to give me for these hos?*)

"They Trinidad hos, already trained. Show the lady what you got, baby doll."

He slaps his fingers on the ass of the girl nearest him. I see now that it's Natsumi, the L.A. boxer. Natsumi doesn't look at me, either, just clatters her bangles and thumbs her nose at Marcus.

"This isn't a talent show," the widow says.

"I am aware of that. But the thing is, these girls have experi-ence. They was working in a house in Port of Spain when I bought them. They all been tested, too. No diseases, not even crabs."

The widow walks past him, heels clicking on the concrete floor. She stops in front of Natsumi. "How old did you say this one was?"

"Don't take my word for it," he says. "Have a pinch. Here . . ." He grabs her ass under the miniskirt.

"Quit it!" Natsumi shouts.

The widow turns to Marcus. "You say these girls are from where?"

"Port of Spain. They Trini hos."

"I see. So if I did this—"

The widow's hand shoots out and slaps Natsumi across the face.

Natsumi doesn't waste a second. "You gonna be sorry you did that," she barks, without a trace of Caribbean accent.

"Leave the merchandise be." Marcus is now plainly nervous. "You can't just lay your hands anywhere you please."

"If I'm buying this merchandise, I can lay my hands wherever I want."

"Do you need help, boss?" The lone guard is agitated. Gunmetal tinks against the zipper on his jacket.

"Stay where you are," the widow says.

She turns to inspect the second girl, and then there is a flash of movement—limbs swirling, sweeping. Marcus fells the widow with a leg tackle. Then shots, one-two-three-four. A body thumps to the floor. The room vibrates with gunfire, and the air fills with concrete dust. Wrists still bound behind me, I drop to the floor and find myself next to the prone, black lump of Maria Herrera's bodyguard. The back of his head has been removed, replaced by a messy hash of hair, blood, and brain. My stomach seizes. I perform a quick self-check: as far as I can tell, I have not been shot. Very carefully I lift my head and see Marcus holding a smoking pistol. Natsumi has one, too, which she is holding away from her body like a bag of stinking dog shit.

"Where she at?" Marcus barks at Natsumi.

"I thought you took her legs out," Natsumi says.

"I did," he says. "But she ain't here now."

I scan the room: the widow has vanished.

44

Marcus pulls a blade from his pocket and cuts my arms loose. He nods toward the door, and I follow my liberators into the hall. The rest of Maria's guard corps is seated against the wall, bound and gagged, weapons stacked neatly out of reach.

"This way," Marcus says. We follow him down the hall until the ceiling opens up. We are in a warehouse of some kind. On the far wall there's a bright aperture where a rolling door opens onto a loading dock.

"There she is!" Natsumi shrieks. She stops and fires two rounds into the sunlight.

"Are you crazy?" Marcus yells as he rushes past her. "Put that thing down. You could hit the others."

We exit the warehouse just in time to see a black Lexus SUV pulling away. A quick honk, and the lights flash on a blue Dodge Charger R/T, freshly waxed, with twenty-inch rims. "Get in," Marcus shouts. We are joined in the car by two more black girls—dressed more modestly than the others, in jeans and short leather jackets. I see pistols in shoulder holsters under their arms. The Dodge is a hunk of American steel with the widest tires I have ever seen on a passenger vehicle. Marcus guns the engine and sets off in pursuit of the Lexus.

The widow takes a left at the main drag, and Tijuana opens

up: just ahead, a man in a grubby hoodie pushes a cart of folded T-shirts across the road. The Lexus zags to avoid him but takes out the cart. Marcus accelerates through the cloud of fluttering white cloth, then takes the next corner without braking, sending the six of us careening against the side of the Charger.

"The fuck!" Natsumi screams.

"Sit tight," Marcus says.

The Lexus turns down an alley that is really an open-air mall specializing in cookware, dishes, and all kinds of glass. The widow's car does most of the damage here, but the Charger is wider by a foot and expands the zone of destruction. The noise of shattering and metal on pavement drowns the cries of the vendors. We emerge from the alley onto another main road, and the widow takes a left across four lanes, narrowly avoiding half a dozen collisions. Marcus follows, hugging the widow's rear end. On the other side of the road the traffic is slower, so the widow cuts onto the shoulder and shoots ahead a few hundred feet before tucking back in. Marcus tries to do the same, but the width of the Charger works against him. The shoulder is too narrow. When we pause at the next intersection, where a ragged-looking cop is directing traffic, we are two cars back of the Lexus. There's nothing Marcus can do to close the gap until we're on the other side.

In this pause—the first since we fled the widow's bunker—I say, "I guess thanks are in order?"

Marcus snorts. "Your girl called last night. She was worried because you didn't reply to the texts she sent after the game."

I pat my pockets. My phone is long gone. Wallet, too.

"Smart lady," Marcus says. "First thing she says to me is 'Know where I can get good sushi in Palo Alto?' Because I have been thinking of opening a Makasu on the Peninsula."

"I didn't know that."

"Ain't your place to know. But your girl is savvy, she antici- pates this kind of thing. Anyway, she says she got an errand for me, to come down here and rescue your ass. After which I would get a line of credit from her fund."

"How did you find me?"

"Don't forget you were in her rental car. Easy to trace if you bug the GPS. Which she did."

I nod, pretending I knew this somewhat disturbing fact.

"So we find the car, but no Adcock. I call up Bethie, tell her the trail went cold. She asks where we at, and I tell her La Jolla. She says you must have gone to see that lady there." He points through the windshield.

"Maria Herrera."

"Correct. Bethie gives me an address two blocks away. Me and Natsumi split up, case the place, expecting we might have to do some ninja shit. But just as we coming round the corner, the garage door lifts up, and this black Lexus pulls out. We run back to the car and follow her all the way to the border."

"Ahem." One of the girls in the back seat clears her throat.

"Oh yeah. We also muscled up."

"How did you know she was buying girls?"

Marcus cracks his knuckles against the steering wheel and says, "We sat in the car awhile, and people kept going in and out of the building, but I didn't put it together until Natsumi's girl LaTasha talked to one of the guards on his cigarette break. I guess he smelled meat, 'cause he asked if she knew anybody selling bodies."

"How'd she take that?"

Marcus grows stern. "You realize that is how our African ancestors ended up on this continent, right? Selling each other out? She said maybe she knew somebody, maybe not. Then she circled back to the car and we cooked up this act. The plan was for me and Natsumi and LaTasha to go in, and the others to wait outside." Marcus cranes his neck around. "What happened with those motherfuckers in the hall? Did y'all tie them up when you heard the shots?"

"We did that as soon as we saw them," says the girl in the middle. "Can't be too safe."

I glance at the back seat, catch a whiff of fruity perfume. "And you had these costumes with you?" I say.

Marcus looks at me. "What costumes?"

Keeping one hand on the wheel, he pulls out his cell, a sad-looking flip phone with a rubbed-down chrome finish. When the person on the other end answers, he says, "Almost there," and hangs up.

45

Marcus tails the car in front of him and makes it through the intersection ten seconds after the widow's Lexus. Then he makes up for lost time, flooring the Charger and switching lanes like Dale Junior. Soon we're right behind the Lexus, close enough that I can see the widow's eyes in her rearview mirror. Road signs announce the last exit before the border crossing. Up ahead, the highway fans out into eight lanes.

"Hold on," Marcus says. A jolt as we bump the rear of the Lexus. We're going fifty or sixty in what must be a thirty-five zone, although these are TJ numbers. The girls in the back seat complain that Marcus is going too fast. He says nothing. The widow's eyes dart to the mirror and back.

Then, suddenly, a Ford van—white, unmarked—cuts in front of Maria. She slows a bit, and the van brakes hard. Maria swerves to the right, narrowly avoiding a collision. Marcus must have known this was coming, because he has eased back so that there are several lengths between us and the Lexus. The widow's momentum sends her careening onto the exit ramp. We follow at a safe distance.

The ramp dumps us into a ragged, burned-out section of town: empty lots behind chain-link fences, weeds strewn with trash. A couple of tarp-and-cardboard shacks stand in one of the lots, but there are no live bodies anywhere. The frontage road continues for five hundred feet and ends in a concrete wall. The highway courses above us, twenty feet up. As soon as the widow senses the trap, she begins a K turn, but by the second pivot she's toast: the white van accelerates past us, kicking up a cloud of dust as it skids into place, closing her off. From the idling Dodge, we watch the driver of the van leap out— he's a black man in jeans and an Oakland A's T-shirt. It takes me a minute, but I recognize him as Marcus's brother Rich, the ex-con turned sushi chef. I've never seen Rich without his rising-sun headband. He looks good in a *hachimaki,* but this outfit suits him better. His right hand dangles a chrome-plated revolver, an old .45. With military precision, Rich runs to the door of Maria's Lexus and pulls it open. He extends the pistol to arm's length. The gun recoils twice. Without a pause, he throws the weapon inside the Lexus and slams the door. Then he jogs back to his van, where he retrieves two jerry cans of gasoline. The man's efficiency is breathtaking. In less than thirty seconds, he douses the Lexus bumper to bumper, makes a gasoline trail along the asphalt, and tosses the cans back in the van. He slams the sliding door. Then, very casually, he looks up and acknowledges us with a thumbs-up. Marcus nods, and Rich drops a match.

The Lexus erupts in flame.

Tijuana sighs.

46

The U.S. border plaza is fortified by concrete barricades and federal officers with bomb-sniffing dogs—more apparatus than the Maginot Line, and about as effective. Ten of the twenty lanes are open at this hour, and Marcus hops the Charger back and forth, testing each lane like a busy Safeway shopper. When a booth on the end changes its light from red to green, he hauls the wheel around, and the car lurches to one side. He accelerates and slips into the line just behind a dark Ford Explorer with Oregon plates. We wait. This time no one speaks. I feel like I might throw up.

A Border Patrol agent steps out of the booth, holding a travel mug of coffee, which he pulls on between questions to the driver of the Ford. The agent is a middle-aged Latino in uniform pants and a federal-issue windbreaker. His hair is still wet from the morning's shower, gelled to preserve the lines of the comb. He has a full-lip mustache, black flecked with gray. He balances the mug in the crook of his elbow and takes a stack of blue booklets from the driver.

Shit, I think. *Passports.*

"Marcus," I say, "we've got a problem. I don't have a passport."

"No problem," he says. He pats his waist, where I see the outline of a gun.

"Are you kidding me? These are federal agents, and they've got cameras everywhere!"

Inexplicably calm, Marcus says, "I saw you on *SportsCenter* last night."

I haven't thought about baseball in what seems like an eternity, although in fact it has been less than twelve hours since I walked off the mound.

"You and Modigliani . . . damn. Motherfucker didn't know what hit him! Always nice to see the good guys win."

Is that what we just saw? I wonder. Do the good guys shoot their enemies in cold blood?

The agent hands the passports back to the driver of the Explorer and waves him through. Now Marcus pulls into position and rolls down his window. "Passports, please," the agent says. He stoops to look into the car, craning his neck to see the girls in the back. He has the tiny, dark eyes of a rat.

"Morning, officer," Marcus says. "Busy day?"

The agent is all business: "I need valid U.S. passports for everyone in the vehicle, please."

"The thing is," Marcus says, "we sort of rushed down here last night, and some of us forgot our passports at home."

I appreciate that Marcus is trying to talk this out, but I really don't want to see him resort to plan B. So I start talking: "Officer, the truth is that I came down for a party after work last night. One thing led to another, and I lost my wallet, my passport, everything. My friends here pretty much rescued me. I promise you I'm an American citizen. I can give you my address, my Social Security number, whatever you need."

The agent is unmoved. "Without proof of identity," he says, "I couldn't let a senator through here unless I knew him personally."

"That so?" Marcus says. "A senator?" Out of the corner of my eye I see him reach for his waistband.

I lean over the console and start pleading: "Sir, I just moved to San Diego for work. My name is John Adcock. I'm from the L.A. area originally, graduated from Cal State Fullerton. My ex-wife and daughter live in Santa Monica. . . ."

Now the agent lowers his sunglasses. "I thought I recognized you," he says. "Adcock, sure. The new lefty. You came over in the Millman trade, right?"

"Yes, sir."

"Hell of a job last night, Adcock. Do you know how many times that bastard Modigliani has torn us up? Sometimes I think he has a vendetta against the city of San Diego."

"I appreciate the confidence, sir."

"Well, keep it up. We may be a losing team, but we're not losers. The San Diego Padres are a proud organization. Do you know what I'm saying?"

"I think so, sir."

"And hell if we didn't need a new setup man! My God, the way Jacoby was stinking up the place, you'd think we were trying to lose games. . . ." The agent shakes his head, apparently lost in Padre Nation. Then, suddenly, he snaps out of it and looks at his watch. "Day game today?"

"Correct," I say. "Sir."

"Well, then, I can't very well detain you." He leans down and scans the cabin of the Charger once more with his small black eyes. "I'm going to assume the rest of you are also American citizens?"

"Every last one," Marcus says. "The rest of us are from Oakland."

"So you're A's fans."

"As you know, sir, American League baseball is an inferior game. The DH ruins everything. But when we must watch AL ball, yes, we do like the A's."

"I once met Rickey Henderson in a nightclub," LaTasha

adds. "His cousin offered me blow, but I'm, like, 'I don't care who you are—you keep that stuff away from me!'" She smiles, certain that this tale of discretion will aid our cause.

A vein throbs on Marcus's temple. I hold my breath, banking on telekinesis to keep his hands on the wheel.

"Well, we could talk shop all morning," the agent says. "But I'm on duty today, same as you." He turns his head, observing the line of cars with a deep, satisfied exhalation. "Guys like us, Adcock, we take pride in our work. Most folks don't understand."

"I just try to give my best effort every night, sir."

"I know it." He steps back and waves us through. "Throw hard today."

47

Don't get me wrong: I am grateful to Marcus. It's just that I'm frightened by the ease with which he has carried out these crimes of self-defense. With Maria and Bam Bam both dead, I know I should feel safe, but I do not. In fact, I have never felt so uneasy. So many questions remain unanswered. Here's one example: Marcus said Bethany called him because she hadn't heard from me after the game. I'm open to the possibility that he might have his timeline mixed up—two murders in an hour will certainly do that—but I distinctly remember speaking with Bethany after the game. She gave me the news about Frankie's blackmail text. It wasn't a long conversation, but it happened. It isn't like Bethany to forget.

But if Bethany didn't send Marcus to San Diego, who did?

I become even more confused after we drop off the girls at LaTasha's place in Chula Vista. I ask Marcus if I can borrow his phone to call the Padres' clubhouse manager. I explain that my stadium keycard was in my wallet, and I will need someone to let me in.

Marcus tosses me his flip phone. "Don't laugh," he says. "I know it's old, but us old folks like to give something a full run before we kick it to the curb. You wouldn't understand."

Before I punch in the Padres' emergency number—every

team has one of these, and you have to memorize it before they give you cleats—I glance at the list of recent calls. There's the call to Rich, sure enough. There are several from the night before, back and forth to a 415 number I recognize as Bethany's cell phone.

I look at Marcus, tapping his thumbs on the wheel. I owe my life to this man, and I can't even trust him to tell the truth about his phone calls. I am a shitty, shitty friend. The fact that my spying turns up nothing only serves to reinforce my shittiness.

I reach the clubhouse guy at home, and he agrees to meet me at Petco in half an hour. My street clothes are at the hotel, but it's a day game. I'll just shower and put on my uniform, then maybe grab some breakfast.

Also, I need to talk to Jerry Díaz.

The ride is tense, to say the least. I have an urge to talk through what just happened but find it hard to describe. "Is Rich okay with the . . . Do you think he'll . . . You know, everything with Maria?"

Marcus raises his brow. "I'll say this about my brother—he knows what to do with a body. Wish it weren't so, but there you go."

"I owe you double now."

"Nah, man," he says. "You would have done the same for me."

"Does Natsumi have my number?"

"Why's that?"

"So she can call me in case you're ever in trouble."

He glances at me, then back at the road. I wonder if he knows I was doubting him a minute ago. Sometimes these things show on your face.

Beyond the windshield, downtown San Diego is alive with the benign business of ordinary folks: secretaries rushing to work in sneakers, hot-dog vendors staking their claims outside the high-rises. Hard to believe gritty, greasy Tijuana is just ten miles south. In the harbor beyond the stadium, a navy ship churns into port, its antennas spinning slowly above the bridge.

"All right, then," I say as Marcus pulls up to the players' gate at Petco. "Drive safe."

The electric fence slides closed behind me. Marcus starts a three-point turn, but the alley behind the stadium is tight, and he loses patience. Three points become five, six, seven. The concrete walls echo the *chugga-chugga* of the Charger's V8, and the air begins to smell like half-burned gasoline. Eventually, he gets close enough and floors it. The Dodge peels out, filling the morning air with an ear-piercing squeal and leaving a pair of wide tracks along the road.

48

A no-hitter in progress is like *Fight Club:* first rule is you don't talk about it. Our starting pitcher, Dan Wheeler, has not allowed a hit through seven innings, and he sits alone at the end of the bench, hat over his eyes, right arm coddled in a warm-up jacket. No one speaks to him. It's exciting but awkward, like riding in an elevator with a celebrity. When Wheeler heads out to start the eighth, the dugout breathes a sigh of relief to have him gone. Then it's all over. On the first pitch of the eighth inning, my former teammate Chichi Ordoñez lines a shot over the shortstop's head into left field, a clean single. There is no call to dispute, no lazy outfielder to blame, just a textbook hit. We still have the lead, 2–0, but as so often happens in baseball, the tiniest shift in momentum changes the balance of everything. Just like that, the air goes out of Wheeler's sails, and the next batter, Julio Cabrera, takes the first pitch he sees over the center-field wall. The ball goes much farther than that, actually, caroming off the "batter's eye" screen and returning to the field. Our center fielder scoops the ball up and throws it back toward the visitors' dugout, in case Cabrera wants to keep it as a souvenir.

In the bullpen we spit our sunflower seeds, cross and recross our legs, and wait for the phone to ring. You can almost feel the heaviness in Householder's dialing finger. Until five minutes ago, his pitcher was totally unhittable, a golden boy. Two batters later, the game is tied, there are no outs, and the Bay Dogs' number-three hitter is stepping up. On deck, in the cleanup spot, is our friend Modigliani.

The phone rings and the bullpen coach picks up. He nods, replaces the receiver, and tells me to get my glove. Fritz DeVries also gets tapped. Fritz is right-handed.

You see where this is headed.

Before I get my glove, I try to touch my toes. My left arm is loose. The problem is my rib cage, specifically the right side, which feels fused. I bend down and hear cracking like knuckles in my lower back. It occurs to me that I am too old to be doing this. Or maybe too old for the other thing. Definitely too old to do both.

"Let's go, Adcock," the bullpen catcher calls. "You're up."

He crouches behind the plate, and I give a few weak tosses from in front of the mound. He looks at me sideways. I ignore him. Fact is, if he were all that, he wouldn't be catching practice tosses in a cage behind the left-field wall. He knows this, of course, so he says nothing. Eventually, I work my way backward to the rubber. Until you are injured, you never realize how many muscles are involved in the simplest tasks. With this particular injury, the act of throwing the ball doesn't hurt too badly; it's the follow-through that kills, when the right side of my body curls in on itself. Now that I'm moving, getting warm, I hear no cracking, just a sort of moan, like Styrofoam flexing.

Then there's a crack, and a loud one: the sound of the Bay Dogs' second home run of the inning. This one is a monster shot onto the grassy knoll in right-center. The stadium falls silent as another of my former teammates rounds the bases. Those fans who are paying attention know that they have seen the last of Dan Wheeler, and when Householder waddles out to the mound, they stand and give Danny the ovation he deserves.

Five minutes later, these same fans have forgotten about the no-hit attempt. All they see is the home team trailing, 3–2. Never mind that ten minutes before they had been ready to nominate Dan Wheeler for governor. A week from now, his seven innings of no-hit ball will be a statistical anomaly, like getting heads in a coin toss seven times in a row, indistinguishable on the page from seven random, nonconsecutive hitless innings. Which begs the question: is it better to have flirted with history and failed, or never to have flirted at all?

Under the falsely optimistic cheer of the ballpark organ, I jog in from the pen. Every step twists the dagger in my rib cage. I wonder what Householder would do if I kept running past the mound and into the dugout, down the tunnel, into the clubhouse Jacuzzi. Among other things, it would vindicate the baseball brass in their conviction that my second career is detrimental to my first. I would never admit they're right, of course, but on a day like this it's hard to argue with their logic.

In the end, I'm too proud to back down. I take the ball from my manager, nod and grunt as required, accept a pat on the ass. "Just like last night," says the catcher. "Let's get him again."

First pitch is wide, and Modigliani takes ball one. Second pitch is the same. Diggy calls time, steps out of the box to check the signs from the third-base coach. I try to guess what he is hoping to see there: a bunt? You never know what the other guy is up against. Could be Modigliani had a hard night, too. He could be angling for a walk, nursing a hidden injury through these last few weeks of the season. A pitcher can hope.

I throw him a couple of sliders away, and he fouls both off—one deep the other way, off the corner of the old warehouse that doubles as the left-field foul pole.

I am pitching from the stretch, even though the bases are empty. This is standard reliever stuff, facing every batter like the bases are loaded. Each pitch must be sequestered in its own universe, each as important as the next. The rhythm of a windup, the economy of motion it provides—all that is useless to me. I will face one batter today. I can afford to burn my last drop of fuel. In fact, if I have anything left when I'm done, I will have failed to do my job.

The count is two balls and two strikes—a pitcher's count. The catcher wants a slider outside, the same pitch we got him on last night. Diggy's weak spot is weak for a reason, not because last week he forgot how to hit breaking balls on the outside corner. This bit of intelligence is culled from years of analysis, from thousands of at-bats. Yet today for some reason I have convinced myself he is expecting the slider. A high fastball, my gut tells me, would be a better choice. I wave off the catcher until he agrees.

Modigliani steps into the box. The catcher crouches down, raises his target. I set my hands at the belt. I stretch. The pitch feels right as it leaves my hand. The arm angle is good, the follow-through doesn't hurt too badly. But this is baseball, not ballet. You get no credit for a beautiful motion. Half a second later, as my pitch rockets into the San Diego afternoon, on its way to becoming the Bay Dogs' third homer in as many batters, I remind myself that often we are just plain wrong. About our friends, about our enemies, and even about ourselves.

49

Nothing like a humiliating loss to show you who your friends are. In the Padres' clubhouse after the game, I am surrounded by a cone of silence. My teammates are talking to reporters, talking to one another, just talking in general, but not near me. I want to tell them I know what they're thinking, that I was asked to do a small job and blew it. I feel awful, but that's part of the game when you pitch to only one batter a night. There's no middle ground; it goes either very well (you get him out) or very poorly (you don't). For years I've been content to take my lumps, but today it hurts. Maybe it's my age. Pitchers tend to lose their confidence like Hemingway said men go bankrupt: gradually and then suddenly. And once the confidence is gone, it can take weeks to gain it back, if it comes back at all. Plenty of guys just retire.

If I were going to chat with my teammates, the topic of the day would be Frankie Herrera's porn film, news of which hit the Twitterverse this morning. By noon, ten different acquaintances had forwarded me the link: "Know this guy???" and "Pst, Adcock, check out GRANMA!!!" In the end, ESPN wouldn't touch the story, so the scoop came from an unauthorized Bay Dogs blog called *DawgPound*. I know the guy who wrote the piece—he hired me to follow his new girlfriend to Vegas during the off season three years ago. (She was what they call a weekend warrior, a stripper who lives elsewhere but flies to Vegas on the weekend for the premium tips. I think he was actually pleased by my discovery.) In his article, my friend pointed out that the Herrera film represents an interesting cultural moment. In an era where celebrity sex tapes have become so common they're almost required for a certain kind of fame, we get a new wrinkle: the tape from beyond. On my phone, I skim the article and some of the hundreds of comments. Most of the talk is about whether or not the black guy is Prince Fielder (I'm pretty sure it's not him), but there is also some discussion of the actress. A couple of people correctly identify her as Herrera's wife. Somebody else says a reporter tried to track her down for comment, but apparently she has gone into hiding. . . .

I'm surprised the writer signed his name to the post. Now he'll have no chance to make the Baseball Writers' Association of America, the members-only body that votes on the Cy Young and MVP awards. The BBWAA remains one of the stodgiest clubs in a stodgy sport, but I guess my friend decided it wasn't worth playing by their rules. The times are changing for all of us. I hope at least he made some money.

I shower quickly, throw on borrowed street clothes, and wait in the hall outside the visitors' clubhouse door. A couple of the Bay Dogs say hello as they leave, but most do not. It's like they can smell the failure on me and don't want to get infected. I have a choice to make. I could stew in my loneliness, or I could reach out and touch someone. In moments of personal crisis, I used to call my mother, but since she passed away, five years ago, I usually end up dialing my ex-wife. Not sure what that says about me and the choices I've made with women, but, for better or worse, Ginny will always be family.

She does not say hello when she picks up.

"What's the matter, John?"

I hear beeping in the background. "Relax, nothing's wrong. I just need your advice."

"I'm at Trader Joe's."

"Okay, I'll call back."

"No, let's get this over with. . . ." She pauses. "Now is fine, I mean."

"I'm thinking about calling it quits," I say.

"Retirement?"

"That's it."

"And what will you do with yourself if you retire?"

"I have some ideas."

"Like what?"

"Marcus wants me to work for him."

"At his bar. Isn't that a cliché?"

"Marcus's place is different, but, yeah, I see what you mean."

"Do you really have to work? You must have some money saved up."

This strikes me as a very Santa Monica thing to say.

"I have some money, yes."

"I'm not digging, you know. Simon gave me everything in the divorce. All he needed was the love of a good man—he said that. Last I heard, he was sleeping under a *palapa* in Zihuatanejo. My point is, don't keep playing baseball for our sake. Izzy and I are doing fine."

I was afraid she would say this. I was hoping for the opposite, that she would berate me into continuing my career, scorching my ear with all manner of vicious threats and belittlements. *You are a fool, Johnny Adcock! What kind of man quits a job that pays a million and a half dollars a year?* But the sad fact about divorce is that even anger falls away eventually. First the good kind of passion dissolves, then the bad. I never thought I would miss her rage, but I do.

"Suppose I retire," I say. "Will you still, you know, respect me?"

She laughs, then apologizes. "I don't mean to belittle your dilemma, but this is not about earning anyone's respect. This is about one thing: do you want to play baseball or not?"

"Fair enough," I say.

I hear the checker ask Ginny if she wants her milk in a bag. "Is that it?" she says.

"Actually, I have one more question. You don't have to answer if you don't want. It's about birth control."

"You're not worried about Izzy, are you?"

"No! Oh, God, no. No—it's a question for you."

"I guess that's a relief."

"Do you know anything about IUDs?"

"A little. Why? Are you shopping around for Bethany's birthday?"

I ignore the jab. "What I want to know is, do they put you to sleep for the operation?"

A pause as Ginny realizes I'm serious. "Okay, my sister has an IUD, and if I remember correctly, it's not even an operation. She said they just slipped it in. Maybe some local anesthesia."

"That's it?"

"That's it. The mysteries of the female anatomy."

"Thanks, Ginny, that's helpful." Out of the corner of my eye, I see that Jerry Díaz has emerged from the clubhouse. "Okay, I gotta go. Kiss Izzy for me?"

She agrees, and we hang up. Another awkward conversation in the past.

Díaz looks as fresh as ever in jeans and an ironed polo shirt, an Adidas tote slung over his shoulder. "Johnny!" he exclaims when he sees me. I must admit that his enthusiasm is especially welcome today. He shakes my hand with gusto.

"Díaz."

"Well?" he says. "You ready to go?"

50

The Aztec Motel in Mission Valley looks pretty much the same as it did when I stayed here in the late nineties as a member of the Cal State Fullerton baseball team: a two-story block of tiny double rooms, external walkways wrapped around the second story, cracked asphalt parking lot with numbered spaces corresponding to the rooms. Off to the side of the parking lot, the motel's office has its own bungalow, an aged swamp cooler chugging away on the roof. Out on the street, a fluorescent signboard reads VACANCY, COLOR HBO, $69+TAX. No extra charge for bedbugs, and no questions asked.

Díaz and I go around the back of the main building and climb up the stairs behind the rumbling ice machine. On the second floor, three doors down, we find Room 16, where Díaz has arranged to meet Rosario. This morning, after Marcus dropped me off at the park, I called Díaz and told him I had another favor to ask, a hunch that needed testing. I said it just like that, "a hunch that needs testing." Needless to say, he was in. After bringing him up to speed on my night in Tijuana and the situation with Maria Herrera, I asked him to call Rosario.

I knock softly, turning sideways so I can keep an eye on the parking lot.

A voice from inside: "Who is it?"

"Barrio El Dorado," Díaz replies. This is the name of his parents' ranch. It means Golden Neighborhood. He said he always thought it would make a good password.

The door opens a crack. When Rosario sees it's us, she unlatches the chain and lets us in. The room is dark and low-ceilinged and smells of stale cigarette smoke. When my eyes adjust, I see that Rosario is not wearing her work clothes. She's in jeans and a Padres T-shirt; without her makeup, she looks much less like her sister.

"Thanks for meeting us," Díaz says.

"We will pay you again," I add.

Rosario shakes her head. *"No money,"* she says. *"This is for Ana."*

Díaz and I sit on one of the two swaybacked double beds, Rosario on the other.

"Last time, you told us Ana wanted to go to university. Did she tell you anything else about her plans in the U.S.?"

"She saved a lot of money," Rosario says. *"Last time I saw her, she said she had enough for two years' tuition. That's why she quit working for Señora Maria."*

"Hold on," I say. "Your sister wasn't working for the Herreras? When did that happen?"

"She quit a month ago. I was at my apartment one night, and Ana showed up unexpectedly. I didn't even know she was in town. She traveled a lot for Señora Maria, but she usually called ahead. She said that she had saved enough money to start taking classes at the university. I gave her my best congratulations, because I knew this was her dream. She said there would be much more to celebrate soon, not just for her but for all of us, because she had convinced Señor Frankie to shut down the business."

"You are talking about Frankie Herrera, Señora Maria's husband."

"That's right." Ana lowers her eyes for a moment. *"My sister and Señor Frankie, they were in love."*

"And he told your sister he was going to shut down the prostitution business?"

"That's what she said. The reason it had not happened yet was because Señora Maria had not agreed. Ana said Señora Maria had a new business partner, someone other than Señor Frankie, and this person would be very upset if Señor Frankie tried to shut down the business."

"I'm sure he would," I say. *"So Ana was worried for Frankie's safety?"*

"She said that even if Señor Frankie agreed to let the business stay open, he would still be in danger because of what he knew. She said Señora Maria's new partner might worry that Señor Frankie would go to the police or something like that. In Mexico, the cartels will kill you for what you know, even if you would never dare to speak. I told Ana that this was America, not Mexico, but she would not listen. She was upset, inconsolable. She was going that night to San José to find Señor Frankie."

"So Maria didn't kill him after all," Díaz says to me. "It was her partner."

"Rosario," I say, *"do you know the name of Señora Maria's partner?"*

Rosario looks at me in horror. *"Why would I want to know his name?"*

I decide to change course. *"You said there were six girls recruited from your village. Are you still in touch with the others?"*

Her eyes go wide. *"When Señor Jerry called me this morning, I was having coffee with Luz—"*

"Luz is one of the other girls?" Díaz says.

"She came north with us, but she got sick and had to stop working for Señora Maria."

I assume she's talking about HIV or another career-ending

disease. I can't imagine there are too many reasons a girl like Luz gets to void her contract. *"I'm so sorry,"* I say.

"I told Luz about you and Señor Jerry, that you believed Ana was killed and were going to find her killer. She gave me something to show you." Rosario digs around in her purse, and then holds out a small glass capsule, about the size of a roll of Life Savers. Inside are an array of densely packed, multicolored electronic components.

"A month after we came to the United States," Rosario explains, *"Luz began to have horrible cramps. Then she developed a headache and a high fever, so I took her to the hospital. The doctor said she had an infection in her womb. He ordered emergency surgery. He saved her life. Afterward he gave her this. He said it caused the infection."*

I turn the capsule over in my hand. My first thought is that it's a bomb, but it seems too small to do anything more than superficial damage. It looks like the remote-controlled firecrackers the pimpito was planting on George Luck's window. That doesn't make sense, either.

I am trying to piece this together—the logic of putting a low-powered explosive inside a human being—when Díaz growls, "Those sick motherfuckers." His choice of words startles me. It is the first time I've ever heard him swear.

"Jerry? You know what this thing is?"

He looks at me. "Of course I do. I'm a cattle rancher."

51

Díaz and I are sitting at a table in one of San Diego's excellent brew pubs. Despite the kid's successes so far, it is clear he has a lot to learn, style-wise, about being a detective. For starters, he asks the waitress if she has Rolling Rock on tap.

"You might as well order a seltzer," she says.

"Rolling Rock *beer*," he says with a flirtatious smile.

"I know what you mean. We don't have it."

"Oh. What are you ordering, boss?"

"Pint of bitter."

"So two Married Woman Bitters?" the waitress says.

Díaz nods. "I guess so. Is it dark?"

"If you want a dark beer, you should try the Fat Madam Stout. It's on the hand pump tonight."

I can tell Díaz wants to chat her up—just to show off his chops—but he can't seem to bring himself to do it. "Fat Madam Stout," he says. "Who comes up with these names?"

"The brewmaster studied creative writing in college."

"Bring two pints," I say.

The waitress nods. "Right-o." She has a kind of sexy belligerence that I can't place. It might come from the way her ass knocks back and forth as she walks. That or the neck tattoos.

As soon as she's out of earshot, Díaz starts to explain: "Do you have any pets, Adcock? Any cats or dogs?"

"I had a dog when I was little."

"Was he chipped?"

"I don't know. Why?"

"This is basically a bigger version of the microchips they implant in household pets." He pulls the glass capsule out of his jacket pocket and holds it between us. "See that? That's the antenna coil. And here's the brain of the thing, the silicon chip." He turns it over and points to a disk about a centimeter thick. "That's the battery, which tells you this is an active RFID tag."

"A what?"

"RFID stands for 'radio-frequency identification,'" he explains. "When you chip your cat, she's given a passive RFID tag. Passive means the tag doesn't have a power source. Using a handheld reader, you can scan the animal and learn its owner's name and address, phone number, that kind of thing. It's all embedded in the chip and transmitted to the scanner. But the range of a passive RFID tag is very small. You have to hold the scanner right over the chip. Active RFID tags are different. They have a battery and actually put out a radio signal that can be picked up hundreds of feet away. Ranchers use them to track their herds. You can even have the device transmit the animal's pulse and temperature."

"Your family uses these?"

"We're starting to, but the equipment is expensive. You need receivers in the barns, in the corrals, even on the range—basically, anywhere you want to count cattle."

"What about the capsules? Are they expensive, too?"

"Compared to the cost of the receivers, the tags are cheap, but you need to pay a vet to implant them." He pauses. "Of course, with cattle you just slip the tags under the skin. I've never heard of putting them deeper inside the body. Definitely not inside organs . . ."

"I'll bet they implanted the tags when they did the IUDs. That's why they put the girls to sleep."

"The girls never knew what they were getting."

"Exactly. The problem is that these things are meant to live under the skin, not inside the womb. I would say Rosario's friend is lucky she lived."

"Do you think they've all been chipped?" Díaz says.

"We have to assume so."

"We need to warn them, Adcock."

"Good luck with that," I say. "It's not like there's a personnel directory. And even if we did contact them, what would we do, line them up at the emergency room for X-rays? You can't do that without answering a lot of questions."

"There's an X-ray machine in the clubhouse," Díaz says. "We could bring the girls there . . . in the middle of night, maybe . . . but we'd need someone who knows how to use the machine." He isn't even convincing himself. "This is fucked," he mutters.

"Rosario told us that business has continued as usual since Maria's death. Someone pays the rent on her apartment, orders her groceries for delivery, sends reminders of her dates. This suggests Maria's new partner is firmly in command. . . ."

I'm at a crossroads. On the one hand, this could be the out I was pitching for—a satisfactory conclusion to a difficult investigation. My clients, the Herreras, are both deceased, and their enterprise has been passed down the line. I might reasonably wash my hands of the case right now. Problem is, my fingerprints are all over this thing. If the Velásquez sisters are correct and people are getting killed just for what they know, then I have a big "X" painted on my back. And I can't afford to die. I can't even decide whether to retire from baseball.

"You need to be careful," I tell Díaz. "Don't go anywhere alone if you can help it."

"What are you going to do?" he asks.

For some reason, a wave of confidence sweeps me up. "I'm going to close this thing."

"Solve the case?"

"And you're going to help."

The waitress arrives with our pints. "What are you guys, like, detectives?" No longer the sardonic tattoo queen, she now appears genuinely interested in us. "Sorry, but I couldn't help overhearing your conversation."

"Actually," Díaz says without missing a beat, "we're major-league baseball players." He smiles ear to ear. He's waited years to say that, and now he's ready to claim his reward.

"Oh," the waitress says, no longer interested. She brushes a strand of dyed black hair off her forehead. "You want anything else or just the check?"

52

The last two weeks of the season continue the losing theme for the Padres, who finish in the cellar of the National League West, thirteen and a half games behind the Giants. After the last game of the World Series (which I do not watch), the club declines its option on the final year of my contract. Translation: the Padres agree to pay me the million five they owe but prefer that I not pitch for them.

Next day, I get a call from Todd Ratkiss. "Listen, Johnny," he says, "I've got an offer I need to run past you. Just came in this morning."

"An offer?"

"To play baseball. Which is your job. Am I speaking Chinese?"

"I'm just surprised. That was fast."

"Well, you're going home."

"To the Dodgers?"

"The Dodgers? Since when is Los Angeles home?"

"Since I was born there."

"Dude," my agent growls, "the fucking Bay Dogs want to sign you. Home sweet San José."

Oh right. *Home.*

"Silence? That's the thanks I get for saving your fucking career?"

"Who says I wanted it saved?"

Todd exhales loudly into the phone. I can practically smell the Doritos. "Look man, do you want to play ball or not?"

It has come down to this. No putting off this decision. I can hang up, but I know that the phone will just ring again and it will be someone else, Ginny maybe, it doesn't matter who, and the conversation will end up here. As my dad used to say, it's time to shit or get off the pot.

"Same terms as last year?" I ask Ratkiss.

"The base salary is lower, but if you hit the performance targets, you get the same total comp. I could probably negotiate a no-trade if you want. They need a veteran lefty in the pen. Apparently, they've got a kid in triple-A they want to bring up, but he needs a mentor. This is what I'm told."

Bottom line, Dad was right: it is easy money.

"Sure," I tell my agent. "Tell them sure."

53

Tonight, after dinner at my apartment, as Bethany and I are sinking into our Scotch, she tells me we need to talk.

"It's about the Bay Dogs," she says.

"My once and future lords," I slur. "You know, when I heard they wanted to sign me, I was kind of disappointed. I had more or less decided to retire. I even called Ginny to get her opinion."

"We bought the team."

It takes a minute to register. "Who is *we*? Your fund?"

"Yep, we took a controlling interest in the ownership group. I know this must be a surprise, and I apologize for not telling you right away. I have been meaning to, but things have been crazy at work. . . ."

"You can't just buy a major-league baseball franchise!" Suddenly I am sober and surprised at the strength of my conviction. "The league has to review the bids first, and then the commissioner weighs in. It can take months!"

Bethany nods. "The great thing about these ownership groups is that when shares are redistributed among existing members of the group, the commissioner's office doesn't need to get involved. It's all in the family, so to speak."

"But you're not a member of the family."

"That's what I have been meaning to tell you. Years ago, the fund bought a small piece of the Bay Dogs partnership, less than one percent. We did a real-estate deal with one of the other investors, and he convinced us to get in. Just a tiny share, as a favor."

"When was this?"

"A long time ago. Before we met."

"Why didn't you tell me?"

"We have hundreds of holdings, Johnny. I couldn't possibly explain them all to you."

"How many baseball teams?"

"You are only allowed to own one."

We sit there a minute. Bethany eyes the tumbler of whiskey sweating on the coffee table, but does not pick it up. Then I say, because it just occurred to me, "The Eberhardts sold out?"

In recent years, Mr. Eberhardt has been held up by baseball traditionalists as the last holdout from an era when families, not corporate investors, owned baseball teams. However, even the stalwart Mr. Eberhardt had to allow outside involvement a few years ago in order to finance the construction of the new stadium downtown. I had assumed the new investors were banks. Guess I should have read the fine print.

"It was a timed divestment," Bethany explains. "The Eberhardts have been trying to diversify into other asset classes, and they structured the ownership group to give their partners regular opportunities to increase their shares over time."

Our eyes meet, and she sees something that makes her frown.

"You're worried. That's understandable, but my partners don't think there is anything fundamentally wrong with the business."

"The business. You mean the team?"

"Tickets, parking, concessions, broadcast rights, merchandise, licensing—it is a remarkably diverse income stream. I had no idea, actually, until Jun showed me some of the analysis he'd done. The stadium alone might be worth the entire purchase price. The land under the stadium, I mean."

Bethany again eyes her Scotch but reaches out and takes my hand instead.

"Nothing will change except on paper," she says.

"So you have no role in personnel decisions?"

"We are retaining the current general manager."

"And you wouldn't call him to put in a good word on behalf of a certain left-handed reliever who happens to be a free agent?"

"Johnny, no!" She laughs, arches her back. I see the outline of her nipples against the silk. "My job is to make sure the Bay Dogs have a strong capital position. That's it. I don't meddle."

"It's just a hell of a coincidence, that's all."

"I can see how you would think that, but I assure you—"

"All this time you owned me. Well, one percent of me."

"You want to guess which one percent?"

I crawl on top of her, smell the alcohol on her breath, the chlorine in her hair. I slide my fingers down under the waistband of her jeans.

"What other investments are you hiding from me?"

"Well, you already know about the chain of sushi restaurants run by a retired baseball player. . . ."

"Do you really expect Marcus to turn a profit?"

"Look, he saved your life—he did—and this was how he wanted to be paid. What could I say?" She pauses, sips her drink. "And he has other businesses besides the sushi bars."

"Like what?"

"Oh, he's all over the map. He once told me about this idea he had for a network of health-care centers for immigrant women. It would be like a combination of an urgent-care center and Planned Parenthood. But no abortions or anything like that, just annual checkups, Pap smears, the occasional gynecological surgery. Do you have any idea how much a hysterectomy costs if you don't have insurance? Anyway, he did his homework before we talked. He knew, for example, about our investments in the fertility-services sector. He said I had the expertise to help him make this a reality."

I sit up, pull my hand out of Bethany's pants. "What else did he tell you?"

"About the clinics? Just that he thought there was a market, and that it was a shame to deny things like diagnostic ultrasounds to women just because they couldn't afford to go to a traditional OB/GYN."

"Bethany," I say, "did Marcus by any chance give you a prospectus for the clinics in a white plastic binder?"

54

Marcus is upset when I tell him I have decided not to retire, but he's glad I'll be playing in San José.

"You can start training at the restaurant," he says. "Mornings, off days—we got plenty for you to do. And in winter you can work full-time."

We are at a tatami table in the front window of Makasu South, as the San José restaurant has been renamed since the opening of Marcus's new location in San Mateo. It is the middle of the afternoon, the restaurant's dead time, and I've caught Marcus between lunch at one restaurant and dinner at the other. Every now and then, a black-clad waitress comes and checks on our tea. Outside the window, a bell heralds the arrival of a VTA streetcar. The side of the train sports a Bay Dogs logo and Malachy Garcia's pixelated face. *Could have been me,* is what I'm supposed to think, but I don't. Maybe because the teacup feels warm in my palm, or maybe because I never wanted to have my face on a bus to begin with, I consider telling Todd Ratkiss I changed my mind about playing next year.

"You ever think about what happens next?" I ask Marcus.

"How do you mean?"

"After sushi. After this gets old. What will you do next?" I understand that with two sushi bars he's got his hands full, but how much can you love a business? There must be a limit.

"I got plans," he says, smiling. "You think you know everything about me?"

"I never said that."

Marcus looks at his watch. "It's gettin' on," he says.

"You headed up to San Mateo?"

Another smile. "You wouldn't know about a full day's work, would you, setup man?"

"I could learn. Need help tonight?"

"Tonight?"

"I could ride up with you and take the train back later."

"If you want, sure. Wait here a minute."

Marcus goes in the back, and I hear him discussing something with his brother. I used to think they were trading tips about sushi when they held their little powwows in the kitchen. Now I know better. I haven't spoken to Rich since he shot the widow and set her car on fire. The guy scares the shit out of me.

I pass the time with one of the sudoku books in the greeter's podium. Marcus requires his employees to solve ten sudoku puzzles every shift. He says it's good for concentration. I'm doubtful about the health benefits, but it definitely passes the time.

Ten minutes later, Marcus signals that he's leaving. I follow him out back to the Charger, parked in a spot marked with a stenciled "51," Marcus's number from his playing days. The big engine growls to life, and soon we're sailing up the 101.

"Let's take the coast route," I say as we approach Mountain View. "We've got time, right?"

Marcus shoots a glance at the dashboard clock. "You mean over the hill?"

"Yeah, cut through Woodside, La Honda, up that way, then

244

back on the Half Moon Bay road. I don't think it will take too much longer."

"Dinner service starts at five-thirty. I got a couple things I need to take care of first."

"Are you afraid of the fog?"

"In this car? Hell, no. Maybe on your little swizzle-dick Honda bike, but not in this machine."

"Fine, then."

"Fine."

As it happens, the fog is severe, maybe even fearsome, with visibility down to maybe twenty feet by four o'clock in the afternoon. Marcus has to drive slower than either of us would have liked, but we pass the time bullshitting about the old days. Marcus tells me that before I came up, back when the Bay Dogs were new in the league, the owners used to have parties on off days at their ranch in the Santa Cruz Mountains.

"Wasn't far from here, actually. There was a Girl Scout camp on the way, and some of the fellas used to joke about stopping for a piece." Marcus shakes his head. "Nasty motherfuckers."

"Wait," I say, "wasn't that the party where DiCamilla met that girl, what was her name?" I vaguely remember a story starring Ken DiCamilla, a lumbering third baseman long since retired, who was known to possess the thickest member this side of a donkey show.

"Yeah, she was the Eberhardts' au pair. Italian, I think, or Swiss—something like that. Anyway, she took it in the ass like a pro."

"According to DiCamilla."

"Right, according to DiCamilla. He called her Butt Nicola."

"What a guy, huh?"

Our conversation goes on like this for the better part of an hour, taking one Bay Dogs legend after another down to its ignominious roots. I don't think either of us finds it especially interesting; it's just how players pass the time on the road. This road or that road, active or retired, it doesn't matter. We could probably drag the conversation out by another fifteen minutes dissecting the Frankie Herrera porn film, but we don't. The story is too fresh. These things need to age for a while to become legend.

When we finally hit the coast highway at San Gregorio, I tell Marcus I have to take a leak. "There's a store up ahead," I say. "I'll be quick."

After the pit stop, we swing right and head up the coast. The road here is straighter and much smoother, but the fog is as thick as pudding. Marcus switches on the Charger's fog lamps. They don't do much but throw a pair of yellow eggs into the soup. This part of the trip would have been the highlight on a clear day—the redwood forest ending abruptly in the coastal meadows and bluffs, churning surf and black rocks. But today we see nothing. Before long we're in Half Moon Bay, a bedroom community known for its annual pumpkin festival and the Sunday buffet at the Ritz-Carlton. It's the kind of place where Silicon Valley types go with their wives when they haven't had sex in six months. How this foggy inlet puts you in the mood for love I have no idea, but if it had been six months since I'd gotten laid, I'd probably do it in a public restroom. At Highway 92, Marcus turns back inland. Makasu North is in San Mateo, on the other side of the mountains. It should take about half an hour from here.

As we climb the hill, the trees get taller and darker—redwoods thrive on fog. Then, near the ridge, the landscape changes. Suddenly the forest breaks and we are in the clear, carving back and forth along the concrete-encased, erosion-proof bluffs near the summit.

"Hey," I say to Marcus, "you know this is where Frankie Herrera went over?"

"Is it?"

"Right around here." I sit up and watch the next couple of curves very carefully. "Pull over, will you?"

"C'mon, Adcock. I got dinner service. We're late as it is."

"I just want to look around. Won't take a minute, I promise."

Marcus pulls into the next turnoff, and I jump out. Looking west across the fog-shrouded highway, I notice that the guard-rail has already been replaced. The rail flashes the reflection of an oncoming car, followed two seconds later by the car itself, invisible until the very instant of its arrival, thanks to the blind curve.

It really is the perfect spot. A car could wait here in the turnoff, watching the lights on the rail. . . .

I bend down, put my head into the Charger. "Get out. I want to show you something."

At the next break in traffic, we cross to the other side of the highway. Marcus and I stand in the shoulder, between the lanes and the rail. Our bodies absorb the flashes from the headlights. "This is the spot," I say, taking a deep breath. "But you know that already."

"Come again?" A van takes the curve a little too fast, tires squealing. A rush of air ruffles Marcus's corduroy sport coat, revealing a leather shoulder holster.

55

"I said you know this is the spot, because you were here the night Herrera died."

"What the hell are you saying?"

"You parked right there, against the hillside. Nobody coming west could see you, and anybody coming east just assumed you were waiting for the faster traffic to pass. You sat there looking for Frankie's car, and when it came along, you put the Charger in gear and crossed the median. You hit the brakes and Frankie's instincts did the rest."

Marcus shakes his head. "I got nothing to say to that."

"The tires gave you away."

"Plenty of cars got tires like that. Trucks, too. You need to get to Oakland more often."

I point to the turnout across the highway. "A truck wouldn't fit in there. As for other cars, you're right, plenty of cars have wide tires. There's the Corvette, the Porsche Carrera, some Aston Martins and Bentleys. . . . But those are all sophisticated vehicles. When was the last time you heard a Porsche peel out? When you laid tracks behind Petco Park, that was all I needed to see."

"I can't believe this," Marcus says. "I saved your life! Not only that, I went down to L.A. for you and almost got capped by that fool Bam Bam."

"Right—just for saying the name Herrera. That made no sense until I realized that Bam Bam never confronted you. You never gave him a chance. You showed up at his office that day intending to kill him, and you did. That's your style."

"My style?"

"I didn't know you had one until I saw how you killed Maria Herrera. It's like pitching—real consistent. I could write a scouting report."

"You don't know shit, Adcock."

"The Herreras were running whores up from Mexico. Lots of profit there, much more than in sushi."

This, finally, cracks Marcus's façade. His face relaxes and his eyes narrow. I recognize this as the face he makes when he's about to tell a joke. "You make me sound like a tycoon," he says.

"I know I'm right. Maria Herrera hired Bam Bam to shoot videos of the johns. But Bam Bam was a big man with expensive habits. One thing about a cokehead, he's always trying to get paid twice. Bam Bam figured that once the Herreras brought him into their circle, he had something to sell. He knew that you had your fingers in all kinds of businesses, so he brought you a business proposition. You grabbed the phone and made a deal with your new friend Maria. You paid Bam Bam a finder's fee, plus some money to let you use his office in North Hollywood. After I helped you dispose of the body, you went back to cover your tracks."

Marcus isn't ready to acknowledge anything, but I see on his face that I'm right.

"You sent text messages to Herrera from one of Bam Bam's computers. It must have been you: how else could you have known Frankie would be driving up here that night?"

"You've seen my cell phone," Marcus says. "You think I could do all that fancy shit?"

"I see it like this: You needed me to keep tabs on Maria. You knew that if Frankie Herrera came to me with a problem I'd try to help him. So you had Bam Bam send him those texts. Once I was on board, Frankie became expendable. You and Maria had already agreed to get rid of him, because he wanted to close down the operation, but she couldn't do it herself. The deal was simple: you took out Frankie, and she gave you part of the business. But you saw the handwriting on the wall with Maria. Turns out she was just like you. She never intended to share her gig with anyone. My guess is that she planned to have Bam Bam cut you down as soon as Frankie was dead. That was your guess, too, and that's why you had to kill Bam Bam."

I watch Marcus's hands. One quick move to his coat and I'm sharing the roster with Frankie and Bam Bam. For now he's quiet, looking over the rail. I wonder if he isn't surprised it turned out like this.

"Once you figured out Maria was going to double-cross you, you had to kill her. It wasn't going to be easy. She had armed guards and plenty of places to hide, with lots of connections in Mexico. But you had a secret weapon. You knew that I would lead you to her when the time was right. All you needed was an excuse to show up. What I don't understand is why she didn't recognize you."

Marcus narrows his eyes. "You serious? That's the oldest play in the goddamn book. I know her, but she don't know me, same as niggas slanging rocks on the street don't know who they dealing with upstairs."

"To prevent squealing."

"I'm not saying you're right, Adcock, but do you really think a jury is going to feel sorry for Maria Herrera? She was smuggling wetback pussy. I didn't start that—she did."

"I wasn't going to confront you until I had a solid case. I knew Maria wasn't going to be a sympathetic victim. The same goes for Frankie and Bam Bam. But there was another option: the girl in the car with Frankie."

"A hooker! You think anybody cares about a dead hooker?"

I hold up the RFID tag. "A surgeon at Scripps Mercy Hospital took this out of one of your girls six months ago. She had a fever of a hundred and five and internal bleeding. The surgeon estimated that if he hadn't intervened she would have died within twenty-four hours. How's that for a case?"

"Great, but it don't stick to me."

"You were using these devices to track the girls, monitoring everything from Bam Bam's office. If it worked like you hoped it would, you could get rid of the local muscle and manage the talent yourself. Nice cost savings there. But you're always thinking ahead." I have to pause here. Stay calm. "But if you could implant cattle tags, why not try putting something more lucrative inside the girls?"

Marcus gives me a dead look. "Like drugs?"

"Whatever it is, you still have to get the cargo out. The IUD procedure was your cover on the Mexican side, but in the United States you can't just set up an illegal operating room in your basement. That's why you proposed the women's health clinics. You did your homework, figured out what it would take to open a site and bring in a doctor or two from Mexico. You could have gotten by with just one location, but as usual you got ambitious. You put together an investment prospectus and started looking for venture funding. I had a copy of the prospectus, but you got it back eventually. You also took back the copy from Bethany's office, but I'm sorry to say they scan everything over there."

Marcus exhales. "I'm impressed, Adcock. That's some nice detective work. You got me on—what—four homicides? But what are you going to do . . . make a citizen's arrest?" He chuckles. "You always had trouble closing."

It's a low blow, but I should have seen it coming. The man has been my mentor for over a decade. A naïve part of me hoped that we could let baseball be baseball, leave our history alone. I should have known he'd dredge up insults he'd been swallowing for years. All it took was me accusing him of murder.

"We always made a hell of a team," Marcus says. "How about you give up this detective thing and work with me?"

"There's a difference between agreeing to work at your sushi bar and helping you run an international prostitution ring."

"Come on, Adcock, let's be smart about this. What are you going to do when you retire, after you're done snooping on people's wives and rescuing kitties caught in trees? I'm offering you the long term. We'll be partners."

"So I can end up like Maria Herrera?"

Marcus shakes his head slowly. Now his hands go under the coat and he unsnaps the holster, removes a .38-caliber revolver. For the second time in a week, my life is elapsing like the penalty time at the end of a soccer match, no way of knowing how long it will last.

I tap my chest, just below the collar. Clear my throat.

"Don't tell me you're surprised," Marcus says. "You can't just lay all that out and expect me to roll over." He cocks the revolver and levels it at my nose. "I've got to finish what I start. I was a closer before they had a word for it."

All of a sudden the air explodes with sirens and flashing lights. A black-and-white squad car accelerates around the curve and does not stop until Marcus is lifted off the ground, caught in the bumper bars. His gun skitters onto the roadway. An officer leaps out of the car with handcuffs. Within fifteen seconds it seems like every cop in San Mateo County is on the scene. With all the pulsing lightbars, Highway 92 looks like a suburban cul-de-sac on Christmas. Somehow, despite the noise, I hear through the wireless bud in my ear the voice of Jerry Díaz: "Sorry, Pops. I might have waited a beat too long there. . . ."

I reach under my shirt and yank out the wire. It has been itching ever since I taped it on at the rest stop in San Gregorio. When I called Díaz from the bathroom stall, I warned him that I would be able to hold off Marcus only so long after I accused him of killing Frankie. He assured me that the cops would step in as soon as things got dicey, that they would be waiting around the corner in the surveillance van, guns at the ready, with plenty of backup.

I probably should have set up a code word. If there's one thing rookies and cops both love, it's a damn code word.

56

It takes months for the dust to settle on the Herrera affair. The state charges Marcus with the murders of Bam Bam, Frankie, and Ana—and of conspiracy to kill Maria, whose body is never found. There are also charges of conspiracy and racketeering related to the prostitution ring, but the big question is whether the prosecutors will charge him with human trafficking, which is a slippery crime and difficult to prove if you haven't caught the smuggler in the act. Ironically, as a sex offender, Marcus will be monitored on a Department of Justice Web site if he ever gets out of prison.

And he may get out. His legal team is excellent, and the newspapers speculate that he will eventually plead guilty to a package of lesser charges, maybe calling the Bam Bam incident self-defense and knocking Frankie's and Ana's murders down to manslaughter of some kind. With luck, he'll go free a couple of years before he dies. It's a disappointing outcome, given how many bodies piled up, but I'm satisfied. Justice is so often subverted in this state that a conviction of any kind for a man so obviously guilty feels like a major victory to me.

The cops never find the computers Marcus removed from Bam Bam's office—another credit, I'm sure, to the yeoman work of Marcus's brother—but they do locate Bam Bam's account with a commercial cloud-backup service. The cache of evidence includes a spreadsheet with the names and addresses of each of the prostitutes, along with the hexadecimal ID of her tracking tag. I find it hard to believe that Bam Bam Rodriguez, a man who couldn't be bothered to use a trash can, backed up all his data, but there you have it: the human brain is a dark and unknowable place, full of contradictions and happy accidents. The police forensics lab also confirms that Bam Bam sent the texts to Frankie, but the most stunning revelation is that the anonymous tip to the *DawgPound* blogger also came from Bam Bam. The e-mail was scheduled on an automatic timer. How's that for a new wrinkle on the celebrity sex tape? A dead player's secret tape, exposed by another dead player. Not sure what it means, but it certainly captures the flavor of this case.

More pressing than Frankie's tape is the fate of the girls he employed. With help from Rosario, the police uncover prostitution operations in every California city with a major-league team, plus a few minor-league towns like Fresno and Bakersfield. With help from the police in Tijuana, the California authorities are able to track down the surgeon Rosario described, and they learn that, yes, he did insert something more than an IUD into each girl's *sanctum sanctorum*. The doctor had no idea what it was—apparently, surgery is a don't-ask-don't-tell proposition down in TJ—but when the cops show him a cattle RFID tag, he says it looks familiar. The police find RFID scanners in all of the girls' apartments, confirming that Marcus and Co. were indeed monitoring their herd from afar. Just as Jerry Díaz thought, the cattle tags have never been tested on humans, so their long-term effects are unknown and presumed potentially hazardous. The state's social workers try to make contact with all the prostitutes listed on the spreadsheet, but of course the girls aren't excited to take calls from the law. A few of the women allow themselves to be scanned by ultrasound, to determine if the implants have put them in danger, and the very bravest ones, including Rosario Velásquez, endure surgery to remove the devices. The whole thing turns my stomach. I'm reminded of a photo I once saw in a magazine of elephant carcasses abandoned on the African savanna, their tusks sawn out by poachers. Beautiful creatures reduced to meat.

Then there are the twin sons of Frankie and Maria Herrera. Possibly because I feel guilty, rightly or not, for what happened to their parents, I have an urge to check up on them. I track down Maria's sister, calling and introducing myself as a former teammate of Frankie Herrera's. Mrs. Pamela Cruz is wary, but her resistance melts when I ask about the twins. She tells me that she and her husband are in the process of adopting the boys, who have been living with them since her sister's disappearance. "Well," I say, "I'd love to have a photo, if you wouldn't mind. We have a corkboard in the clubhouse where players put up kids' art projects and school photos, that kind of thing." I don't tell her that the board is labeled "Birth Control Reminders" (because this is baseball and not a daytime talk show). But that's just swagger. Even the hardest players stop now and then to take a look. Pamela Cruz says she would love to send a photo, and we exchange addresses.

That's why, when a letter arrives a few days later sporting a San Diego postmark, I assume it's from her. I even take care in opening the envelope to avoid tearing the contents. But the envelope contains no photos. In fact, it is not even from Pamela Cruz, but from Frankie Herrera's lawyer. I unfold the letter and find a check, drawn on a trust account, in the amount of $250,000. The letter explains that this is payment for professional services rendered by me. Apparently, Frankie wrote his lawyer the day before he died, requesting a payment in this amount.

As far as I can tell, the lawyer has no idea what "professional services" I provided his client, but he appears determined that I accept the payment.

"It is crucial," the letter explains, "that all debtors acknowledge receipt of funds in writing so that the corpus of the estate (which will be placed in trust for the deceased's heirs) can be declared free of claims. Please reply at your earliest convenience."

I'm conflicted about accepting Frankie's payment. For one thing, it's way too much. I usually charge my clients only a nominal fee, or ask that they buy me dinner. In an era where the average salary for a major-league player is well into seven digits, it feels pointless to take money for something I'd probably do for free. My big hang-up with accepting Frankie's money, though, is that I didn't deliver what he paid for. Quite the opposite: I blew up his life. I sit on the problem for a few weeks, and then, one day, the answer comes to me. I am walking across the campus of San José State University, a public college downtown with something like thirty thousand students. It is a commuter school, part of the same university system as my alma mater, Cal State Fullerton. This afternoon I am making an appearance at a kids' pitching clinic run by Kenny Glidewell, an old Bay Dogs teammate. The ball fields are on the far side of campus, fifteen minutes from the parking garage. As I am crossing in front of the student union, I notice a pretty young Latina rushing toward the automatic doors of the campus bookstore. She trips on a step and spills a handful of change. She looks around, embarrassed, then crouches down to gather the coins. I understand that this handful of nickels and dimes may have meant nothing to her—she might have been stopping in for a Coke, nothing more—but it gets me thinking.

That night, I write an e-mail to George Luck: "I am setting up a scholarship fund at San José State named for Frank Herrera and his wife. The fund will support Latina girls, first-generation kids like Ana. Why don't you do the same at Fullerton? Name the fund for Ana. I can't imagine a better way to honor her memory—can you?"

Going through the widow's black book (lifted from her house because you never know when these things might come in handy . . .), I pick out the johns I know, ballplayers who came through Cal State schools. It's not hard to do. The California State University system might be the impoverished stepchild of higher education, but it churns out two products better than any other institution in the world: first-generation college graduates and professional baseball players. My request to each of these lucky gentlemen is simple: Match or exceed the quarter-million our late colleague Frank Herrera is putting up. And do it fast.

As I sit at my kitchen table, typing out the appeals, it occurs to me that some of these players may never have spent a quarter-million on anything, let alone something you cannot lock, drive, or screw. But by two in the morning, when I finally close my laptop, I feel pretty sure they will write the checks.

I don't need to tell them what will happen if they don't.

57

The off season: Some of the Caribbean guys play winter ball in their home countries, but American players generally go wherever their kids are in school and sit around the house, trying not to go crazy. Working out helps some. Modern contracts stipulate that you must arrive at spring training in reasonable physical condition—and, to be honest, the best players make it a point to improve their game in some way every winter, so they come back the next year with an edge. It's never been that way for me. I have always struggled to stay in shape during the winter. Mostly I'm just lazy, but I do believe that working out by yourself will eventually crush your soul. Which is why I'm trying something new this year: keeping up with Bethany.

So far it's killing me. The woman is indefatigable. The other day we were on a jog—an "easy" ten-mile loop through the foothills of South San José—and around the eighth mile my legs went wobbly and I fell down. I wasn't hurt, and Bethany teased me into finishing the course, but it got me thinking. I realized that at some point this will happen every time I go running. I will have to retire. It's just a matter of time. Not many people have careers that end before they reach middle age. Aside from the obvious financial trouble this presents, there is also an existential dilemma: How do you remake yourself when you quit the game that has been your identity since childhood? *What are you going to do when you retire?* Marcus asked me that night on the mountain. He ought to know what he was talking about; he certainly forged a new life after retirement. The newspaper stories about his trial all claim that he was driven by greed, but I'm not so sure. Fear of obsolescence probably played a big part.

One thing I will say for Bethany's workout regimen: she knows how to pamper herself afterward. This evening we are at Watercourse Om, a Japanese-style bathhouse in Palo Alto. The Stanford kids call it Intercourse Om, and that's a nice thought, but I doubt many of them can afford the price of admission when the dorm shower is free. For two hundred dollars an hour, Beth and I get a private room with our own spa, sauna, and cold plunge. The decor is maxed-out Asian, with Buddha heads everywhere and fresh jasmine flowers in rectangular bud vases. Hidden speakers emit soothing Japanese harp music. We sip from cups of iced pomegranate green tea as Bethany shows me the proper way to alternate between dry heat, wet heat, and cold. "It's just like working out," she says. "You have to find your red line."

She means, I think, the point at which you are about to pass out. I can only stand so much Jacuzzi before I start to feel like a lobster being boiled alive, so I take my tea and lie down on the wooden cot in the corner. Ten minutes later, Bethany emerges from the sauna, naked and gleaming with perspiration. She leans over me and kisses my neck.

"Maybe we should get married," I say.

She looks at me. "What's this?"

"I've been thinking about it."

"Why didn't you say something?"

"Why didn't you tell me you owned the Bay Dogs?"

"That's fair. But I'm afraid I can't marry you."

"Why not?"

"I thought we had an understanding about marriage."

"Remind me what we said?"

She shoves in close. The cot is narrow, and we just fit.

"You're worried because I own you," she says.

"That doesn't bother me."

"No?"

"I'm serious, Beth."

"I know you are, but do we have to be married to love each other?"

She takes my hand and slips it between her legs. I want to finish the conversation, because I feel there is more to say, but Bethany is persuasive. By the time we are finished making love, I can't remember what was so pressing. I drift off.

The door to the room opens and shuts. Bethany stands before me with two plastic cups of ice water. She hands one to me and sits down next to me. Knees up, with our backs to the wall, we might be high-school kids catching our breath after a romp behind the field house. I have a warm feeling in my stomach that I don't want to mention, in case it goes away.

They say a second wife is more like a friend than a lover. In most ways Bethany Pham is a better match for me than Ginny ever was. My fear is that I blew my load, love-wise, on Ginny. What Bethany and I have is wonderful, even enviable. We are the best of friends. The sex is prizewinning. Is there more to love than that? I once felt like there was. But look where that got me.

"Are we going to do this?" I say.

"You're going to make me close the deal." The look she gives is incredulous but not really surprised.

"You know I'm a horrible closer."

"We're not on the baseball field. This is different."

"Not really. This is what I do. I get close, but I don't close. I've made a whole career out of it."

"That would look funny if you wrote it down," she says. "Close and close."

"Marry me, Bethany."

"There you go! Be bold. I like that."

"Marry me now, or I will marry Glenn Close."

"Keep it coming!"

"Marry me and I will pitch for your baseball team. But I don't come cheap. It will cost you a million dollars plus incentives."

This routine gets us both pretty worked up, so we knock another one off. Afterward it's time to get dressed. The room is starting to smell, and our two hours are almost up.

Bethany finishes her water in one long gulp. "Can I tell you how much I love owning a baseball team?" She hurls her cup into the trash can. "So far, it's all about sex."

I wish that was the first time I heard someone say that.

Acknowledgments

Thanks to my editor, Rob Bloom, who has the filthiest stuff in publishing. Thank you, Rob, for seeing the potential in this project and helping me draw it out. Thanks also to my agent, Jennifer Carlson, for taking an unexpected manuscript in stride. Thank you to the generous friends who commented on drafts: Dave Kern, Jeremy Resnick, Victoria Dougherty, Nathan Oates, and Bob O'Connell. Thanks to my wife, Jessica, for seeing me as a big-leaguer, and to my kids, Violet, Raymond, and Rose of Sharon, for understanding that they are too young to read this book.